FORGIVEN

THE WATCHERS TRILOGY
BOOK 3

BY
INTERNATIONAL
BESTSELLING AUTHOR
S.J. WEST

S.J. WEST

COPYRIGHTS

Cover Design by Paper and Sage Designs, all rights reserved.
Formatting and Interior Design by Carolina Silva, all rights reserved.
Proof Reader by Kimberly Huther.

Published by Watchers Publishing: November, 2012.
www.Sjwest.com

Writer. Storyteller. Daydreamer.

Books in the Watcher Series

The Watchers Trilogy

Cursed

Blessed

Forgiven

The Watcher Chronicles

Broken

Kindred

Oblivion

Ascension

Caylin's Story

Timeless

Devoted

Aiden's Story

The Alternate Earth Series

Cataclysm

Uprising

Judgment

The Redemption Series

Malcolm
Anna
Lucifer
Redemption

The Dominion Series

Awakening
Reckoning
Enduring

Other Books by S.J. West

The Harvester of Light Trilogy

Harvester

Hope

Dawn

The Vankara Saga

Vankara

Dragon Alliance

War of Atonement

Vampire Conclave Series

Moonshade

Sentinel

TABLE OF CONTENTS

ACKNOWLEDGMENTS

I would like to express my gratitude to the many people who were with me throughout this creative process; to all those who provided support, talked things over, read, wrote, offered comments, allowed me to quote their remarks and assisted in the editing, proofreading and design.

I would like to thank Lisa Fejeran, Liana Arus, Karen Healy-Friday, Misti Monen, and Erica Croyle, my beta readers for helping me in the process with invaluable feedback.

Thanks to Kimberly Huther my proofreader for helping me find typos, correct commas and tweak the little details that have help this book become my perfect vision. Thank you to Carolina Silva for creating the Interior Design of the books and formatting them.

Last and not least: I want to thank my family, who supported and encouraged me in this journey.

I apologize to all those who have been with me over the course of the years and whose names I have failed to mention.

CHAPTER 1.

Can any sin be forgiven?

As I looked at the three fallen angels around me, I had to wonder. I knew Brand, the love of my life and soon-to-be-husband, yearned to be forgiven by God for going against His law. Yet, knowing what he knows now, would Brand have chosen a different path, or did he feel as though he made the right decision all those years ago?

If he hadn't fallen in love with Abby's mother, I knew for a fact we wouldn't be together now. As selfish as it might sound, I was glad he had fallen out of God's grace, because I couldn't imagine living my life without him. I would have been left living a half existence, not knowing why I felt so incomplete.

People say we each have a soul mate, that one person whose ethereal essence matches the ragged edges of our own. I guess when I was younger I always thought that person would be Will, one of my best friends since childhood. It wasn't until I met Brand that I came to realize what it truly meant to find your other half. He made me stronger and braver than I could ever be on my own. If there was a way to discover the true reason Lucifer needed me before it was too late, I knew Brand would be the one to help me find it.

For the last two weeks, my small troupe of angels has been trying their best to figure out Uriel's cryptic message to me. Just when I thought the archangel had me cornered, and was about to hand me over to Robert to be butchered, he let me go with the promise that he would cease trying to orchestrate *accidents* leading to my untimely demise. Still, I couldn't stop thinking about the implications of one of his statements to me: *"There is no sin in a martyr's death."*

His meaning was clear. He thought I should kill myself before becoming Lucifer's pawn. When I questioned why he decided to abandon his attempts to end my life, he simply said God had intervened on my behalf. He didn't seem to know the exact reason why, after all these years, God ordered him to end his attempts. He assumed it was because I had already chosen to do something that would ultimately lead to the failure of Lucifer's plans. I had no way of knowing what it was I had chosen to do, but I sincerely hoped I hadn't changed my mind about it unwittingly. As Uriel had said, humans are fickle creatures who often stray from the right path.

"So, what do we know so far?" I asked.

Brand, Will, Malcolm, and I were sitting around the dining room table in Brand's house. Will was still on his laptop, combing the Internet for clues to Lucifer's plans. Malcolm was searching through an old book of legends, and Brand was helping me stuff Jordan almonds into little red and white silk pouches. On top of everything else, we were still preparing for our wedding that was only a week away. Considering the world as we knew it might be on the verge of collapse, it seemed like an inconsequential activity to be performing. That is, until you factored in my mother, who practically ordered us to fill the more-than two hundred silk purses before the end of the weekend.

"We don't seem to know much, dearest," Malcolm said, closing the book in his hands. When he looked up at me, I could see his worry about my fate clearly in his eyes.

"I haven't been able to find anything going on in the world during the timeframe we were given," Will said. "There just isn't much happening in December."

"What about the Mayan Doomsday thing everyone seems to be talking about?" I asked.

"It's a bunch of hogwash," Malcolm said dismissively, "something public media has sensationalized."

"So nothing is supposed to happen? Nothing at all?" I asked, desperate to have some clue as to what Lucifer's real plan for me was.

"Not that I can find," Will sighed. From the slight drooping of his shoulders, I knew Will had spent endless hours searching for something...anything that would shed more light on what we could expect to happen.

I felt a pair of warm hands cover mine. I looked over at Brand and tried to muster up a smile for him.

"Have faith," he said to me, squeezing my hands. "God knows you will do what's right. If He has that much faith in you, we need to trust Him too."

"Brand's right," Malcolm said. "We're probably worrying over nothing. Everything will work out in the end, dearest. Don't worry."

I tried to smile and put on a brave face for them, but I felt sure it looked as strained as I felt.

"Anyway," Malcolm said, "aren't you supposed to be going out with the girls today?"

"That's the plan," I replied, piling my share of the almond purses into a white basket festooned with artificial red roses. "They didn't tell me where we're going, though."

"It's your *bachelorette* party," Malcolm shrugged. "I don't think you're supposed to have all the details. Some of it needs to be kept a surprise."

From the broad smile on Malcolm's face, I had a feeling he knew more about my party than he was letting on.

"Well, it's just going to be the four of us," I said. "I doubt it'll be anything too elaborate."

"Abby's been pretty tight-lipped about what they have planned." Brand looked down at his watch. "In fact, it's about time for us to head over to Allan's house."

"So, he's really coming over here?" Malcolm asked. "I never thought I would see the day he willingly stepped out of his house."

"He's stronger than he knows," I said, needing to come to Allan's defense. "He proved that when he followed Robert to that forest after he kidnapped Angela."

My protectors fell silent and found somewhere else to look.

They all felt as though they had let me and everyone else down Halloween night, when Robert orchestrated his game of Bait. Robert had only been able to force me to be a part of his sadistic game because he kidnapped Abby, Angela, Sebastian, Tara, and Malik all at the same time. I never would have been able to forgive myself if Brand, Malcolm, and Allan's children had consumed the blood of my best friend Tara and my fairy godfather, Malik. If they had, their souls would have been deemed unforgivable in God's eyes, a fate all of my Watcher friends had been feverishly protecting their children from since their birth.

Even though Malcolm had only recently started abstaining from giving in to his bloodlust, I knew he had been protecting his son from following in his footsteps and facing a doomed fate. He wanted Sebastian to have a chance of reaching Heaven, a privilege he himself had lost long ago.

Will and Malcolm made excuses to leave shortly after.

Brand took me into his arms and held me tight. "You know we'll never forgive ourselves for what happened that night."

"It wasn't your fault," I said, looking up into the warm gray eyes of my future husband. "If anyone should feel blame about what happened that night, it's me."

Brand shook his head. "You can't think like that, Lilly; it wasn't your fault, either. You've been an innocent pawn in all of this. You didn't choose how you came into this world, and I can't imagine anyone else who could have faced what you have and still be sane."

"I wish Uriel had at least told me who my father is. Maybe then we would know more."

"We'll find the answer to that," Brand said, full of confidence. "I have faith in Him. He'll show us the right path."

Even though God refused to let Brand and the other Watchers back into Heaven because they fell in love with human women, the man who held my heart still believed his father would aid us in our quest. I myself have never been very religious. Yes, I have always believed in a higher power, although I couldn't tell whether that was just ingrained in my genetic code, or because Utha Mae had me sit in a pew at her church every chance she got. Considering I now knew for a fact He exists, it didn't much matter.

When Brand and I phased to Allan's home, we found him and Angela waiting for us outside the front door of their fortified castle, a fact that, in itself, seemed to be a small miracle. As far as I knew, Allan hadn't stepped outside his home except for the two times he visited me in the hospital, and when he helped me get my friends away from Robert that night in the forest.

As soon as Allan saw me, he smiled his relief, and his shoulders visibly relaxed. Angela waved to us, holding tightly to her father's hand as they walked towards us. I began to wonder if I was sorely underdressed for my bachelorette party, since Angela was wearing a sleeveless white cocktail dress and high-heel shoes.

"We thought we'd get some fresh air while we waited," Angela explained. Her happiness at the newfound strength her father recently discovered within himself was written plainly on her face.

"So, I don't suppose you'd be willing to tell me what's on the agenda for today?" I asked Angela.

"Nope," she said, "I promised Tara I wouldn't say a word. You'll find out soon enough."

"Is it something I'm going to like?"

"If you don't, the rest of us will." Angela's smile was so bright with enthusiasm it immediately made me suspicious.

"Angela hasn't even told *me* what's happening," Allan said, "and she usually tells me everything."

Angela's cheeks took on a rosy hue. "I couldn't possibly tell you, Dad. It would just be too embarrassing," she confessed. "I'll let Lilly explain it to you later when you pick me up, if you still want to know."

"From what you're saying, I'm sort of scared this might be something that will scar me for life," I said in all seriousness. What did my best friend have planned that would make Angela's cheeks flush so hotly?

"It won't be that bad," Angela giggled. "But, just remember, it's all in good fun."

It was then I knew I should have badgered Tara into divulging the details of her plans to me. The only reason I hadn't was because I still felt guilt over her involvement in Robert's deadly game. She would forever be marked with a nasty scar as an eternal reminder of how close she came to dying because of me. For that reason alone, I knew she would have carte blanche to whatever she wanted from me for the rest of her life.

We phased Allan and Angela to the living room in Brand's home. Since angels can only phase to places they have either been to before or followed another angel's phase trail to, Allan's personal catalog of phasing locations was extremely limited. Bringing him to Brand's home in Lakewood was a monumental step forward for both him and Angela. Now he would be able to phase Angela to Brand's anytime she wished to visit us.

Allan studied his surroundings critically. I knew his compulsive disorder made him acutely aware of the cleanliness of his environment. It was the sole reason I had Brand hire a cleaning crew to scrub down every nook and cranny of his home the day before. Allan's attention was soon drawn to Brand's painting of me, hanging in the dining area.

"You captured her completely," Allan said in awe, staring at the painting of me, in the dress I wore to the Black and White ball.

Brand had hung it up on the wall the day before, after the cleaning crew was done.

"If I can't have you in my arms tomorrow," he had said to me. "At least I can have your picture hanging up to keep me company."

He was always doing that, saying things only a romance novel hero could get away with. It was only because of the sincerity of his declarations that I knew he truly meant them.

"Wow, that really is a good painting of you, Lilly," Angela said, going to stand closer to it. "Did you do this, Brand?"

"Yes, he did," I answered for him, hugging his arm tight. To me, Brand's portraits of me didn't quite look as I thought I truly looked. The girl in his paintings held an ethereal beauty I just couldn't see in my own reflection.

"It looks just like you," Angela said, seeming to have a hard time dragging her eyes away from the picture.

"Do you have a painting of Lilly I could have?" Allan asked.

"Why would you want one?" I questioned. It seemed like an odd request.

"Am I out of line for asking?" Allan stammered, making me immediately regret questioning his motives.

"No, of course not," Brand was quick to reply. "I have plenty of similar paintings for you to choose from, old friend. Why don't you come up to my studio and pick one for yourself?"

Allan visibly relaxed again.

Brand bent his head down to mine and kissed me lightly on the lips.

"Why don't you girls go on ahead? I'll show Allan the rest of the house while you're gone."

"We'll be back before sunset," I promised.

I had to have Angela and Abby back before they were due to change into their werewolf forms. That was the curse of the Watcher children. They were able to live a normal life, with the exception of nighttime, when the moon rose and forced them to transform into the nightmare beasts of legend.

Not completely satisfied with such a simple peck on the lips, I turned to our guests and asked, "Would you please excuse us for just one moment?"

Without waiting for them to answer, I tugged on Brand's hand and walked us out the French doors leading to the back porch, which faced the lake. Brand closed the door behind us, and I immediately wrapped my arms around his neck, pulling his lips down to mine for a proper kiss. The silky texture of his tongue against mine melted my will to leave him for even a minute, much less an entire day. As if feeling my resolve to leave him completely dissolve under his touch, Brand pulled away, albeit reluctantly.

"If you don't go now," he said huskily, "I'm afraid I won't be able to let you leave at all. Then I would have the wrath of Tara Jenkins to deal with, and that's not something I would willing inflict upon myself."

I groaned in frustration. "I don't know why I agreed to do this. I'm not really a party person."

"You agreed because she wanted to do it for you."

Brand put his hands on my shoulders and promptly turned me back around to indicate I needed to re-enter the house and leave, before his own will to let me go crumbled alongside my own.

Angela informed me that I was to phase us to Tara's house first.

After the near-fatal events on Halloween, Brand and I talked Tara into taking up residence in what was once Abby's house on Brand's property. At first, she refused, because she said she would feel like a kept woman, since Brand refused to let her pay rent or any of the utility bills.

"You're part of my family now," he told her, "and I take care of my family."

It wasn't as if Brand couldn't afford it. I didn't ask him to fully disclose how wealthy he was, but I knew he had more than he could possibly spend in a hundred lifetimes.

I phased Angela and me to Tara's front door. Tara hated for people to phase in on top of her, mostly because it scared her to death. I couldn't blame her. I could still remember how scared I was when I first saw Malcolm phase the night he and I first met. However, to be fair, he had been sent to kill me that night. The only reason he didn't follow through with his mission was because my blood seemed to hold a special quality that soothed his bloodlust. Now I couldn't imagine not having Malcolm in my life. He had quickly become one of my closest friends. Even though I knew he thought he was in love with me, I couldn't stop myself from caring for him deeply.

The house Tara now stayed in had been a barn on the property until Brand had it completely remodeled for Abby, but she had no use for the house anymore. Abby, and Malcolm's son, Sebastian, had fallen in love, and spent their days and nights together at Malcolm's house. At first, Brand and Malcolm were resistant to the idea of their children pledging themselves to one another. From what I was told, they were very much like real wolves, in the sense that, once they chose a mate, it was for life. At first, the mere concept of having to be in each other's lives for such a long time had disconcerted both Brand and Malcolm. I knew they only suffered through having to be around each other for my sake, but now they would be forever bound to one another through their children.

"Come on in!" Tara called after my knock.

As we entered the house, Tara was walking down the steps from the upper level, where the bedroom was. She wore a short, blood-red strapless dress and carried a pair of black high-heels in one hand. The only thing marring her ensemble was the large white bandage she had to wear over the wound on her neck.

"I feel sorely underdressed," I said, looking down at my jeans and plain white blouse.

"Don't worry, girl. Abby's got your dress." Tara leaned against the rail of the stairs to slip her shoes onto her feet. "I told you I would have everything handled for today, and that includes your outfit."

Tara walked to the couch in the living room and picked up a sheer black scarf, which she wrapped once around her neck, to hide the bandage.

Next, we phased to Malcolm's home. Malcolm promptly directed us to Abby and Sebastian's suite of rooms.

"They're so in love it makes me a bit nauseated at times," Malcolm confessed as we walked to the west wing of his house. "I thought it best if they had a private spot to paw at one another."

"Did you really just say 'paw'?" I asked him, amused he would use werewolf humor.

"Well, if you had to watch them all the time, you wouldn't fault me for my observation, dearest."

Abby was waiting for us in her bedroom. I was surprised to see she wasn't wearing a wig. She wore her natural white hair down, allowing her glittering mane a chance to shine.

"No wig today?" I asked her.

"Nope; I won't need it where we're going. I should fit right in, actually. At most, people will think I'm an entertainer of some sort."

"Ok, so is anyone going to tell me where we're going?" If it was a place where Abby's natural hair color wasn't conspicuous, I wasn't sure I wanted to go.

"No," the three of them said in unison.

"Girl, just chill your heels and let us pamper you," Tara said, directing me to sit down in the chair in front of Abby's vanity.

For the next hour, the girls curled my hair, gave me a manicure, a pedicure, and applied my makeup. Once perfectly coifed, they showed me what I would be wearing.

"You're kidding, right?" I said, looking at the hot-pink dress. "Where's the rest of it?"

"This is the last time you'll be free to flirt with any guy you want," Tara told me. "Do you really think we would put you in something normal? Now, just go put it on."

"But..." I began to protest.

"No buts!" Tara said, turning me in the direction of Abby's bathroom, and pushing me forward. "Just go in there and put it on, Lilly Rayne Nightingale."

It wasn't so much that the dress was extremely skimpy, but I couldn't remember ever showing so much of my legs in my life. The top hung from one shoulder, by way of a rhinestone-bejeweled strap. It draped down loosely to a snug miniskirt that made me wonder how I would be able to sit in it without flashing everyone who might be watching. I made a mental note to keep my legs crossed whenever I had to sit down.

When I stepped out of the bathroom, the girls seemed extremely pleased with themselves.

"Now put these on," Tara said, handing me a pair of rhinestone T-strap stilettos.

"Are you trying to kill me?" I whined.

Tara just waved her hand at me. "Stop complaining and just put them on. If worse comes to worst, you can always phase yourself somewhere safe."

I knew in that moment I loved Tarajinka Shovanda Jenkins very much. Only for her would I risk my life in a pair of heels so high.

"Are you girls ready?"

I looked up to the doorway of Abby's room and saw Malcolm leaning against it, casually watching me. He was dressed in a very well-tailored, black double-breasted suit, with his hair pulled back into a ponytail and wearing a fedora. I had never seen him with so many clothes on before. He usually wore only pants and button-down shirts opened to the waist, to show off his well-defined chest.

"Ready for what?" I asked. "And why are you dressed like Fred Astaire?"

"I'm escorting you to your first location," he told me, a lopsided grin on his face.

"We're ready," Tara said, grabbing her purse that lay beside me on the bed.

Malcolm strolled into the room and offered me his hand to help me stand. I instantly felt myself start to topple, but a pair of strong arms caught me. Malcolm held me close to him until I regained my balance.

"Be careful, dearest," Malcolm murmured.

When I met his eyes, I could see the mask Malcolm usually hid behind falter for a split second, showing me his true concern and love for me.

"Thanks," I said. "Stupid high-heels."

"They may be hard to walk in, but they do wonderful things for your legs," he teased, instantly bringing up the roguish personality I was more used to dealing with.

"Shall we go?" he suggested, holding out his arm for me to take.

When Malcolm phased us, I felt the heat of the place instantly. A crowd of people walked by us, as though we had been there all along, never consciously realizing we had materialized out of thin air.

When I looked up and down the street, I instantly knew where we were.

"Las Vegas?" I asked Tara.

"Yep, thought you needed a little Sin City before you swore off all other men forever."

Malcolm patted my hand, which was still lying on his arm. "Come, dearest; I've arranged something special just for you."

I won't lie. When I walked into the Rio Hotel and Casino on Malcolm's arm, it made me feel like I owned the joint, partly because that's just how Malcolm seemed to think about everything. He was the most confident and self-assured person I knew. Not to say Brand didn't brim with a self-confidence of his own, but Malcolm never tried to temper his with the same humbleness Brand did. Malcolm knew he was the most looked at and sought-after man in any room he entered and didn't try to shy away from it. In fact, he reveled in it.

We were escorted by one of the casino guards to the nightclub on the top floor.

"Are we seeing a show?" I asked, noticing billboards that had been covered up with black velvet material.

"Yeah," Tara said. "We asked them to hide everything so it wouldn't give it away before you saw it. I need to see your eyes pop out of your skull for myself."

"I must leave you ladies here at the door," Malcolm said. "Only women are allowed beyond this point."

"Thanks, Malcolm. I owe you one." Tara grabbed my arm and practically dragged me into the dark room beyond.

I could hear the whispers and giggles of women in the room, and could faintly see them seated in a line of chairs in front of a stage. A woman with a flashlight escorted us to a group of seats that were front and center of the stage. They were the best seats in the house for whatever it was we were there to see.

"How come Malcolm had to arrange a special showing?" I asked as what remained of the lights in the room were extinguished, and music with a rhythmic thump started to play.

"Just watch," Tara said. "Watch the stage, Lilly Rayne Nightingale, 'cause you've never seen anything like this before."

Five spotlights flashed on the stage, illuminating male figures in long, black trench coats. At first, the sight alarmed me, reminding me of the cloaked figures of the Watchers who gave into their bloodlust. When the men began to dance in unison to the beat of the music, my hand involuntarily flew to my mouth, and I indeed felt my eyes begin to bulge out of my skull. I heard Tara cackle with glee beside me.

Abby leaned in towards me and had to yell in my ear to be heard over the music.

"Welcome to the Las Vegas Chippendale show!"

I sat there for a while, at a complete loss for words, though I think I was the only one. The array of women in the room soon got up out of their seats to cheer and/or leer at the dancers performing in front of us. As the men began to tease the crowd by revealing one muscular shoulder after another, you would have thought the women around me had never seen the skin of a man before. The men suddenly turned around all at once to face us, and allowed the trench coats they were wearing to dramatically fall to the floor in unison.

Malcolm was the only man I'd ever seen who overtly displayed his rather large, well-toned muscles. But the five men standing in front of me proved humans could indeed have similar physiques. I felt flushed all of a sudden. Tara soon stood up, joining the raucous crowd around us, yelling to the men to take more of their clothes off. I seriously thought about hiding underneath my chair until the show was over, but the girls wouldn't let me. Tara and Abby soon pulled me up to stand with them as they began to dance to the music.

I'm not sure how many dance routines followed, but, by the middle of the show, I'd joined in on the frivolity of it all and found myself enjoying the role reversal. Usually people associate striptease shows as being men watching women. I found it interesting that women could turn such an event into a party without even having to see the men strip down past their underwear. The men came out dressed in a plethora of costumes for each routine. Once they were dressed as firefighters, once as bikers, once as clones of Tom Cruise from the underwear dancing scene in *Risky Business* and once as hip-hop dancers. Near the end, the boys were dressed up as cowboys and seemed to know exactly where I was in the crowd, as though they had been tipped off that it was my bachelorette party. Before I knew it, they had me up on stage, wrapping a white rope around me like they were lassoing me for safekeeping. As the song ended, they took the rope off me and asked that I sit in a chair directly in the middle of the stage. I didn't have much choice. It was either sit or stumble my way off stage in the dark, an act I felt sure would lead to my untimely demise at the hands of my own clumsiness.

A song I recognized began to play, and a single spotlight illuminated the solitary male figure on the stage. I felt, more than heard, my sharp intake of breath.

As I hear a woman's husky voice sing the lyrics to the song "You Can Leave Your Hat On", the familiar muscle-bound figure in front of me began taking off the suggested clothing.

It was then I realized I should have known something was suspicious when Malcolm showed up with so many clothes on to bring us to Las Vegas.

As he performed his striptease in front of his enamored female audience, he would turn to face me, as if making sure I was watching every undulation of his body. Malcolm's striptease was in a completely different league from that of the Chippendale dancers. He moved each of his muscles with confidence, knowing, without a shadow of a doubt, that every woman in the room desired him. His fluid movements left no doubt about his prowess in the bedroom, yet somehow he maintained his dignity even when he stood in only a pair of black nylon underwear while gyrating his hips in front of me in a completely sexual way.

Like every other female in the room, I couldn't take my eyes off Malcolm. However, unlike every other female in the room, I knew the reason wasn't because of the overpowering pheromone all Watchers produce to attract the females of the human species. Of anyone in the room, I knew the real Malcolm best, and I knew exactly what he was trying to do: seduce me.

I felt my body begin to quiver slightly, of its own accord. Breathing became harder as Malcolm continued to stare into my eyes, as if daring me to look away from him.

By the end of the song, as the woman crooned her last words to the song, Malcolm straddled my thighs and placed his fedora on my head.

He leaned down and whispered in my ear, "I haven't forgotten. You still owe me a day alone with you, Lilly."

The lights went out, plunging us into complete darkness, and I felt him place a gentle, wet kiss on the side of my neck.

Then he was gone.

CHAPTER 2.

When the lights came back on in the room, the girls came up on stage to help me down.

"I can't believe that big lug did that," Tara said, shaking her head. "I swear to God, Lilly Rayne, I didn't know he was planning to do that to you. You know if I had, I wouldn't have let him."

"Can I suggest," Abby said, "that we not tell my father about Malcolm's… demonstration? Their relationship isn't the strongest as it is. Plus, I really don't want to have to tell my boyfriend that his father just got me completely flustered in a good way."

Angela was waving a hand in front of her face, like she was trying to cool herself down. "I agree; that information should remain secret between the four of us."

"I'm not going to lie to Brand," I quickly said.

"Well, you don't have to lie exactly," Abby said. "Just don't offer the information freely; surely you're allowed to keep some secrets to yourself."

"I have to say I agree with Abby on this one." Tara nodded. "We don't need to add gas to an already-burning fire. However, I can't say I minded seeing the big boy strut his stuff up there. And, boy howdy, do I mean *big*."

Tara's admission soon had us all remembering the one stand-out feature of Malcolm's performance. I think Angela was the first to start giggling, which soon became contagious.

After that, we all decided to go eat at the Bellagio Hotel. Of course, they had a buffet big enough for a king, and Tara tore into it. I never understood how such a small person could eat so much food and not weigh fifty more pounds afterwards. I stuck to the crab legs and shrimp for the most part, only allowing myself a sweet treat at the end. After all, I did have to fit into a couture wedding dress in less than a week.

As I was battling with myself on whether I wanted the strawberry shortcake or the fruit tart, I heard a familiar voice say, "I would go with the fruit tart myself; sweet and tangy, just like me."

I turned to face a fully-clothed Malcolm. He only wore the slim-fitting tailored black pants and white shirt open at the chest, but that was definitely more than the last time I saw him.

"What were you thinking?" I asked, pulling him off to the side before the other girls could see him. "Have you completely lost your mind? Brand will go ballistic when he hears about what you did."

Malcolm smiled. "I'm not really concerned about what he thinks. You should know that by now, dearest. I would, however, love to know what you thought about it, or do I even have to ask from the way you were breathing at the end?"

I took a deep breath and tried to wipe the picture of a virtually nude Malcolm straddling my lap out of my mind.

"You know you're gorgeous," I told him. "And I'm still half-human. It was a natural reaction."

Malcolm took one of my hands into his and twined our fingers together intimately.

"I would be more than happy to give you a private show on our day together," he said softly, his voice filled with suggestive undertones.

I closed my eyes, no longer able to look at the promise of sensual delights in his gaze and whispered, "Stop."

"But do you really want me to?" He pressed his body in closer to mine.

"I need you to," I sighed, opening my eyes and looking into his handsome face. His jet-black hair fell like a curtain, shielding us from those around us. He bent his head down even closer to mine.

"Why deny yourself the pleasure you know I could give you, dearest? You know how much I care for you. I would make it a moment you would never forget. Even you can't deny you have feelings for me."

"Malcolm, please," I begged.

"Lilly," he murmured, saying my name as he placed a gentle finger under my chin to tilt my face up, forcing me to look at the desire he held for me in his eyes.

He began to lower his lips to mine.

I stepped away, trembling. I stared at him for the space of a second and quickly turned my back to him, no longer able to stand looking at the desperate longing in his eyes.

When I got back to the table, I told Tara I needed to go to the bathroom. As is the unspoken rule among females, Tara stood to join me. Once we reached the bathroom, I pulled her into the same stall as me.

"What's going on?" Tara asked. "Are you sick?"

"Tara, I almost let Malcolm kiss me," I confessed, feeling as though I might faint.

"When?"

"Just now." I went on to explain the scene.

"That man will not give up," Tara said, shaking her head. "Listen, you're only human, Lilly Rayne Nightingale. Hell, I'm not sure I wouldn't drag that man into my bed after the show he put on in front of you. And I know you love him in your way, for your own reasons. But, girl, you're *in love* with Brand. Of that I have no doubt in my mind, or I wouldn't let you marry the man."

"But why did I almost let it happen?"

"I can't answer that for you," Tara said. "But don't start doubting your love for Brand. He's the right man for you. Malcolm's just a hormonal accident waiting to happen. My advice is to stay as far away from that man as you can for a day or two."

"But what if I'm not able to do that? The night of the Halloween dance I promised him I would spend one day alone with him before I married Brand."

"What the hell for?" Tara almost shouted.

"I accused him of something he didn't do, and he said if I spent a day with him before I was married, he would forgive me for it."

"Can't you get out of it?"

"I promised him, Tara."

"And you don't break a promise," Tara sighed, knowing me all too well. "Well, girl, the only other advice I can give you is take a cold shower before you go off with him, because he's not going to make things easy for you. I can tell you that right now. Now that he knows he can have that effect on you, he won't give up so easily next time."

"Next time?" I asked in alarm.

"Girl, you know there'll be a next time. That's just a fact of life. You just need to figure out what you're going to do when it happens."

Soon after, I was instructed to phase us back to Tara's house. When we arrived, Will and Malik were just stepping out the front door, with what appeared to be empty cardboard boxes in their hands.

"Are y'all done?" Tara asked, walking up to Malik and giving him a kiss on the cheek, so naturally it almost didn't register in my mind. It was the first time I ever saw her do such a thing with him.

"Everything is as you instructed," Malik said, beaming down at her, as if she was the most important person in the world.

When we brought Tara home to recover from her injuries, Malik had been instrumental in her care. Since he was a fairy, his knowledge of herbal remedies helped her heal faster than she would have naturally. He even found a poultice which would diminish the scar from her wound to be almost unnoticeable in time. I would always see it though. I would never be able to forget how close I came to losing my best friend.

"Don't blame me for the decorations," Will said to me, seeming to want complete absolution for the décor. "I just did what I was told."

"See you later?" I heard Tara say to Malik.

"Just call me when you're done, and I'll be right over," he answered before giving her a chaste kiss on the lips.

I raised an eyebrow at the pair, not realizing their relationship had progressed so far in such a short amount of time.

When Malik saw me staring at them, he said, "I promise, Lilly. She made the first move, not me."

Tara slapped Malik playfully on the arm. "Why did you have to go and tell her that? Now I can't pretend it was all your idea."

"Because I made a promise to Lilly that you would have to make the first move," Malik said, putting the box down and bringing a playfully-reluctant Tara into his arms, "and I always keep my promises."

"Well, I'll forgive you this time," Tara put her arms around Malik's neck, "but just remember who butters your bread."

"I didn't need to hear that," I said, shaking my head in dismay.

Tara giggled before giving Malik a full-on kiss in front of God and everyone standing around her. It was one of the few times I'd seen Tara so unabashedly happy.

While Tara was otherwise engaged, I walked over to Will as he was putting his cardboard box in the trunk of his car.

"So, do you have an answer for me yet?" I asked him. "The wedding is only a week away."

Will looked up at me. "I don't think I can give you away at the wedding, Lilly. I want to make you happy, but that's the only reason I would be doing it."

"I wish you *could* be happy for me."

Will sighed. "I wish I could, too," he said, closing the trunk and leaning against it. "But I still think it should be me and you getting married, not you and Brand."

"Will…" I began to protest before he held up a hand, as if asking me to hear him out.

"It's not just because I've known you pretty much all your life," Will said. "But the fact is I could provide you with a more normal life than Brand can. I can grow old with you, Lilly. I can give you children."

"What do you mean? I thought you said your kind couldn't have children with humans."

"Lillith was able to give birth to children from my kind. If you're her descendent, then that means you should be able to also. Don't you see how much more sense it makes if you and I are together? You loved me once not that long ago, Lilly. I think you could learn to love me like that again if you gave us half a chance. I would treasure you just as much as Brand. Better probably, because I know all of you."

"What is it with you and Malcolm today?" I muttered.

"Malcolm just wants to get in your pants," Will stated hotly. "I want to see you have a full and happy life. Our motives are completely different."

I looked down at the ground, no longer able to meet Will's gaze. His earnest expression just wasn't something I could handle at that moment.

"Are you going to at least come to the wedding?" I asked.

"I can't make any promises. I haven't decided if I'm going or not."

"I want you there," I said, looking back up at him. "You know how little family I have."

"I know, Lilly. All I can promise is that I'll try, even though I think you're making a mistake."

As I watched Will and Malik pull away from Tara's house in Will's Honda Accord, I had to wonder if what he said was true. Could he and I have children of our own? I *was* Lillith's only remaining descendant. If she could bear children from the rebellion angels, then the chances I could too were very good. At one time in my life, I would have wanted nothing less for myself, but, since I met Brand, he was the only one I could see building a future with.

After the boys left, the girls made me close my eyes as they escorted me into Tara's house.

"Surprise!" they yelled in unison.

"You can open your eyes now," Tara told me.

I took a deep breath before opening my eyes, fearing what I might see. I was mildly surprised to see what looked like any normal party. The room was decorated with colorful balloons and streamers; a chocolate heart-shaped cake with 'Lilly –n- Brand' piped on it in red icing was laid out on the coffee table, as well as a couple of presents.

"I don't understand," I said, looking around at things, expecting something to jump out at me at any moment. "What was Will apologizing for?"

"Uh, take a closer look at the balloons, love," Abby suggested coyly.

I walked over to a cluster of them tied to the arm of a chair in the living room. Almost every color of the rainbow seemed to be represented. I thought the balloons seemed a bit more transparent than normal ones, but was still clueless as to what I was supposed to be seeing.

"Ok, you girls have completely lost me," I confessed.

Tara threw something small at me, and I caught it. When I looked down at what was wrapped in the clear cellophane, I felt my cheeks grow warm. It was a red condom. I immediately let go of the bunch of balloons in my hand.

The girls began to giggle uncontrollably at my reaction.

"Just thought you might need a reminder," Tara said, her arms crossed over her chest. "I know what can happen if you guys have an accident, and I'm not about to lose you like that."

"None of us want to lose you like Angela and I lost our mothers," Abby said, sobering up from her giggles

"You taking those birth control pills the doctor gave you?" Tara asked, like a mother hen.

"Yes, I'm taking the pills," I told them all, "and Brand will be careful."

I didn't think I should mention I had already made Brand promise we wouldn't use a condom the first time we made love. I knew it wasn't something he wanted to do, but I also knew he would do anything to make my first time as memorable as possible. I would be on birth control, and I felt sure that would be enough to protect me.

After we ate a piece of the red velvet heart cake Tara had made, the girls gave me their gifts.

Angela and Abby gave me a large box of rainbow-colored condoms that I thanked them for. I tried not to blush too much as I set it aside.

"This one is from me and your mom," Tara said, handing me a pink-wrapped package.

"You picked it out together?" I asked, sure I had misunderstood.

"Yep. Your mom's been a lot better lately. I guess all this wedding business has made her easier to get along with."

After peeling away the pink wrapping paper from the white box, I found an ivory-colored tulle and satin baby doll negligee inside. Only the underwire bra and little panties were silk, the rest was made out of the transparent tulle.

"Oh yeah, Dad will like that, love," Abby said with a knowing nod.

I quickly put the lingerie back in the box. It felt odd to have Brand's daughter so involved in my future sex life with her father. Apparently, she sensed my discomfort.

"Don't feel like you have to hide it, Lilly," Abby said. "I know my dad hasn't been with anyone else since my mom. If you ask me, it's about damn time he was. I'm just glad it's with someone who makes him so happy."

"I love your father with everything that I am," I told her, suddenly finding the events of the day slip away from me. All I wanted to do now was go home to Brand and feel his warmth.

After taking Abby back home, I phased Angela back to Brand's house, and was pleasantly surprised to find Allan still present, watching a football game on the big screen TV over the fireplace, with Brand.

"Have you been here all day, Dad?" Angela asked, not trying to hide the complete astonishment she felt from her voice.

"Yes. Brand was showing me American football," Allan said, having a hard time taking his eyes off the game to answer his daughter. "I find it quite stimulating in its brutality."

Brand came to me and took my packages out of my arms. As soon as he turned back around to me, I pulled him closer.

"I missed you today." I hugged him close, reveling in the warmth of his body, not wanting to let him go.

"We should be getting back home, Dad," Angela said discreetly.

I reluctantly pulled away from Brand so I could say goodbye to our guests, secretly wishing they would hurry up and go already.

Once Allan and Angela phased back home, I phased Brand and me to his bed.

"What's gotten into you?" he asked, smiling at my aggressive behavior.

"Can't a woman want some alone time with her fiancé?" I kissed his neck, running my hands down over his chest.

Brand rolled me over onto my back, plundering my mouth with his tongue, infusing my senses with the scent of him.

"I like this dress," he murmured against my lips, sliding his hand up my thigh to just above the hem of the skirt and just below where I really wanted his hand to be.

I moaned in aggravation. "Could we just pretend this is our wedding night?"

Brand laughed against my throat as he nibbled his way across my bared shoulder.

"We're almost there," he reminded, slowly pulling his hand away from my thigh. His movement did little to lessen the torturous pleasure of having him so close, yet so far away.

If I'd had my way, we would have made love right then and there. But I made a promise to Brand that we wouldn't make love until after we were married. It was important to him that we do things right and not tempt God to withdraw His faith in us to follow the right path. Mentally, I understood his desire not to go against his father again, but physically all I wanted to do was show the man of my dreams just how much he meant to me in every way possible.

"Once we're married, you're going to have a hard time getting out of this bed," I warned him.

Brand pulled away from me with a pleased smile on his face. "I'm definitely ok with that."

"You'd better be," I said, rolling Brand over onto his back and straddling his hips. "I don't plan to give you any other choice."

CHAPTER 3.

After taking what had become a routine cold shower, I went downstairs to find Brand speaking with Malcolm in the living room.

Brand smiled at me with a hint of amusement on his face. He thought my habit of taking a cold shower after our intimate time together was cute. I just found them an irritating necessity. Otherwise, I wouldn't be able to keep my promise to him to wait until after we were married.

"Malcolm has an idea I think we should follow up on," Brand told me as I came to stand by the pair.

I kept my eyes averted from Malcolm, not wanting to face him just yet. Our last meeting had left me shaken in my resolve to keep him at arm's length. I wasn't sure how Malcolm was feeling about how we left things, but I could sense his eyes on me as he watched my every move even more closely than usual.

"What is it?" I asked Brand.

"I may have thought of a way for you to take control away from Lucifer, dearest," Malcolm answered instead, forcing me to look his way, since staring at Brand while he talked to me would look suspicious.

"How?" I asked him, grabbing hold of Brand's hand beside me, needing to feel his touch.

"King Solomon's ring."

"That was the king who said he would cut the baby in half when two women claimed they were its mother, right?"

"Yes, that's the one. He was given a ring that gave him the power to control demons, or the rebellion angels if you prefer, and the jinn. If we can find that ring, it may give you power over Lucifer. Since we know he plans to use you in whatever scheme he has cooked up, you may be able to use the ring to at least make sure he can't possess you."

"Where is the ring?" I asked.

"That's the problem," Brand answered. "We don't know, but I might be able to find the person who does."

"Samyaza?" Malcolm asked Brand. "Do you think he will talk to us?"

"I doubt he will talk to you, Malcolm, but I might be able to gain an audience with him."

"Who is Samyaza?" I asked.

"He was the leader of the Watcher angels when we were first sent here to Earth," Brand said. "If any of our kind knows where the ring is, he might."

"If he was your leader, why wouldn't he talk to you?"

"After our fall, he stayed distant from the rest of us. I think he still feels like he led us all astray and that's why we have the lives we do. He was close to one Watcher in particular, though, his second-in-command. I know where he lives, and can ask him to help us locate Samyaza."

"You mean Isaiah?" Malcolm asked. "I haven't seen him in ages either."

"He lives here in America. I saw him not so long ago. I think he probably still lives in the same place. Would you mind staying with Lilly for a little while, Malcolm? I should probably go speak with Isaiah as soon as possible. If he doesn't know where Samyaza is, he might be able to track him down for us."

"I don't need a babysitter," I protested, not wanting to be alone with Malcolm so soon after our last encounter.

"I don't mind, dearest," Malcolm said, a slow suggestive smile spreading his lips.

"I won't be long," Brand leaned down and gave me a kiss, "and I would feel better if you weren't alone."

Reluctantly, I nodded my head. "All right; if it will make you feel better."

"Keep her safe," Brand told Malcolm, as if his life depended on it.

"I will keep her close to me at all times," Malcolm promised.

Brand phased to points unknown, and I turned my back to Malcolm and headed to the kitchen.

"Would you like something to drink?" I asked him, opening the refrigerator to find something for myself.

"Would the sweet nectar of your lips count?"

God. And I thought only Brand could come up with those types of lines. When they came from Brand, they were sweet with sincerity. Coming from Malcolm, they were drenched in innuendo.

"No, that does not count," I answered. "We have water and ginger ale. Pick your poison."

I felt, more than heard, Malcolm come stand behind me. He leaned his head down over my shoulder, making a pretense to look in the refrigerator.

"Well, now, let's see," he said, his breath tickling my ear, he was so close. "I guess I'll take a bottle of water then."

Not waiting for me to grab one for him, he reached under the arm I was using to prop the fridge door open, and slid his arm against my side as he pulled the bottle out for himself.

I closed the door, not feeling like drinking anything now. I walked to the other side of the large kitchen island, trying to put as much of a barrier between us as I could.

"So, do you really think this ring will help us stop Lucifer?" I asked, hoping to distract Malcolm from his mission of seducing me.

"I hope so," he said, watching my retreat with amused eyes. "Why are you running away from me, dearest?"

"You know perfectly well why," I said, feeling my temper start to flare.

"I've never tried to hide my feelings for you," he said. "You've always known that I want you. Why does it make you feel uncomfortable now?"

I looked down at the granite counter in front of me, unable to meet Malcolm's gaze.

"I don't know," I admitted.

"I think it's because you're starting to feel the connection between us that I've felt all along. You're starting to have feelings beyond friendship for me, aren't you?"

I shook my head, but couldn't quite make myself say the word 'no'.

"Do you remember asking me if what I felt for you was love?"

I looked up at him, and saw the mask he usually wore fall for the second time that day.

"Yes, I remember," I said.

"I do love you, Lilly; I have since the night we first met, and always will."

"Why are you telling me this now?" I whispered.

"Because I think you have a right to know where I stand before you marry Brand. If you love me in the slightest bit, I have to know. I'll fight for you if I have a chance of winning your heart for myself."

I didn't know what to say. The Malcolm standing in front of me wasn't the Malcolm I was used to dealing with. He usually hid behind his sarcasm and wit, but now he stood before me filled with raw emotion, letting me see how he truly felt about me.

"Am I interrupting something?"

I turned to see Brand, in the same spot in the living room he had just phased from a few minutes earlier.

"Did you find him?" I asked, choosing to ignore his question, not knowing how much of the conversation he had heard.

"Isaiah says he'll help us. He doesn't know where Samyaza is exactly, but he seems to think he can track him down within a couple of days."

"Let me know when you hear something," Malcolm said, before phasing without saying goodbye.

"What happened while I was gone?" Brand asked, coming to stand in front of me.

I wrapped my arms around his waist and laid my head on his chest.

"Just hold me," I begged, feeling tears trail down my cheeks, but not knowing exactly what I was crying about.

Once I regained some semblance of calm, Brand sat me down on the couch. He asked me to tell him everything and I did. Whether it was right or wrong for him to know what had transpired that day, I didn't care. I needed him to help me sort through my feelings because I felt confused by them. If our marriage was going to have any chance at all, I felt we had to be completely honest with one another, about everything. It was hard to admit how attracted I was to Malcolm, but it seemed like a moment of embarrassment was worth gaining Brand's insight into what might be causing it.

"You've always cared about him, against my better judgment," Brand added, remaining much calmer than I expected he would, after everything I just told him. "He means something to you."

"But I don't think it's love," I said, "at least not the type of love I feel for you."

"There are all different types of love. You just need to figure out which one you feel for him."

I leaned in to Brand, hugging him around the waist and resting my head against his shoulder.

"Why aren't you mad?" I asked. "I thought you might go over to his house again, like you did the time he saw me naked in the shower."

"That was disrespectful of him to do."

"And doing a striptease in front of me isn't?"

"That was more an act of desperation."

I was surprised to hear the pity in Brand's voice. I never thought he would feel such an emotion for Malcolm.

"I think he wants to make you second-guess your decision to marry me, and the easiest way he can do that is by making you feel attracted to him. I suppose I am a little upset with him for playing on your emotions and hormones, but I can't say I wouldn't have done the same thing if our roles were reversed."

"Hmm," I said hugging him tighter, "would you have done a striptease for me?"

I would have paid good money to see that.

Brand laughed. "I'm not sure I could have kept a straight face through it all, but if I thought that was the only way I could gain your attention, I might."

"I promised Malcolm the night of the Halloween dance that I would spend one day alone with him before you and I married."

"I think that's a good idea."

I looked up at Brand, completely shocked by his statement. "Why?"

"Because I think you need to prove to him, and yourself, that you can't be anything but friends. Whether I like it or not, he is a good friend to you, and he treats Abby like she's part of his family now. We might not like each other much, but we will have to put up with one another for a very long time. The sooner you deal with whatever it is he's brought to the surface inside you, the better off we'll all be."

"How are you so rational about all this?"

"I love you. I know we are meant to be together, and I don't think Malcolm has a chance in hell of ever changing your feelings for me. However, I want you to be as sure about your feelings for me as I am. I want you to stand at that altar with me, completely certain that you're making the right decision."

"I love you," I said, feeling the love I held for the man in my arms with all of my heart.

"I know," he replied, gently bringing my face up to his with a warm hand, pressing his lips against mine with a tenderness only someone who truly loves you can show.

CHAPTER 4.

The next day was Sunday. Early that morning, I received a phone call from Utha Mae.

"Lilly, honey, I wanted to invite you and Brand over to my house for supper tonight."

"Sure, Utha Mae. What time?"

"Let's say six, baby."

"Will it just be us three?"

"No, I invited your mom and her new boyfriend too."

I paused, trying to think if my mother had mentioned a new boyfriend.

"Who is he?" I asked.

"His name is Lucas Hunter. He's a doctor of some sort."

"Did you say Lucas Hunter?" I asked, sitting up straighter.

"Yes, baby. Do you know him?"

"Is he good-looking, with wavy blond hair?"

"That's him. Has your mother already introduced you to him? I was under the impression she hadn't yet."

"I met him in a jewelry store here in Lakewood, before Halloween. When did she start dating him?"

"Around that time, now that I think of it; what a small world it is."

A small world, indeed; I knew then, for a fact, my first meeting with Lucas Hunter hadn't been by chance.

"I hate to talk ill about someone," Utha Mae said hesitantly, "but that man just doesn't seem right to me. That was one reason I wanted you and Brand to come meet him. Maybe I'm just an old woman who imagines things, but there's just something wrong with the man that I can't quite put my finger on. Your mom is head over heels in love with him, though; I've never seen her so happy."

And here I thought it was the wedding which was making my mother happier lately. I should have known a man figured into the equation somewhere.

"Mind if we bring Tara and Will with us tonight?"

"I've already called them, baby. They'll all be here. I told Tara to bring her new man along too. Malik, right?"

"Yes, ma'am, that's him. You'll like him, Utha Mae; he's good for Tara."

"Well, that's good to know." I could hear the relief in Utha Mae's voice at my reassurance about Malik. "I'll see you tonight, baby. Give Brand my love."

After I got off the phone, I told Brand what I had just learned.

"Good; now we'll be able to find out who this Lucas Hunter really is."

"What if he's dangerous?" I asked, now filled with worry. "How will I get my mom away from him?"

Brand sighed. "I don't know, Lilly. Let's meet him first; then we can decide what needs to be done."

"Utha Mae doesn't like him," I said. "She's usually spot-on with her judgment of people."

"But when you met him, you felt good in his presence, right? You didn't feel any danger."

"Yes, I know, but I also knew there was something not quite right about him too."

"Let's not worry just yet. We'll meet him and go from there; no need to stress over something that might not mean anything in the long-run."

Malik drove us in his Lexus RX hybrid to Dalton, my hometown. Will followed in his Honda Accord.

"I hope your grandma likes me," Malik said, nervously tapping his steering wheel with his thumbs.

"She's gonna love you," Tara reassured him.

"How do you know that?" Malik asked.

"'Cause you make me happy."

I watched Tara smile at Malik, and couldn't help but smile myself. I knew, then, that Tara's heart had finally been captured by a man.

When we reached the trailer park Utha Mae and my mom lived in, I immediately noticed the brand new black Mercedes Benz parked in front of my mom's place.

Malik knocked on Utha Mae's door, holding a pot of his homemade chicken and dumplings. I knew his desperation to make a good first impression had led him into dangerous territory. I almost wished he had contacted me first before making the dish. I knew Utha Mae set a high standard with her own recipe for dumplings, and hoped she didn't squash Malik's pride into dust if she didn't like his version. Even though I had tasted his before, I wasn't sure if Utha Mae would appreciate someone else butting into her culinary niche.

When Utha Mae opened the door, she smiled.

"Come in, come in," she said, "don't stand out there like strangers."

After we all walked in, Tara said, "Grandma, I'd like you to meet Malik. Malik, this is my grandma, Utha Mae."

Malik set his pot of dumplings on the kitchen island and held out his hand for Utha Mae to shake.

"It's a pleasure to meet you, Mrs. Jenkins. Tara and Lilly have told me a lot about you."

"Nice to meet you, too, hon, but you have to call me Utha Mae like everyone else does. I don't stand for too much formality in my own home."

"Yes, ma'am."

Utha Mae eyed Malik's pot with open curiosity. "And just what did you bring in that pot, hon?"

"Chicken and dumplings, ma'am; I hope you like them."

"Well," Utha Mae's eyebrows shot up in surprise, "I'll let you know after I taste them."

There was a knock at the door. Will was the closest one standing to it, so he turned to open it. I saw Will's shoulders tense all of a sudden, as if he had just received a blow to the gut. Brand seemed to notice the same thing, so we watched the door to see what had caused the change in Will's stance.

"We're not late, are we?" I heard my mother ask before she stepped inside.

I almost passed out when I saw what my mother was wearing: a well-tailored white shirt, blue blazer, slacks, and penny loafers. Her hair was completely straight and styled in a layered bob, which made her look age-appropriate. The ensemble was a far cry from the usual go-go dancer mini-dresses she normally wore. I assumed that was what made Will's body tense up, but I soon felt Brand's body stiffen when my mother's new boyfriend walked into the trailer behind her.

"If we are, I take all the blame," Lucas Hunter said to us all. "I wanted to show Cora pictures of the new house I just bought, and completely lost track of time."

Brand discreetly took my hand, tightly holding it. Will backed away from the door and came to stand on the other side of me. I wanted to ask what was wrong, since they both took up a protective stance around me, but knew such a question would draw the unwanted attention of my mom and Utha Mae.

Both Brand and Will kept their eyes locked on Lucas's every movement.

Lucas's eyes found me easily, and he smiled at me, as though we were old friends.

"Haven't we met before?" he asked me.

"Yes," I answered, feeling Brand squeeze my hand even tighter, as if warning me not to say too much. "We met at Clive Jewelers in Lakewood, right before Halloween."

Lucas held his index finger in the air. "Ahh, that's right, I remember now." His eyes shifted to Brand. "Is this the lucky man you're supposed to be marrying?"

Brand held out his hand to Lucas. "Brand Cole."

"Lucas Hunter," he said, shaking Brand's hand. "Glad to finally meet you, Brand. Cora's told me a lot about you."

"All good, of course," my mother said, wrapping a possessive arm around one of Lucas's.

"I heard you were a doctor," Brand said, his voice not betraying the strain I knew he actually felt.

"Pediatric oncologist," Lucas answered. "Though, I've been taking a break from my practice the last couple of weeks." Lucas looked down at my mom, like he only had eyes for her. "Cora and I have been spending the time getting to know one another better."

And then something happened I never thought I would see in my lifetime. My mother blushed.

"Well, since everybody knows everybody now," Utha Mae said, "let's sit down and eat. Malik, honey, you can use my stove if you need to heat up your dumplings."

Brand turned into me and whispered, "Make up an excuse for us to leave for a minute."

I quickly wracked my brain to think of something.

"Mom, would you mind if I grabbed my baby book from your place? Brand wanted to see some pictures of me when I was younger."

"Sure, sweetie; the albums are still on the bookcase in your room."

Brand and I stepped out of Utha Mae's trailer and headed to my mom's trailer right next door. Once we were inside, Brand sat down heavily on the couch in the living room, putting his head in his hands, like he had a headache.

"Who is he?" I asked. "Why did you and Will act like he might eat me alive in there?"

Brand looked up at me. I could see the shock on his face and worry in his eyes.

"That's Lucifer."

All I could hear after that was my own ragged breathing. Brand came to me just as I lost feeling in my legs. He sat me down on the couch beside him and held me tight.

"He won't do anything to you tonight. We still have over a month," Brand said. "We'll find a way to stop him, Lilly."

I couldn't reply. I was having a hard enough time just trying to remember to bring oxygen into my lungs. I'm not sure why I was so surprised. I knew this day would come. I knew I would have to face him eventually, but to have him take on the guise of my mother's new boyfriend was something I hadn't prepared myself for.

"What are we going to do?" I asked, not seeing how I could possibly stay in the same room as him now, knowing who he actually was.

"We need to stay strong and face him together. Maybe this is what we've needed to happen. He may slip up and reveal something to us unintentionally."

"He wouldn't be that stupid, would he?"

"Lucifer's vanity has always gotten in his way. He may end up bragging about something during supper that will give us the hint we need to figure out what he wants with you."

I focused on Brand's plan. If I let myself think about Lucifer too much, I knew I might faint from shock. I couldn't let him see me weak. I wouldn't let Lucifer think I was going to let him win without a fight. I had too much to live for, and I wasn't about to let him take it all away from me.

I did go into my room to fetch one of my baby albums, just to make our excuse to leave truthful. When we returned to Utha Mae's trailer, everyone was already sitting around her table, ladling food on to their plates.

Lucas a.k.a. Lucifer stood from his chair at the table when I entered, and smiled at me. I knew I should feel uncomfortable by his presence, but I could sense an inner light within him that I just couldn't ignore. I knew he was evil incarnate, but, for some reason, it didn't seem that way to me. It was just like when he touched me at the jewelry store. I felt comfortable in his presence, as if he was an old friend. I chalked it up to being part of his power. He *was* the great deceiver, after all.

All throughout the meal, I couldn't help but notice how happy my mother was. She looked at Lucifer in a way I had never seen her look at a man before. How was I going to get her away from Lucifer, without telling her the complete truth? Would she believe me even if I told her? I highly doubted it. She was completely under his spell, and I couldn't think of a thing to say to bring her back to reality.

"Sweetie," my mom said to me, "did you happen to bring those silk purses back with you?"

"Yes; they're in Malik's vehicle. We filled them all."

"Oh, yes," Lucifer said knowingly. "You two are supposed to be married next Saturday, right?"

"Yes," I answered, "we are."

"Your mother invited me to come, but I'm afraid I won't be able to make it. I have a symposium that weekend in Chicago. I'm sorry I'll miss it. I'm sure you'll make a beautiful bride, Lilly."

"I'll miss you while you're away," my mother said, putting one of her hands on Lucifer's arm. "I wish you didn't have to go."

"I won't be gone long," he reassured, patting her hand. "I'll be back before you have a chance to miss me too much."

"So, have you decided who will give you away at the wedding, baby?" Utha Mae asked me.

I glanced at Will but answered, "I'll probably just give myself away."

"Well, why not have Will stand in for your father?" Utha Mae suggested. "He's about the closest thing you have to a brother."

I didn't know what to say. I didn't want Utha Mae to think badly of Will. He simply couldn't bring himself to walk me down the aisle to someone he didn't think I should be marrying.

"Don't you think that's a good idea, Will?" Utha Mae asked.

All eyes focused on Will as he rolled a dumpling on his plate over and over, avoiding direct eye contact with Utha Mae. He knew as well as I did that if he looked at her directly he would end up doing whatever she told him to. It was like in *Star Wars* when the Jedi used their mind tricks to make you do what they wanted with just a few coercive words. Utha Mae didn't have to use tricks, though; just guilt.

"I can't do that, Utha Mae," he finally said.

"Why not, baby?"

"Because," Will sighed, "I'm still in love with Lilly. Why would I willingly give her away to someone else?"

The rattle of dinnerware on dishes ceased, and an uneasy silence permeated the room.

My mother cleared her throat. "Well, if Lilly's father hadn't abandoned us, you wouldn't have been placed in such an awkward position, Will. You can't help the way you feel. I think we all understand that."

"Malik," Utha Mae turned her attention to my fairy godfather, "I swear I've never tasted chicken and dumplings as good as yours. You'll have to give me your recipe."

"Oh," Malik smiled shyly, knowing Utha Mae had just given him the highest of praises, "I'll definitely do that. I'll bring you a copy the next time I see you."

I was thankful for Utha Mae's quick change of subject. She and Malik talked for the rest of the meal about his variations on classic dishes Utha Mae had made all her life. I kept my eyes on my plate, but I felt Brand place a comforting hand on my thigh underneath the table. When I looked over at him, he smiled and winked at me, making me feel more at ease. I chanced a glance in Will's direction, and immediately regretted it.

He was staring at me with intense longing. I knew he wanted nothing more than to be where Brand was right now. If he could have possessed Brand like he could any human body, I felt sure he would have. I quickly looked away and tried to concentrate on Malik and Utha Mae's conversation.

Will's eyes weren't the only ones staring holes into me, though. I felt Lucifer's eyes on me, and couldn't prevent myself from glancing in his direction. His expression was indecipherable, but I got the distinct impression he found Will's confession amusing. It was he, after all, who had placed Will in charge of keeping me safe all these years. Now that he knew for sure Will loved me, he had to wonder how divided Will's loyalties were. Since I was marrying someone Will didn't approve of, perhaps Lucifer felt Will was back on his side. I had no way of knowing for sure if he was right.

While I was helping to clear the table, Lucifer asked, "Lilly, could I speak with you privately for a moment? I have something I would like to ask you."

Both Brand and Will quickly set their dishes down, turning their full attention to Lucifer.

"Why?" I asked. It seemed a logical question. I wasn't supposed to know this Lucas Hunter guise Lucifer was wearing very well. Why would he want to have a private moment with me?

"I have something I wish to ask you, but it's something I would like to keep as a surprise for Cora."

"Go ahead, baby," Utha Mae said. "We've got the dishes."

Feeling like a lamb led to slaughter, I couldn't think of a polite or non-suspicious way to refuse Lucifer's request. Besides, my mother looked beside herself with pent-up anticipation. I followed Lucifer out the door, but saw both Will and Brand take up positions at different windows to keep watch over me.

Once outside, Lucifer leaned his back against the wood railing of Utha Mae's front porch, and faced me. I stood close to the door, just in case I felt a need to make a hasty retreat.

"I assume you know who I am now," he said to me.

"Yes," I answered. "I know."

Lucifer smiled. "I couldn't pass up the opportunity to meet you in person. When I took over this body, it was easy to charm your mother into thinking someone like him could be interested in a trollop like her."

"Don't you dare call her that," I hissed, surprising myself at how protective I felt over my mother. "She's a good woman. Her life only got screwed up because she got pregnant with me."

As soon as I said the words, I realized how true they were. My mother had, at one time, wanted to stay in the Amish community my grandparents belonged to. It was only because she fell in love with my father and conceived me that she ended up where she was now.

"Well, I for one am glad she did spread her legs so easily for the first angel she met. It certainly helped me out."

From the pleased look on Lucifer's face, a question popped into my mind and out of my mouth. "Are you my father?"

Lucifer's brow furrowed in consternation before he let out a billowing laugh, as if I'd made the joke of the century. Once he got himself under control, he chuckled, "Now, that would be interesting, wouldn't it? But no, dear Lilly, that would just be too cliché. It sounds like something you would read in a bad dime store novel. Oh, no, my dear, your father was someone else. But, I did help your mother pick up the pieces when he unceremoniously kicked her to the curb."

"But my grandmother said she met my father. My mother brought him to meet her after I was born."

"Once your mother learned she was pregnant, she came looking for your father, but by that time he was long gone. I represented myself to her as being your father's best friend, and told her he didn't want anything to do with her or you. She needed a shoulder to lean on, and I provided it. After she was shunned by her parents, I helped give her a new life so I could keep an eye on you."

"You're the one who blackmailed Mr. Landry into giving her a new identity. You killed his wife to prove you could, and then you threatened the life of his daughter."

Some of the pieces were finally falling together. It was no wonder Mr. Landry chose suicide over having to face Lucifer again.

Lucifer shrugged. "Humans are easily manipulated through their feelings, especially through the safety of their children."

"Then who is my father?"

Lucifer shook his head. "If I told you that, your fallen angels would have too many pieces of the puzzle and might figure out what I plan to do with you. I'm not that stupid, Lilly."

But he was prideful. That's what Brand had told me. If I could play on his vanity, maybe he would slip up and reveal some shred of a clue to me.

"We'll never let you win. I won't let you use me. I'd rather die first."

Lucifer came at me and grabbed me by the arms. Before he could say anything, I saw a vision inside my head so clearly, I knew it had to be what Lucifer was thinking in that moment. His anger at my threat had caused him to let his guard down. He had been intentionally hiding his thoughts from me, much like Uriel had the last time I met with him.

In the vision, I saw myself standing on a snowy plain, the body of Lucas Hunter lying dead at my feet. It was daytime, and I had my arms raised to the sky. Streams of fire shot from my hands into the sun-filled sky, and a white ribbon of light formed at the point of their convergence.

Lucifer let go of me as quickly as he grabbed me, but, by that time, it was too late. I felt his rage at my having seen what was inside his head, and knew that, if he could have afforded my death, he would have killed me on the spot.

"You're lucky I need you," he spat, slowly backing away from me. "Tell your mother I had to leave. Oh, and by the way, I'm asking her to move in with me."

Lucifer turned and practically ran away from me.

I stood on the porch and watched him get into his car, squealing the tires as he spun out of the trailer park, running away from the only human on Earth he was afraid of.

When I stepped back into the trailer, I told Utha Mae and my mom that I was feeling a little sick and needed to go home. In truth, I needed to speak to my friends about what just happened as quickly as I could.

We didn't even bother to drive back to Lakewood. Brand and Will phased us all to Brand's house. I called Malcolm to come over so he could hear what I had to say too.

Tara about lost it when we told her who Lucas Hunter really was.

"And you didn't find a way to tell me?" she yelled at Will and Brand. "What the hell were you thinking, letting Lilly Rayne go out there alone with him?"

"Tara," I said, desperately wanting her to calm down, "he didn't do anything to me. I think I scared him more than he scared me."

"It did look that way," Brand agreed. "What happened when he touched you? He seemed frightened, which is an expression I've only seen on Lucifer's face once before."

"I saw myself," I told them, visualizing the scene clearly in my mind. "I was standing in snow. Lucas Hunter's body was lying at my feet, and I knew he was dead. I had my arms stretched out and projecting streams of fire into the sky. I saw a ribbon of white light begin to form, but then he let me go because he seemed scared that I might see more of his plans. I don't think he thought I would be able to breech whatever mental dam he had built up to hide his thoughts from me."

Everyone was silent, trying to think through what I had just told them.

"Do you know what it means?" I asked my angels. Of anyone in the room, they would be the only ones who could decipher my vision's meaning.

"It sounds like Lucifer plans to possess you to cause a cosmic event of some sort," Brand said. "What the ribbon of light you saw is exactly, I'm not sure. But, it still doesn't answer why he needs you specifically to make it happen."

"He wouldn't tell me who my father is," I said. "I asked him if he was my father, but he laughed and said no." I looked at Malcolm. "Do you still think the ring will work on him?"

"What ring?" Will asked.

Malcolm explained to everyone about King Solomon's ring, and how it had the power to control demons and jinn.

"Do you think it will work on Lucifer?" Brand asked Will.

"I don't know for sure. He was never around Solomon while he had the ring. That might be one reason he left him alone. I say anything is worth a shot at this point."

Even I knew it was our Hail Mary pass, a last ditch effort to thwart Lucifer's plans for me. I just hoped we would be able to find it in time.

CHAPTER 5.

After breakfast the following morning, Brand and I had an unexpected visitor.

We were just putting the last of the dishes in the dishwasher when a man phased into our living room. He was tall and muscular like Brand, with skin the color of creamy milk chocolate. His hair was cropped close to his head and his eyebrows were low, almost hooding his striking hazel eyes. He wore a blue t-shirt with a picture of Jimmy Hendrix playing a guitar, with angel wings spread wide on his back.

I knew he had to be a Watcher, not only because of his ability to phase, but because of how handsome he was. For whatever reason, every Watcher I had met so far looked like a male supermodel. Not that I was complaining, but I made a mental note to ask the reason later.

"Isaiah," Brand said, walking over to greet our guest and shake hands with him. "So glad you could make it. Have you had any luck finding Samyaza?"

"Yes. He says he'll meet with you." Isaiah looked directly at me, like he sensed me in the room. "Is this Lilly?"

I walked over and extended my hand to him. "Hi. Lilly Nightingale."

"Soon to be Cole, though, right?" Isaiah said with an easy smile. "Brand told me about the wedding. Congratulations."

"Thank you."

"When will he meet with me?" Brand asked anxiously.

"Today. He told me you should wait for him at my place. He didn't give a specific time, though, so I'm not sure when he'll show up."

Brand looked down at me and said, "Why don't you call Malcolm? Today would be a good day for you to spend time with him, especially since classes are cancelled for Veterans' Day."

My heart sank a little. I knew Brand wanted me to keep my promise to Malcolm to spend one day with him before I got married, but facing Malcolm so soon after I almost let him kiss me seemed like something a masochist would do.

As if sensing my dilemma, Brand reminded me, "You only have four more days until the wedding. It's probably best if you go ahead and get it over with."

I nodded and went to get my phone to call Malcolm.

He answered on the first ring.

"Dearest, is anything wrong?"

"No. Brand needs to spend the day waiting to speak with Samyaza. He thought it might be a good time for me to keep my promise to you."

"I'll be right there."

Before I knew it, Malcolm was standing in the living room too.

He was wearing a white shirt, unbuttoned to reveal his chest, and a pair of white twill pants. His long black hair hung loosely around his face, giving him the appearance of an untamed god of romance novel covers.

"Malcolm," Isaiah said, looking at my friend like he was a curiosity. "I heard you've sworn off drinking human blood."

Malcolm's lips twitched into a smile, but the twinkle in his eyes never appeared. "Dearest won't let me if I want to keep her as my friend. So it's either abstain from making any more human sacrifices, or not have her in my life. I can't live without her."

The way Isaiah looked at Malcolm, I knew he was surprised to hear those words come from my friend.

Brand took me in his arms and gave me a kiss, which literally took my breath away. It was so unexpected, I had to grab onto his arms, and felt his hands fold in behind me to support my back so I wouldn't fall. Usually in front of company, Brand was reserved in his physical affections, never wanting to make people uncomfortable around us.

I knew instantly what was going on.

Brand wanted to make sure Malcolm understood who I truly belonged with, and that Malcolm might try to sweep me off my feet that day, but the love of my life knew without a shadow of a doubt that I would return to him, steadfast in my resolve to become his wife.

When Brand finally let me come up for air, I felt light-headed and slightly euphoric.

"Have fun today," he said before he and Isaiah phased to wait for Samyaza.

"I will try my best to wipe that image from my mind," Malcolm said, taking hold of one of my hands.

Before I knew it, we were standing in Malcolm's house in Hawaii. The glass wall in front of me faced the scenic view of the ocean. The wall had been slid open to catch the cool, gentle breeze gliding off the blue water, bringing with it the smell of salt and sand.

"Have you had breakfast?" Malcolm asked me.

"Yes," I told him, keeping my eyes on the undulating currents of the waves beyond the black sand Malcolm's house was built next to.

"Dearest, look at me."

I took in a deep breath and forced myself to look up at Malcolm. He smiled down at me, not trying to hide his joy at having me all to himself for one day.

"Thank you for this. I know I might not deserve it because of how I've been acting lately. You had every right to refuse to be alone with me again, and I promise to be on my best behavior while we're together today."

"You promise?" I asked, just to get clarification.

Malcolm held up his right hand and solemnly pledged, "I promise to not do anything you don't want me to do today. You have my word as your friend."

I felt my defenses go down, knowing Malcolm would never make a promise to me he didn't intend to keep.

"So, what's on the agenda?" I asked.

"Do you like the beach? I know you said you didn't like water, but surely you like to go to the beach."

"I don't like deep water," I said. "As long as I can stand up in it, I'm fine."

Malcolm grinned from ear to ear. "Perfect. Why don't you go up to my room and look on the bed. I bought some swimsuits for you to choose from. At least one of them should fit," he said, eyeing my body up and down, as if taking a mental measurement.

When I went to Malcolm's bedroom, I found ten bathing suits positioned carefully on his circular, white satin-sheeted bed. It was almost as if Malcolm had expected me to choose this day to spend with him.

Half of the suits I immediately discarded because they were two-piece bikinis. Some of them were skimpier than the baby doll negligee Tara and my mom had bought me for my wedding night. I surveyed the remaining suits and picked out the one that would cover the most flesh. It was a simple strapless dark blue suit. A white robe cover-up, matching sun hat, and flip-flops completed the ensemble.

When I went back downstairs, I found that Malcolm had changed into a pair of red-hot swim trunks. He stood with his arms akimbo, staring out at the ocean view. I noticed a brown wicker picnic basket sitting by his feet.

"I'm ready," I said, breaking his concentration.

He turned to me and smiled. "Which one did you pick? Please tell me it was the itsy bitsy tiny yellow bikini."

"You wish," I laughed. "The blue one-piece."

Malcolm rolled his eyes and groaned. "I knew you would pick that one. It barely shows anything, dearest. At least give a heartbroken man a break and flash a small bit of flesh."

"Do I have to remind you about seeing me naked in the shower? Don't try to act all deprived. You've still seen more of me than Brand has yet."

"That day is scorched into my memory forever, dearest. If I were human and allowed to die one day, it would be the last image in my mind to carry me on to the next world with a smile on my lips."

I just shook my head at Malcolm, which made him chuckle.

"How do we get down to the beach?"

"Oh, we're not going out there. The black sand makes it too hot to have any fun." Malcolm held out one of his hands to me, while picking up the picnic basket with the other. "I'm going to take you somewhere else."

Malcolm phased us to a secluded beach within a rocky cove. The sand was pinkish in color and the water an emerald green. A tall rocky cliff at our back shielded us from unwanted company. In fact, I wasn't sure how a regular human would reach the area we were in without a boat or rock-climbing gear.

"Where are we?" I asked, looking out at the clearest water I'd ever seen. It was so clear you could still see the white sandy bottom of the ocean floor even far in the distance.

Malcolm walked over to a solitary oversized blue umbrella with two lounge chairs shaded underneath.

"The Bahamas."

I joined him under the umbrella and took off my robe and hat. I felt, more than saw, Malcolm's eyes on me, but chose to ignore his ogling.

"You probably shouldn't go out until you put some sunscreen on," he said to me, pulling out a bottle of it from the basket he brought.

I held out my hand for the bottle and Malcolm pulled it back. "Why not let me put it on you, dearest? You might miss a spot."

"I think I can put it on myself," I said, seeing through his obvious ploy. "But I'll let you put some on my back. I don't want to get burnt right before the wedding."

Malcolm sighed in disappointment, but handed me the bottle. After spreading it on everywhere I could reach, I gave the bottle to Malcolm and pulled my hair to the front so he could spread it on my back.

His warm hands glided smoothly against my skin, massaging the lotion into my back and shoulders.

"You have the fairest skin I've ever seen," he said, "silky smooth to the touch."

I stood up abruptly and tossed my hair back.

I looked up at Malcolm and squinted.

"Last one in is a rotten egg," I said, and took off running towards the water.

Malcolm phased into the water up to his navel.

"You cheated!" I yelled, causing him to laugh.

"If you're going to play a game with me, dearest, you had best set the rules in place first. Otherwise, I'll always find a way to win."

I ran to Malcolm full throttle, and unceremoniously pushed him into the water. He came up sputtering, his long hair completely matted to his face.

"And that's what you get for cheating," I told him.

He slung his hair back away from his face and slapped the water in front of me, causing it to spray in my direction. Not to be outdone, I did the same, which set off another contest of who could make the largest splash. Malcolm won, of course, when he phased into mid-air and did a belly flop into the water, completely drenching me.

For over two hours, we played in the surf, looked for sea shells along the shoreline, and then finally lounged underneath the blue umbrella to eat the food Malcolm had brought. After the meal, I laid down on the lounge chair, letting the gentle ocean breeze and the sound of the water rushing in over the shore lull me into a sound sleep.

Sometime later, as I began to wake up, I felt someone gently trace the outline of my face with the tips of his fingers. As I cleared away the fog of sleep, I knew that someone had to be Malcolm. His fingers languidly traveled across my forehead, circling around to lightly brush one cheek, and then continue down to my chin and up the other cheek. He slid his fingers across the bridge of my nose, and then lightly passed them over one lip and then the next. He let his hand slide down the slope of my neck, stopping at a point just above my breast. I felt his hand tremble slightly against my skin.

My eyelids fluttered open. He was leaned over me with one arm propped above my head, staring at his hand as if he were trying to decide what my reaction would be if he explored my body further. He must have felt me watching him, because his gaze soon found mine. I knew what he was about to do as he leaned down into me, but couldn't seem to muster up the will to make him stop.

When his lips touched mine, I heard him release an excited whimper of pleasure. He plunged his hands into my hair on either side of my head, tenderly holding me as he gently tasted my lips. His silky tongue parted my lips, intent on deepening the kiss, and I felt the first of my tears fall from the corners of my eyes. Malcolm pulled away, having felt the hot wetness of my cries against his hand. He bent down and tenderly kissed the tears away.

"Lilly, why are you crying?"

"This isn't right, Malcolm," I said, shaking my head.

"Of course it is," he murmured, planting small kisses all over my face. "You love me."

"But I love Brand more."

Malcolm looked down at me. I wanted to wipe away the hurt and disappointment I saw in his eyes, but didn't know how to.

"If we still had four years, do you think you could come to love me more than him?"

Without even having to think about the answer, I shook my head. "No."

Malcolm sighed in resignation, resting his forehead against mine, accepting my answer as the truth.

"May I have one last kiss, dearest Lilly, before I make my heart let you go?"

I nodded, not trusting my voice to not betray me.

Malcolm leaned down and pressed his lips to mine, but not before I saw the sparkle of his own tears in his eyes.

Malcolm phased me back to Brand's home soon after. We found Brand starting supper in the kitchen.

"Any luck with Samyaza?" Malcolm asked him.

"Yes, he'll help us find a way to locate the ring, but he said it would probably take him a week or more to gather the information he needs to find it."

"Well, at least that will give you and Lilly time to get married and enjoy something of a honeymoon afterwards," Malcolm said with a melancholy smile. "I'll leave you two alone. I'm sure you have a lot to talk about."

When Malcolm phased, Brand came up to me and took me in his arms.

"How did it go?" he asked.

"I think I broke his heart," I cried, burying my face in Brand's chest and letting my own heartache over my friend's pain come out.

When I had finally exhausted my tears, Brand brought me a box of Kleenex. I saw him watching me as I blew my nose over and over again. I was sure I looked a hot mess.

"Stop watching me," I said, sniffling.

Brand smiled. "I can't. You're just too cute."

I looked at him like he'd lost his mind. "I'm a complete basket case, and you think I look cute? You must *really* be in love with me," I laughed.

"Yes," he said, coming up to me and cradling me in his arms. "Yes, I am definitely in love with you, Lilly Rayne

Nightingale. I love you for a lot of reasons, but your loyalty and compassion for your friends is at the top of the list."

I took a deep breath and asked, "Do you want to know what happened today?"

"Only if you feel like I need to know. Otherwise, I'm not that worried about it. You did what you had to do today. You finally proved to Malcolm that you love me more than you do him. I don't think he'll try to seduce you as often anymore."

"As often?" I asked.

"He will always want you. I have no delusions about that, but now he knows your heart belongs to me, and that he doesn't have a chance of ever winning it. I saw that in his eyes before he left. He had the look of a defeated man."

I began to cry again, which only made Brand chuckle harder.

"Stop crying, my love. You proved yourself a true friend to him today. You let him go."

I leaned into Brand and found strength in the comfort of his love. I truly hoped one day Malcolm would come to a place in his life where he found that one person who made him whole. I knew without a shadow of a doubt I had only been a transient visitor to that part of his soul. I felt sure Malcolm would one day find his own soul mate. I just hoped I lived long enough to see him find his happily ever after.

That night, I got a phone call from my mother.

"Sweetie, Lucas told me he asked how you would feel about me moving in with him. Thank you for giving us your blessing. It means a lot to me."

I didn't know what to say. I certainly hadn't given them my blessing, and I sure as hell didn't want my mother shacking up with Lucifer.

"Are you sure you're ready to move in with him?" I asked, hoping to plant some seed of doubt in her mind that what she was thinking about doing was wrong. "You haven't known him very long, Mom. It seems like you're rushing things."

My mother laughed, but not politely. "You're one to talk, Lilly. You've known Brand for less than three months and you're getting married. I'm not marrying him, for God's sake. We're just moving in together. Weren't you the one who told me I should date a better class of man? How much better can someone like me get than a doctor?"

"You shouldn't sell yourself short like that, Mom. You're a good person. Is it because you're in love with him?" I braced myself for her answer.

She sighed. "I don't know, Lilly. He makes me feel good about myself, which is something I haven't felt in a long time. You know, he reminds me a lot of your father. He made me feel like someone special, too, even though we were only together for a few days."

It was the first time my mother freely gave up any information about my father. Whenever I asked her questions about him, she would shut down and refuse to say anything. I felt like this might be my only chance to learn more about him from her.

"What was his name, Mom? What was my father's name?"

"Mick," there was a long pause, and I heard my mother sniff, like she might be crying. "His name was Mick, Lilly."

"Do you know where he is?" I asked breathlessly, as a hollow part of my past was finally being filled. "Is there any way I can contact him?"

"I have no idea where he is, sweetie. The last time I saw him was in his apartment in Chicago on South State Street. When I learned I was pregnant, I went back there and found out he had already moved away. He didn't even leave a forwarding address, and I only knew his first name. It was like your father completely disappeared off the face of the planet. I was young and impressionable at the time, not worldly at all. But when I was with Mick, he made me feel like I was the only woman on the planet. I wish I could tell you more, but that's all I know about him. His best friend was the person who helped me the most when your grandparents threw me out of their home."

It wasn't much to go on, but at least I had a name and a street now.

"Just promise me you'll be careful when you're with Lucas," I said, knowing there wouldn't be anything I could say, barring the truth, to reach my mother. "I don't want to see you get hurt."

"I'll be careful, sweetie. Don't worry about me."

When I got off the phone, I told Brand what I learned.

"It's not much to go on," he said. "I'll contact the private investigator who found your mother's parents in the morning. Maybe she can dig up something."

I tossed and turned that night, finally finding sleep sometime around 2:00 in the morning.

When I found myself back in the house Malcolm built for me, I instantly knew I wasn't in a regular dream.

"You seem to be changing my children for the better."

I turned to find the owner of the voice. A girl of around eight, with long straight brown hair and large hazel eyes, stared at me. She wore a simple blue sundress, which fluttered against an invisible wind.

"How can you have any children? You're a child yourself."

The little girl looked down at herself and then back up at me.

"I thought this form would please you most. If it just confuses you, I can be whatever you want."

The little girl began to morph into a variety of different people, from men to women, of different races and ages. The longer I stood there, the faster the form changed.

"Stop," I finally said, not caring what form the creature in front of me took.

The final form was of a black man in his late forties, with a shiny bald head and serious, penetrating eyes. He wore a thin gray sweater underneath a black pinstriped suit.

"Is this better?" he asked in a low, masculine voice.

"It's fine," I said, not really having an opinion one way or the other. "Am I having a dream?"

"Yes," he said, cocking his head to the right, "and no."

"How can it be a dream and not be a dream at the same time?"

"Your body is sleeping but your mind has traveled to this place," he said, looking around him. "You feel safe here. Malcolm did a good job building something which brings you so much comfort."

"How do you know Malcolm?"

"He's my son. They're all my children."

I felt my blood begin to race, causing my heart to pound inside my chest at the implications of his statement. I swallowed hard, finally realizing Who it was I was talking to.

"God?"

He smiled. "Like I said, you've been good for My children, Lilly. They've felt more connected to Me since you came into their lives. Even Will has changed for the better, and I never thought I would see him willingly go against Lucifer. Thank you for showing him a different path. I have hope for him now."

"How could you abandon them like that?" I asked, having a hard time reconciling a benevolent higher power with someone who could do what my grandparents had done to my mother, shun them. He cut them out of His life completely, just because they made a mistake.

"I never abandoned them," God said. "I've always been with them."

"How can you say that? Look at Malcolm. He became a vampire because he didn't see the point in denying what you made him into."

"Yes, but look at Malcolm now. He's grown so much since meeting you. The Malcolm I knew would have never let you see him so vulnerable. Even though you turned away from the love he was offering you so freely, he remains loyal to you. He's learned to swallow his pride because of his love for you."

"Why do I have such an effect on them?" I asked. If anyone could give me the answers I needed, who better than God?

"They see your father in you. They sense his essence inside you."

"Who was he?" I asked, taking a step forward. "Who was my father?"

"You'll learn the answer to that on your own soon."

"Why can't you just tell me?"

"Because only through learning the answer for yourself can you awaken your true potential."

"Why did you let me be born at all? If you knew Lucifer was going to try to use me, why allow me to exist at all?"

"All life is important to Me, Lilly. Yours is no exception. Plus, I felt you could help bring my children back to Me. You've shown them how precious life really is. That it's not to be taken for granted. Their pride was their downfall in the past. You've given them a chance to show how much they've changed. They care about you more than they do themselves."

God began to fade, his body becoming completely transparent.

"I will help guide you when I think you need it," God said. "Don't lose faith."

And then I woke up.

CHAPTER 6.

When I first woke up, I immediately told Brand about my dreamscape visitor. He wanted to know what God said, word for word. I talked him into waiting until Will and Malcolm could be with us. I didn't want to have to tell the same story three separate times.

I phoned Will to invite him over for breakfast, but felt I owed Malcolm an invitation in person.

When I phased into his house and called out for him, he was instantly at my side.

"Good morning, dearest," he said, a genuine smile of surprise on his face. "Don't suppose you came to tell me what a horrible mistake you made yesterday, and how you've left Brand to pledge your undying love and loyalty to only me?"

The twinkle of amusement in his eyes told me he was joking. I breathed a little easier, knowing our relationship would forever stay as it always had been -- him making suggestive remarks and me gently turning them down. Even though I knew in his heart he meant them, to a certain extent, I also knew he now understood that our relationship could never go beyond the love of friendship.

"I had a talk with your father last night," I told him, immediately wiping the smile from his face.

"What did He say?"

I held my hand out to Malcolm. "Come on. We'll all talk about it over breakfast."

I told my angels what God said. They all sat transfixed by my retelling of the conversation, and didn't attempt to interrupt me until I was completely done.

Malcolm sat back in his chair at the table, crossing his arms over his chest and letting out a deep sigh.

"He's still as obtuse as ever," he grumbled.

"So He didn't tell you exactly how you're supposed to find out who your father is?" Will asked.

I shook my head. "He seems to think I have to learn that on my own to awaken something inside me. What that is, I have no idea. I hope it's not anything bad."

Brand covered one of my hands with his, underneath the table. "There is nothing in you that could ever be bad."

I smiled at him and looked away, feeling shy all of a sudden from his praise. I met the gazes of my two other fallen angels and noticed them staring at me, like they completely agreed with Brand's statement.

"Who besides me makes you feel like you do right now?" I asked them, hoping the question would spur an answer which would help me figure out who my father was.

"I guess," Brand said, "I feel like I did when I was with my brothers in Heaven. When you're around, I feel a calm and happiness I haven't experienced since then."

"He's right," Will said. "I've always felt it around you, but could never quite put my finger on it until now."

"You bring out the best in us, dearest," Malcolm attested. "We would do anything for you, no matter how outrageous a request you might make."

"He still loves all of you," I told them. "And He's proud of how far you've each come in trying to right the wrongs you've done in your lives. He seems to want to forgive you and bring you back closer to Him."

No one said anything. They each seemed to consider my words and how they related to their own stories.

"If you'll all excuse me," Malcolm said, "I would like some time alone to think about things."

"Me too," Will said.

Both of my friends phased away.

Brand and I decided to try to keep things as normal as possible for the rest of the week. There really wasn't anything else for us to do until Samyaza contacted us with new information on the whereabouts of King Solomon's ring. We went to all our classes during the day, and came home in the evenings to spend time with one another. I think I was averaging two cold showers a night, and desperately prayed for the ability to warp time to make Saturday come more quickly. Unfortunately, time is a stubborn thing, and moves at its own irritatingly slow pace.

On Thursday afternoon, I received a phone call from Will.

"I was talking to Malcolm today," he told me. "He said you spent a whole day with him not too long ago, and I was wondering why I wasn't given the same opportunity to spend time with you before you got married."

"He asked me to," I said, simply stating the truth. The idea of Will wanting the same opportunity as Malcolm had never even crossed my mind, quite honestly.

"Well, I'm asking you. Can I have some time alone with you before the wedding?"

"Of course," I said, silently wishing Malcolm had kept his big mouth shut. All I needed was to have another emotional day with someone who proclaimed he was in love with me. "When would you like to get together?"

"Considering your wedding is the day after tomorrow, I would like to do it now, if you have the time."

I didn't have a good enough excuse not to go, but I did ask him to give me half an hour to get ready.

"How should I dress?" I asked.

"Casual, but bring a light jacket; the wind might make it chilly."

When I told Brand, he seemed to take it all in stride.

"So, you don't mind?" I asked him.

"No," Brand answered. "If I were Will, I would probably feel a bit slighted if you refused to do for me what you did for Malcolm."

"Does it make me a bad person to say I don't want to go?"

Brand smiled. "No, it doesn't make you a bad person. I know this will be hard for you, because you don't want to hurt Will any more than he already is. However, apparently he needs this just as much as Malcolm did. You were able to let Malcolm know the two of you can only be friends. I think you need to let Will understand that too. It'll be better for all of us in the long-run."

When Will picked me up in his car, he instantly phased us to a spot I'd never thought I would see again.

The sun glared off the water of the Gulf Coast, almost blinding me with its brilliance. There were a man and a woman on the beach, flying a box kite, using the breeze coming off the ocean to their advantage. Will got out of the car without saying a word, and I followed him.

He stared out over the water as I came to stand beside him.

"Do you remember this spot?" he asked me.

"How could I forget it?" I said, remembering this was where Will had given me my first kiss; a kiss which had broken my heart with its tenderness before Will shattered it by acting afterwards like it had never happened.

"I'm sorry I wasn't stronger back then, Lilly," he said in a low voice. "To be honest, you scared me a little."

I looked over at Will. "I scared you? How?"

"I'd been feeling something grow between us for a while before we kissed, but just chose to ignore it. I told myself it was ridiculous to think I could be in love with a human. I think Lucifer knew my feelings for you were growing too, and he would make condescending jokes about how I must think I was a human. After we kissed, he told me that if I ever tried to do it again, he would force me to leave you and put another demon in my place to watch over you. By that time, I couldn't afford to lose you, Tara, or Utha Mae from my life. You had all become too important to me."

"That's why you stopped talking to us?"

"I had to. Even if I couldn't be with all of you like before, at least I was able to watch over you from afar. It was better than not being near you at all. I thought I should tell you the real reason I acted the way I did before you married Brand. I never stopped loving you, Lilly."

"Thank you for telling me," I said, knowing what Will said was hard for him to say. "But it doesn't change anything. I still love Brand. I'm still going to marry him."

Will nodded his head. "I know. I thought you should have the whole truth, though. I hope it makes it easier for you to understand why I can't give you away at the wedding."

We both stared across the calm ocean surface, not sure what to do next.

"Hey," he said, "do you remember old Ms. Cane, the principal's secretary back at Dalton Elementary?"

I remembered Ms. Cane well. Who could forget that head of hair?

"What about her?"

"I found out she got married not too long ago."

"What? I thought she would stay an old maid for the rest of her life."

Will shrugged. "Guess not. She ended up marrying Principal Wright. You know, his wife passed away a couple of years ago."

From then on, Will and I spent at least two hours reliving events from our childhood, and laughing over things that had happened to us as kids. They were things that help build a person's life and form them into the adult they eventually become. It made me realize how similar Will and I were, because most of our lives had been shared with one another. I knew I would never again love Will as I did the night he first kissed me, and I was alright with that fact now. It took me a long time to get over him breaking my heart, but I had finally found the one person in the world who my heart had always truly belonged to.

After classes on Friday, Tara and Malik rode to Dalton with me and Brand. We were supposed to meet Utha Mae and my mom at the church, to help put up the decorations. For the most part, the sanctuary was already bedecked with the church's own Christmas décor. Two 12'-high Douglas fir trees stood on either side of the choir section, behind the pulpit. Each was tastefully decorated with twinkling white lights, red and green mesh ribbon, glass balls with gold filigree, red and white glittery poinsettias, and gold-painted sprigs. At the altar there was a classic white sweetheart arch, festooned with white gauze, red and white roses, and greenery. Basically, all we had to do was put the finishing touches on the pews and reception area.

Pastor Ryan also wanted us to do a run-through of the ceremony, just to make sure we knew what to expect. It was going to be a simple, quick wedding. I didn't think my heart could take anything too drawn out. The sooner Brand and I were married, the better.

Brand asked Abby to stand in as his best man. As she and Tara walked down the aisle, side by side, I stayed at the back of the church, waiting for the bridal march music to begin. I felt a familiar hand grab one of mine hanging at my side. When I looked behind me, I saw Malcolm.

"Abby told me Will refused to walk you down the aisle, dearest." He came to stand beside me. "I would be honored to do the job if you'll let me."

I reached up and hugged Malcolm tightly around the neck, realizing he had just officially reached best-friend status.

"Thank you," I told him, knowing what he was doing couldn't be easy for him. To hand me over to Brand would be just as hard for him to do as it would have been for Will. However, unlike Will, Malcolm was putting my needs first. God was right; Malcolm had indeed changed.

After the rehearsal, we put the final touches on the sanctuary decorations and finished decorating the reception hall. Brand and Malcolm decided it would look nice to drape white lights from the exposed cedar rafters in the room. I distracted Utha Mae and my mom while the guys used their phasing ability to make quick work of what would have been a time-consuming job.

I stepped outside to the back of the church to dispose of some trash, when I felt a presence behind me. I turned quickly and found someone I thought I would never see again, staring straight at me.

Robert stood at the edge of the woods. Before I knew it, he phased in right next to me and grabbed one of my arms.

"I couldn't let you get married without giving you my wedding gift," he hissed.

I immediately tried to phase, but Robert counteracted it with one of his own, not allowing me to reach my destination. While we played a tug of war to see who could phase faster, he pulled me to him with what seemed like the strength of a hundred men. I tried to wiggle out of his hold, but found it impossible. For a few minutes, it seemed like we were stuck in a white misty cloud, as each of us tried to keep the other one from phasing to their destination. During that time, he ripped my shirt open at the front and grabbed the back of my head, forcing me to face him while he tried to cover my mouth with his own. I felt the savage intensity of his hate as he forced himself on me. I tried to fight, but found myself nowhere near strong enough to fend him off.

When I felt him try to undo the front of my jeans, a burning rage I'd never had reason to feel before consumed me. My whole body suddenly felt like it had been lit on fire from the inside out. I grabbed Robert's arms with my hands, and heard the sizzle of burning flesh. He immediately let me go, and stopped trying to prevent me from phasing. I phased us to the one place I knew we would be alone: the forest where he'd tortured my friends on Halloween night.

A holy righteousness burned deep within my soul. Even in the dark, I could clearly see the fear in Robert's eyes. Within his dark pupils, I could see the flames lighting my own eyes reflected there.

"You can't be one!" he screamed at me. "You can't be one!"

I tightened my hold on Robert and watched as he burst into flames, falling into a black pile of ash at my feet.

I held my burning hands out in front of me, but didn't feel frightened by the sight. Instead, I felt a strange sort of comfort by the fire's presence. I brought my hands to my face and let the flames flicker against my skin. They felt like a warm wind on a summer day. They didn't burn hot against my flesh, but, instead, brought a sense of calm.

"Lilly?"

I looked up, and saw Brand staring at me with an expression I'd never seen on his face while in my presence: fear.

"What am I?" I asked him, hearing my voice, but realizing it sounded different, slightly deeper, infused with power.

I saw Brand's chest move up and down quickly, as if he was having trouble breathing.

"What am I, Brand?" I asked again, demanding an answer.

"The child of an archangel," he said breathlessly.

After he said the words, I knew he was right. The forest around me suddenly began to fade away. I collapsed to the forest floor, losing consciousness.

I felt a cold wet cloth resting against my forehead. When I opened my eyes, I found all three of my angels standing around my bed, watching me. I immediately sat up.

None of them said anything, just staring at me as if they were waiting for me to sprout horns out of my head.

"Why are you all staring at me like that?" I asked, sitting up and removing the small washcloth from my head and laying it beside me on Brand's bed. "Haven't you ever seen an archangel's kid before?"

I meant it as a joke, but none of them laughed.

"Stop staring at me. You're starting to freak me out."

Brand sat down on the bed beside me, while Malcolm and Will continued to watch me carefully, like they weren't quite sure if I was still the Lilly they knew.

"Lilly," Brand said, "tell us exactly what happened."

I told them about what Robert tried to do once again.

"I knew in my heart," I said, "even if I was able to stop him this time, there would be another attempt. I'm not really sure what happened. It was like a power that's been buried deep inside me all this time suddenly erupted. Before I knew it, Robert was just a pile of black ash at my feet."

"The slimy bastard deserved what he got," Malcolm snorted. "I won't lose much sleep over his loss."

"But how can she be the child of an archangel?" Will questioned.

"She's not the child of just any archangel," Brand said, understanding finally lighting his eyes. "She's the child of Michael."

The room went completely silent. The line 'you could hear a pin drop' came to mind.

"Is that bad?" I asked, needing to know.

"Unexpected," Malcolm answered. "But it makes sense."

"Why does it make sense?"

Brand touched my face tentatively, letting the palm of his hand cup one of my cheeks in its warmth.

"I see it now," Brand said, his voice full of wonder. "That's what we've all been seeing in you, Lilly. We just didn't know it."

"Seeing what?" I asked, realizing we were finally solving the mystery of what made me so special to the fallen. "What do you see?"

"God was right," Will said, staring at me as if he was seeing me for the first time. "We *can* see Michael's essence inside her. That's why she has the effect on us that she does. Why are we only now realizing it?"

"Because none of us have known the archangels to procreate with humans," Malcolm answered. "Why would we even think of such an absurdity?"

"There must be a reason God let it happen," Brand said. "But what could His purpose be?"

"Michael didn't have a child with just any human, though," Malcolm pointed out. "He had one with a descendant of Lillith. That can't just be a coincidence. It has to be divine intervention."

"Malcolm's right," Will agreed. "It had to be planned."

Becoming frustrated, I said, "Will anyone answer my question? What do you *see* when you look at me?"

"Michael's job was to banish fear inside others," Brand told me. "That's what made him such a good warrior and leader in the fight against Lucifer when he rebelled. His strength helped guide us through the darkest hour in Heaven. You have his strength, Lilly. You have his power to make us reach above what we fear most and strive to be better. I think you're meant to guide us through whatever it is Lucifer has planned."

"If I'm supposed to stop Lucifer, why did God let Uriel keep trying to kill me? That makes absolutely no sense."

"I think it was because of me," Will said, realization bringing tears to his eyes. "God told you He still watched over us. I think He knew you were never in any real danger, because

I was always there to keep you out of harm's way. My relationship with you, Tara, and Utha Mae is what changed me from being someone who hated humanity to someone willing to do anything to protect the humans I love. You were never in any danger of dying in those accidents Faust orchestrated, because I was always there to save you."

"But what am I supposed to stop Lucifer from doing?" I asked.

The room fell completely silent again for a second time. No one had an answer.

"It may be time to gather the Watchers together," Brand said, standing to face Malcolm and Will. "Maybe, with our combined knowledge, we can figure out Lucifer's plan before it's too late."

"You know there's only one way to get them all together," Malcolm said, sounding like that in itself might be an impossible task too. "Our sides hate each other too much to do it willingly."

"What are you talking about? What has to be done?" I asked.

"Samyaza will have to order it," Brand said.

"Well, he's already helping us, right?" I said, not thinking this was an impossible task. "Doing us one more favor shouldn't be too hard, should it?"

"I don't think he will do it if I'm the one who asks." Brand looked down at me. "But he might do it if you ask him, Lilly. He's a Watcher, and we've already established those of us you know would do anything you asked."

"But he doesn't know me."

Brand smiled. "I didn't either. Yet, you captured my heart with one glance in my direction." He looked at Will and Malcolm. "You made the outcasts of Heaven yearn for a better life. You are your father's daughter, Lilly. I believe it's your destiny to lead us through this dark time."

"I'm not a leader," I whispered.

"You're wrong, my love," Brand smiled at me, his eyes filled with certainty. "You were born to be a leader."

After Will and Malcolm left, Brand lay down in bed and held me in his arms. I began to tremble.

"What's wrong?" he asked, holding me tighter.

"I'm no one special, Brand," I said. "How am I supposed to lead a legion of angels?"

"You brought three of us completely under your control, and you didn't even know you were doing it. I wouldn't worry about a couple hundred more of them. They'll see what we do in you and follow you into battle, if it comes to that."

I buried my face in the side of Brand's neck, wishing I could just forget everything I'd learned that night. It was the night before my wedding. I should be excitedly anticipating the ceremony and the wedding night, instead of worrying about the fate of the world.

As if sensing my dilemma, Brand rolled me onto my back and straddled my hips, lightly pressing his body into mine. Looking into his eyes was like delving into the ocean of his love. I felt drenched to the bone in his love for me, and knew in that moment I would do whatever I needed to defeat Lucifer. I wouldn't let him rip my world apart when I had just found the one piece that made it whole.

"You're glowing," Brand said, a hint of a smile touching his lips. "What are you thinking about?"

"That I have too much to live for," I confessed. "I won't let him win, Brand. I won't let him take you away from me when I just found you."

"We'll find a way to stop him," Brand promised. "It's our destiny. Just like it was our destiny to meet one another and fall in love. I don't think you were made to just defeat Lucifer, Lilly. I think you were born to show me how to love again too."

He bent his head down and gave me a tender kiss, not meant to awaken my passion but to demonstrate without words how much he treasured and adored me for who I was. After a while, he pulled away and held out his hand to me.

"I don't want to," he said. "But I promised Tara you would spend tonight at her place. You know it's bad luck for the groom to see the bride before the wedding."

Reluctantly, I placed my hand in his.

"If there's anything we don't need," I said, "it's bad luck."

Brand phased me to Tara's front door, giving me a kiss meant to tide me over until we could be together again the next day.

"Meet you at the altar," he whispered before phasing back home.

I stood there for a minute after he left, needing to have a moment to myself to absorb everything I'd just learned that night. All my life I'd thought myself to be no one special; simply the illegitimate child of a woman who would rather spend her nights with strange men than her own daughter. Now I knew I might be the most important person on the planet.

How are you supposed to deal with that knowledge and not let it change you? Vanity had never been a problem for me, and I didn't really feel like it was a problem now. Yet, I couldn't lie and say knowing I might be the only person who could put an end to whatever Lucifer had planned didn't make me feel powerful. I felt almost drunk on it. I was no longer someone a creature like Robert could push around and frighten. Now I was able to harness the power my father passed down to me, and use it against anyone who might try to get in my way. I felt pride in myself, knowing I could put an end to those who would try to harm me or those I loved. I would no longer let anyone hurt me. If they tried, I knew I could strike them down as I had Robert, disintegrating them into a pile of ash, never to be heard from again.

CHAPTER 7.

After I went in and told Tara everything I now knew about myself, she decided it was a good enough excuse to dive head-long into the pan of chocolate pecan fudge she had just made. It wasn't quite cool enough to cut into little squares, so we grabbed a couple of spoons and sat in front of the blazing fire in the fireplace, spooning out scoops of the gooey chocolaty goodness.

"What did it feel like to murder someone?" she asked.

Her question caught me off-guard.

"He was trying to hurt me," I defended. "It's not like I planned to do it. It just happened."

"I know you, Lilly Rayne Nightingale. You're kind-hearted to a fault. You can't sit there and tell me killing someone didn't affect you, even if he deserved it. Hell, he deserved worse. He got off easy, if you ask me. However, I don't care about him. I care about you."

I sat there for a moment, trying to think of a way to explain to Tara how I felt. There was really only one way to put it.

"I know I should feel some guilt over what I did, but, if I'm being honest, it made me feel unstoppable. It was a rush of power to know I could destroy him with just my touch."

The disappointment on Tara's face from what I admitted forced me to look away.

"You know that's wrong, don't you?" she asked.

"It may be wrong," I said, chancing a look at her, "but it's the truth."

Tara sighed heavily. "Listen, girl. I don't pretend to know what you're going through, but I don't think you need to let this new-found power go to your head. I kinda doubt that's what the Lord had in mind. You know He's not much for arrogance. Be careful, Lilly; you don't need to piss off God."

I smiled. "Did you really just say that? I don't think those two words belong in the same sentence."

Tara waved her hand in the air, as if flinging away my admonishment. "He knows what I'm saying. I'm just a plain talker is all. Anyway, the point is you need to keep Him in your corner. Don't do something that makes Him turn His back on you."

Tara and I went to bed soon after. All I needed were bags under my eyes on my wedding day.

I found myself back in the house Malcolm built for me, looking out the large picture frame window at the snow-capped mountain and lake far in the distance. When I looked beside me, I saw the form God had chosen the last time I spoke with Him.

"I know who my father is now," I told Him.

"Yes, I know you do. I also know how it's changed you."

"Is it wrong to feel powerful?"

"Yes and no."

"Do You always think like that?"

God cocked his head to the side. "What do you mean?"

"It seems like You keep seeing both sides of a coin even though You're looking at it on its edge."

God smiled. "Almost nothing is always one way or the other."

"I think I know why it's good to feel powerful," I said. "It gives you strength. But, why is it bad to feel this way too?"

"It might be easier for you to understand if I showed you an example of what arrogant power can lead to."

I found myself standing in a completely white space. I looked around and said, "What is this place?"

"Heaven."

"But I don't see anything."

"Heaven is different for everyone. It's whatever they make it into. When you die, you'll understand. But right now, I'm going to show you what happened here to tear my children apart."

"When Uriel came to speak with me, I wasn't able to see him clearly because I'm only half-angel. Will I be able to see what you want to show me?"

"Give me your hand."

I placed my hand into His and felt a tiny spark.

God smiled. "Your vision of Heaven and angels is beautiful, Lilly. I will show you things in the way you see them, so you can fully understand."

I found myself transported to the top of a small hill. The earth beneath my feet was hard-packed and reddish in color. A solitary tree, bare of leaves, stood in front of me, and two male figures with large white wings on their backs were staring into the flames. One was lounging casually against a large boulder, while the other sat crouched before the fire.

"You look troubled, my friend," the angel sitting against the rock said.

The other angel looked across the fire at his companion.

"I don't understand why He loves these vile humans of His more than He does us, Michael. *We* are His first-born. *We* should be the ones who garner His favor."

I stared at the angel by the rock, realizing I was looking at my father for the first time in my life. Even though I knew God had transformed the scene to meet my expectations of how I thought they should look, I felt myself start to tremble at the sight of Michael.

"How can you say He loves them more than us?" my father asked. "He loves us all."

"How can you sit there and say that He loves us when He's asked us to bow down to them like servants?" Lucifer sprang to his feet, wings spread out. Pacing agitatedly before the fire, he continued, "Why do *we* have to spend an eternity working to keep His precious humans safe?"

Michael studied Lucifer silently, as if considering his friend's words carefully.

"You should not question His orders, Lucifer. You know, as well as I, that He sees beyond what we know. He always has good reasons for the things He asks us to do."

"I don't think He realizes His mistake," Lucifer tightened his hands into fists at his sides. "I'm tired of being a servant to those things. They should be serving us, not the other way around!"

Michael looked at Lucifer warily. "What are your intentions, Lucifer?"

Lucifer's eyes narrowed to pinpoints in the firelight. "I intend to find out who He loves most. The humans are like a disease. They should be taken care of now before they are allowed to evolve any further. You know that given enough time, they will corrupt everything He has created."

"You can't know that!" Michael yelled back, standing to face Lucifer's wrath. "Do you think yourself better than our father? Do you find that your wisdom has expanded so much that you, Lucifer, first of the archangels, knows more than the One Who made you?"

"Where the humans are concerned, yes, I believe I know them better than He does. We're the ones who have to spend time down here among them! We know what they are capable of better than anyone!"

Taking a steadying breath, Michael calmly said, "I don't want to lose you, old friend. Not like this. Please, think about what you're saying before you make a rash decision."

"Join me, Michael," Lucifer urged. "I'm not the only one who feels this way. If we all band together, we can force Him to change His mind."

"I can't join you, Lucifer," Michael sighed. "Even if I thought you were right, I couldn't turn my back on our father."

"Fine," Lucifer gritted out through clenched teeth. "But heed my warning to you, Michael. If you try to get in my way, I won't hesitate to destroy you."

God let go of my hand, and we were back in the white space.

"So the war in Heaven started because Lucifer wanted You to destroy humanity?"

"Lucifer's pride has always been his weakness. He was too proud to do what I asked him to do. He always felt I loved humans more, and I couldn't seem to do anything to convince him he was wrong. I love all My children equally. Angels were the first of My creations, and I felt they had the most to share, like a parent to a child. Lucifer just didn't see it that way. After the battle in Heaven, I convinced him to stop the fighting so we could talk things through. I hoped to give him one more chance."

God took my hand again and said, "We all gathered in the Hall of Angels."

A vision of such a place flashed in my mind, and God smiled.

"Quite pretty, Lilly," he said, before transforming my surroundings into the place in my mind.

Lucifer was pacing in front of God, Who was sitting on a golden throne. Seven angels stood on either side of Him like a holy protectorate. All seven of the angels standing by God and Lucifer wore glowing crowns on their heads.

"It's time You made a choice," Lucifer said. "Either You prove we mean more to You by destroying the humans, or we will rain fire on their world and destroy them ourselves!"

Lucifer turned to the angels standing behind him in the gilded white marble coliseum, raising his arms urging them to show their support of his demand. Half of the angels cheered him on. The other half remained stoically silent.

"You are asking the impossible, Lucifer," God said, weariness in his voice. "They are the first of their kind, as are you. Asking Me to destroy them would be like asking Me to destroy you."

Lucifer angrily rushed up to God's throne, with wings flared out. He gripped the throne's arms tightly and pushed his face in close to God.

"Why do You love them more than me?" Lucifer questioned quietly, searching his father's eyes for an answer. "Haven't I done everything You have ever asked of me? Why do You refuse the only thing I've ever asked of You?"

God raised one of His hands and gently touched the side of Lucifer's face. Lucifer's eyes closed and his wings lowered at the show of affection.

"My love for you has no limits," God said, looking at Lucifer like a father knowing he is about to lose his child. "But I will not do what you ask of Me." Lowering His hand back to

His lap, God said, "If you are determined to continue on this path, I have no other choice but to banish you and your followers from My sight."

Lucifer's eyes opened, drenched in madness. "You would forsake us for those things?" Lucifer hissed. "How can You choose them over me?"

"I love you all, Lucifer. But do not test My patience," God warned. "I will not destroy those precious to Me for the sake of your bruised vanity."

"Well, if You won't destroy them," Lucifer angrily pushed himself away from God, turning his back on his father, "we will!"

Lucifer stepped away from God's throne, seeming intent on returning to the world of humans to wreak as much havoc as he could.

All of a sudden, Lucifer fell to his knees and cried out in agony as his wings were ripped from their sockets by an unseen force. Blood poured from the freshly-opened wounds. The once-glowing crown on his head lost its light, and now looked simply like a regular crown made of silver. Cries of pain came from the congregation of angels, and I watched as almost half of them fell to their knees, their wings torn from their bodies. Lucifer lifted his head and watched as the angels who had cheered him on earlier now found themselves doomed to the same fate as him. The blood of the fallen soon covered the hallowed floors of Heaven.

God slowly stood from His throne. "From this day forward, Lucifer and those who followed him into battle are banished from Our presence. They will live on Earth with the humans until such time as I see fit."

God looked to Michael standing beside him and ordered, "Take them to the world below. Perhaps in time they will learn to accept My children there."

I watched my father as he gently lifted Lucifer into his arms and did as God instructed.

Cradled in Michael's arms, Lucifer remained silent. I had to wonder if the pained expression on Lucifer's face was physical or emotional.

Michael phased to a soft patch of grassy earth and gently laid Lucifer's prone body upon it. Kneeling behind his friend, Michael placed his hands on the open wounds and healed them.

"In time He may forgive you, Lucifer," Michael said. "You should not have tested His patience like that."

Lucifer remained silent. Finally, he lifted his torso with his arms, but refused to look back at Michael.

"Leave me, Michael. I don't want your pity. Go back to your God."

Michael took a step towards Lucifer, reaching his hand out, as if to console his friend.

"Go!" Lucifer ordered.

Michael brought his hand back to his side and disappeared. The pain of loss I saw on my father's face made me want to reach out and comfort him.

God let go of my hand, and I found myself back in my Colorado home.

"Sometimes power can lead you down the wrong path," God said. "It can blind you to the needs of others, and distract you from your real purpose."

"Is it wrong of me not to feel guilt over Robert's death?"

"Yes."

I felt my heart sink.

"You should always pity those who lost their way like Robert did. I know what he tried to do to you was wrong and that you were only defending yourself against his actions, but you should not take joy in taking the life of another, no matter how much they might have deserved it. If you decide to go down the path of vengeance, all will be lost, Lilly. It is only your great love for those around you that will save you."

God took my hand again.

"I have a wedding gift for you," He said, turning to look at the set of stairs just outside the living room that led to the second floor.

I followed His gaze and found my daughter standing on the stairs, dressed in a pink princess costume with a rhinestone crown perched precariously on top of her head.

"Come play with me, Mommy."

My free hand flew to my mouth as tears clouded my vision and stung my eyes.

"How is that a gift?" I questioned, my throat tight from trying not to cry. "You know I can't have a child with Brand and survive the birth."

"Have faith, Lilly," God said to me. "Have faith in the love you and Brand have for one another. It will protect you when the time comes."

"Protect me from what?" I asked, dragging my eyes away from the vision of my daughter.

But God was already gone.

CHAPTER 8.

"Lilly, wake up!"

When I opened my eyes, Tara was shaking my shoulders.

"You were crying in your sleep," she told me. "It's your wedding day. You shouldn't start it out crying."

I wiped the tears from my face and sat up.

"Is it morning already?" I asked, feeling like I hadn't gotten any sleep during my time with God.

Tara smiled. "Yep. Now get out of bed, sleepy head. We've got a lot to do before you can walk down that aisle and marry Prince Charming."

A lot to do was right. After we each showered, I phased us over to Malcolm's home. Apparently, it was going to take an army to make me presentable that day. If I had been a lesser person, I guess I would have taken offense at the amount of work my friends deemed necessary to transform me into the perfect bride. As it was, I just let them pamper me into perfection.

Tara placed Malcolm in charge of my hair, which completely tickled me. She would never have passed the reins down so readily if she weren't one hundred and twenty percent positive he would do a better job than she. Malcolm decided my hair should be styled in an up-do, since I would be wearing a veil.

Tara, of course, did my makeup. You would have thought she was painting the *Mona Lisa* the way she would stop and survey her work before continuing. I'm pretty sure I was poked and prodded for over two hours. Once they got through with me, my friends got themselves ready.

Tara had to wear a red scarf to cover her still-healing wound, but it didn't distract from how beautiful she looked in her dress.

Tara and Abby helped me get into my wedding dress. I heard Tara sniff when she put the veil on my head.

"Don't you dare cry," I told her. "If you start crying, I'll start to cry."

"Oh, no, you don't, Lilly Rayne Nightingale," Tara placed a hand over her mouth, tears still in her eyes. "That might be the last time I get to call you that," she realized.

"Lilly Rayne Cole," I said aloud. "Doesn't quite pack the same punch, does it?"

Tara shook her head. "Just 'cause you're marrying him doesn't necessarily mean you have to take his name. It's the 21st century, not the Middle Ages."

"Well, let's just get me married first, then we'll worry about the semantics."

Instead of taking cars, I decided we should all just phase to the church. There would be so many people present, I didn't think anyone would notice one way or the other.

Utha Mae had warned me when I first told her I planned to marry Brand that she wanted to invite a few of her friends. I just didn't realize she was going to invite everyone in the county, plus a few in the neighboring one. I did know a lot of them, but there were a lot I didn't know too. All in all, there were supposed to be 200 people at the wedding. In lieu of gifts, we asked people to donate to their favorite charity.

We phased into one of the church's Sunday school rooms. It was outfitted with some chairs and a full-length mirror for me to use.

"I'll go see if your mother and Utha Mae are here," Malcolm offered, stepping out of the room.

"Lilly," Abby said, coming up to me. She was wearing a red dress similar to the one Tara wore. "We all divided up the 'something old, something new, something borrowed, something blue'. I picked the borrowed." From Abby's little black handbag, she pulled out a short strand of white pearls.

"Thank you," I said to her while she put the necklace on me.

"They belonged to my mother," Abby said with a sad smile. "I think she would be really happy Dad found someone to share his heart with again. He's been so lonely all these years. I'm just happy he finally let someone in."

I hugged Abby and said, "Thank you for making me a part of your family."

My mother and Utha Mae stepped into the room. The smile on my mother's face made me wish I had a camera to keep the picture forever.

"Oh, sweetie, you look beautiful."

Utha Mae reached into her handbag and pulled out two tissues; one for her and one for my mom.

"Take it, Cora," Utha Mae said. "You know we're gonna need it."

"Is it my turn yet?" Malcolm asked, coming into the room after them.

"I gave her something borrowed," Abby told him.

With a smile, Malcolm put his hand inside the inner pocket of his coat and pulled out a blue garter.

I just rolled my eyes at him. "I should have seen that one coming," I laughed.

Tara and Abby helped me hold my dress up while Malcolm knelt and slid the garter up my left leg to mid-thigh.

Malcolm sighed. "Would you like it higher, dearest?"

I laughed. "No, that's quite high enough."

Malcolm stood up and kissed me on the cheek. "I truly am happy for you, even if you chose the other guy."

"Thank you for being here," I told him. "You'll never know how much it means to me."

"I think I do," Malcolm replied, trying to smile. "And if he doesn't make you happy, you know where to find me."

All of a sudden, Malcolm let out a yelp and started to rub the back of his head. When he turned around, I saw Utha Mae standing behind him, holding her purse like a Billy club.

"No talk like that," Utha Mae told him sternly. "Lilly's made her choice, just like I did when I married my Harry. Now move on over; I have something old I need to give my baby."

Utha Mae stood in front of me. "I hope you know how proud I am of you, baby. I told them I wanted to give you something old." Utha Mae opened her purse and brought out a silver bracelet with a heart-shaped charm attached to one of the rings.

"My Harry gave me this on our wedding day. Every year he would add another charm to it to mark something special in our lives. I took off all the charms except for this one, because that's how he first gave it to me. Now you tell Brand he has to add to it for you during your life together, so you can remember all the special moments when you get to be as old as me."

With age-trembling hands, Utha Mae put the bracelet around my right wrist. I hugged her close afterwards.

"Thank you, Utha Mae."

"We just figured the dress would count as something new," Tara told me. "So don't expect any more surprises."

"I won't," I told her.

There was only one thing, or person, who could make the day any more complete, and I knew I would just have to forget about Will coming to wish me luck in my new life with Brand. It made me sad that I wouldn't be able to share one of the happiest days of my life with my best friend, but knew his feelings for me would prevent it.

Finally, it was time for the ceremony to begin. Malcolm and I stood at the back of the church, behind the closed doors leading into the sanctuary. I held my bouquet of red roses, white calla lilies, and red holly berries in one hand, while Malcolm held my other hand in the crook of his arm. Just as the wedding march began to play and the doors to the sanctuary opened, I felt a light touch on my left shoulder. When I turned to see who it was, Will came to stand on the other side of me, offering his arm.

With no time for words, I took his arm and let the other two men in my life walk me down the red rose-petal-strewn aisle, both giving me their blessing to marry the man of my dreams.

Once inside the sanctuary, I finally saw Brand for the first time that day. My heart felt like it suddenly dropped down into my stomach as I looked at the gorgeous man waiting to make me his wife. He was dressed in a black tuxedo, and was standing between Pastor Ryan and Abby, smiling at me as I walked down the aisle to meet him. I felt like I had a million butterflies in my stomach by the time we reached the altar.

"Who gives this woman to be wedded to this man?" Pastor Ryan asked, looking pointedly at Malcolm and Will.

"We do," they said in unison, letting go of my arms, so I could walk away from them and begin a new chapter in my life as Brand's wife.

As Pastor Ryan began to tell us how we were entering into a blessed union, his voice seemed to veer to the background of my mind, because all I could think about was the man standing in front of me.

Brand's soft gray eyes twinkled with his happiness, and I knew this day would be the first of many happy days to come for us. He was everything I'd always needed, but never knew I did. He made my life whole, and I held no doubts about his love for me.

"Lilly," Brand said, bringing me out of my reverie.

"What?" I asked, smiling up at him in my euphoria.

He smiled at me and whispered, "This is the part where you say 'I do'."

I looked at Pastor Ryan and saw him nodding his head, urging me to say those two little words.

"I most *definitely* do," I said, loud enough for the entire congregation to hear.

There were a few laughs, but I didn't care. I was marrying Prince Charming, and I wanted the world to know he was all mine.

My mother hired a photographer to take pictures after the ceremony. After almost 30 minutes of posing, we were finally allowed to go to the reception hall to partake of the food and festivities. To be honest, all I wanted to do was take Brand home and finally put an end to having to take cold showers, but, I knew how hard Utha Mae and her friends had worked to provide food for everyone in attendance, and couldn't bring myself to do something so selfish.

A small band had been hired to play some music, and Brand and I were directed to start the first dance. A familiar song began to play.

I smiled up at Brand. "This is the first song we ever danced to."

"I thought you would remember," he said, bending down to kiss me on the lips lightly.

I remembered it well. It was "Time in a Bottle" by Jim Croce. It was playing the night we danced in the gazebo right after my car accident.

Brand began to hum the tune in my ear, and I remembered what a beautiful singing voice he had.

"Will you sing to me later?" I asked him.

"If it would make you happy, Mrs. Cole."

I smiled. "It would make me very happy, Mr. Cole."

"Then your wish is my command."

After the prerequisite toasts to our marriage, and the cutting of the cake, Brand made good on his promise to sing to me, and asked one of the band members if he could borrow an acoustic guitar.

When Brand stood up to the microphone, he said, "My wife has requested I sing her a song. I think she'll remember this one, because it was playing the first time she ever told me she loved me."

Brand began to strum the strings of the guitar and sing. I did indeed remember the song. The first time I told Brand I loved him was permanently etched into my memory as one of the most glorious nights of my life. After I declared my love, we spent the first of what would become many nights in his bed holding, kissing, talking, and laughing with one another. He knew this song held a special meaning for the both of us, and I reveled in his thoughtfulness. I could remember lying in bed that night, asking him what the name of the song was and he told me it was "Afterglow" by INXS.

Brand changed the lyrics slightly, to make it more personal, but I could tell from the way the girls at the reception were riveted by him that they all wished they were me, even if it was only for one night.

By the end of the song, I felt desperate to finally get Brand home, and didn't see any reason for us to stay longer than we had to.

"You've got to throw the bouquet and Brand has to throw the garter, or we're gonna have a mad crowd, Lilly Rayne," Tara said, refusing to let me leave before we did those two customary things.

Tara gathered all the single women together, and I tossed the bouquet over my shoulder, not really caring who caught it. When I turned around, I met the stunned eyes of Tara, now holding my bouquet squarely in her hands, like it had just landed there of its own free will. I glanced at Malik sitting at one of the tables, and saw a slow smile spread across his face. I didn't have to be a mind-reader to know what he was thinking.

Brand made quick work of taking my garter off and throwing it into the crowd of single men. Apparently, it had a will of its own, and journeyed back to its original owner. Malcolm held the blue garter to his nose, and inhaled deeply while giving me a wink.

Now that our duties as the newly-wedded couple had been completed, we made our goodbyes and got into Brand's car to drive away from the church. As soon as we were far enough away, Brand phased us to his driveway. Grabbing one of my hands, he phased us directly to his bedroom.

We fell against one another, drinking in each other's lips as if we would die of want. Reluctantly, I pulled away just to take a breath.

"I have to get out of this dress," I said, turning my back to him for his help.

Brand lowered the zipper with one hand while letting his other hand trail down my back as more of it was revealed. I held the dress against my chest so it didn't just fall to the floor. After the zipper was down, I felt Brand's hands slide inside the opening, seeming intent to peel the dress off me, but I turned around before he could explore any further.

"Give me one minute," I said to him, bringing his lips back to mine for another kiss to tide me over before I went to the bathroom to prepare for the rest of our evening together.

I reluctantly pulled away and walked to the bathroom. Before entering, I turned and said over my shoulder, "Stay in your tuxedo."

"You know things would go much faster if I disrobed while you're in there," he said. "Or are you planning to torture me all night?"

"I don't want fast," I told him. "I want to do everything I've always wanted to do to you for the past few months, and one of those things is to undress you myself." I smiled at him. "Just do what I ask; I promise you'll like it."

Brand smiled back and bowed, "Whatever your heart desires is my command."

When he stood back up, the hunger he held for me smoldered in his eyes, silently telling me I should probably hurry up, or he wouldn't be able to keep from just throwing me down on the bed as soon as I reappeared.

I quickly took off my dress and everything underneath to slip into the baby doll negligee I received at the bachelorette party. I wasn't sure if I was ever going to get all the bobby pins Malcolm put in my hair out, and silently wondered if he did it on purpose to slow me down. Once my hair was completely free and loose, I looked at myself in the mirror. The negligee did very little to hide my body, but I wasn't as self-conscience about it as I'd thought I would be. I wanted Brand to see me. I wanted to watch his eyes as he discovered every inch of flesh on my body. I wanted to feel his hands explore all that I had to offer him.

When I opened the door to the bathroom, Brand was lighting the last of the white candles in the room. He set his lighter down on the table by the window and turned to face me. I saw his lips part slightly as he caught his breath. I stepped further into the bedroom.

"Do you like it?" I asked, slowly spinning around so he could see it from every angle.

"Do you really have to ask?" he replied in a hoarse voice.

I walked over to him and slowly ran my hands down the lapels of his tuxedo jacket, feeling the silky texture against the soft skin of my palms.

"Your turn," I whispered to him, running my hands in between his jacket and shirt, and up over his shoulders until the coat fell to the floor behind him.

I tugged on the bow tie at his neck and pulled the knot free, sliding it from around the stiff collar of his shirt. One by one, I undid the small buttons of his shirt, exposing his chest inch by glorious inch. Once the shirt was open at the front, I ran the palms of my hands over his chest muscles, slipping the shirt off his shoulders so it could join the jacket. I let my fingers make maddening trails down the length of his arms, bringing our torsos closer but never quite touching. As I glided the tips of my fingers back up his arms and across his chest, I felt his muscles tighten as I slid them down over the tight muscles of his abdomen, finally finding the top button of his slacks.

Brand's breathing had become shallow by this point. When I looked up at his face, I saw he was watching my every move.

He swallowed hard before saying, "I can't take much more, Lilly."

"Wait," I said, begging him to be patient while I released the button on his pants and planted small, distracting kisses across his chest. I quickly found the tab for the zipper and pulled it down, allowing gravity to do the rest of the work for me, leaving Brand standing in only a pair of form-fitting black boxer briefs.

"Lilly," Brand moaned, closing his eyes, "please…"

"Just one thing left," I said, running my hands under the black elastic band and then pulling downward.

"Why, Mr. Cole," I said, standing back up with a suggestive smile on my face, "I do believe you're happy to see me."

Brand opened his eyes and looked at me like he couldn't believe I'd just said what I did.

A pleased smile spread his lips as he replied, "Yes, Mrs. Cole, I am *very* happy to see you."

Before I knew it, he had me cradled in his arms, carrying me to bed. He laid me down gently on the already-turned-down covers and slid in beside me.

"My turn," he murmured against my ear, nibbling the tender flesh there and kissing his way down the curve of my neck.

"Mine's simple," I said, trembling slightly under the soft pressure of his warm lips against my skin. "Just undo the bow."

Brand's lips passed over the tops of my breasts and quickly found the silky bow tying the two halves of the bra together. He pulled on one end of the bow with his teeth, instantly releasing the fabric, exposing me to his eyes for the first time. I heard his sharp intake of breath just before he lowered his head and made love to every inch of my body for the very first time.

CHAPTER 9.

I woke up the next morning to find my husband no longer in bed, but I heard the distinct rattle of cookware coming from downstairs. I hugged his pillow to me, breathing in the scent of him, which still lingered there. I couldn't stop myself from smiling from ear to ear. Of all my school girl fantasies about how my first time making love to a man would go, I never imagined the experience would shake me down to my very core.

Brand had been gentle and attentive in his lovemaking, always seeming to know how to bring me to the brink of passion with his hands and mouth. When we joined our bodies for the first time, he held me gently to him, waiting for my pain to subside before we went any further. He kissed my tears away and promised it would be the one and only time he ever intentionally hurt me. He withdrew from me then and worked to reawaken my passion, to a point where I begged him to come back into me.

Throwing off the sheet I was under, I went in search of the bow tie Brand wore the night before and quickly tied it around my neck. I quietly slipped out of the bedroom and down the stairs. Brand, wearing only his black boxer briefs, had his back to me checking on something he was cooking in the oven. I tiptoed to the kitchen island and struck a relaxed, and what I hoped to be a sexy, pose.

"What's for breakfast?" I asked.

Brand closed the oven door and turned to face me. I watched his eyes travel from the tips of my toes to the bow tie around my neck.

"I thought it was quiche," he said, sauntering up to me and taking me into his arms, "but now I think it's you."

For the next four days, Brand and I hid away from the world. We divided our time between his home in Lakewood and his London residence. The world could have been on the brink of destruction, and we wouldn't have known or cared about it. We didn't contact anyone, and no one tried to contact us. We made love in every room of both houses and even ventured outside once, completely naked while it rained, only coming in when we needed to warm up in each other's arms while making love in front of the fireplace. I knew if I died, I would die a fulfilled and happy woman.

I also became very thankful for the large box of condoms from Abby and Angela.

But, like all things must, our honeymoon had to come to an end. Just married or not, Utha Mae would have killed me if I missed spending Thanksgiving Day with her. Since she did so much to help us prepare for the wedding, Brand and I told her we would handle the Thanksgiving meal to give her some much deserved rest. I worried she might protest, so I was pleasantly surprised when she didn't.

When Malik and Tara made it to Brand's Thanksgiving morning, Tara knocked on the door and opened it slightly.

"You two decent?" she yelled. "I don't want to see more of y'all than I have to."

I went to the door and yanked it wide open.

"Get in here, crazy," I said, giving her a hug.

"Well, we haven't heard from y'all since the reception. It doesn't take a rocket scientist to know what y'all been up to."

I felt my cheeks blush red hot.

"See?" Tara said knowingly, pointing to my face. "Told ya."

"Stop picking on my wife," Brand said good-naturedly to Tara. "She can't help it if she finds me absolutely irresistible."

I turned into my husband's arms and kissed him.

"Guilty as charged," I confessed with a dramatic sigh. "I do find my husband completely and totally irresistible."

Tara averted her eyes from our lovey-dovey show of affection, and found the painting of me hanging on the wall.

"Is that supposed to be Lilly?" she asked, walking over to it.

"Can't you tell it's me?" I asked.

"Well, yeah, but it makes you look like the supermodel version of you. I mean, don't get me wrong," Tara amended, "you're beautiful, but the girl here is drop- dead gorgeous."

"It looks exactly like Lilly," Brand said, disregarding Tara's observation. But I couldn't disregard it so flippantly, because I had thought the same thing when I first saw Brand's paintings of me.

"Well, anyway," Tara said, turning away from the painting, "what do we need to start on first?"

By the time noon rolled around, we had completed the cooking of our Thanksgiving feast. Just as we were putting the finishing touches on the table, our guests began to arrive.

The first to arrive were Malcolm, Abby, and Sebastian.

When Malcolm came in, he pulled me into his arms for a hug, and kissed me on the cheek.

"You're positively glowing," he told me, no malice or jealousy in the statement. "Are you happy, dearest?"

I nodded, having a hard time repressing a smile. "I'm the happiest I've ever been in my life."

"Then I'm happy," he told me, kissing the top of my head before walking to the table to examine what we had prepared.

Will brought Utha Mae with him. When she saw me, her face lit up and she said, "Baby, I've never seen you so happy. You look like you're glowing."

I felt my forehead furrow, wondering why Malcolm and Utha Mae had said almost the exact same thing, but quickly discounted it as being coincidence.

I gave Will and Utha Mae kisses on the cheek while Brand took Utha Mae's overnight bag up to the spare bedroom. I had invited her to stay the night because I wanted to take her shopping the next day. If there was anything Utha Mae loved more than food, it was finding bargains, and Black Friday was *the* day to go shopping for them. I had already gone to the little convenience store up the road and picked up the newspaper with all the fliers advertising what would be on sale the next day. As was tradition, I knew Utha Mae, Tara, and I would plan our attack strategy later that afternoon.

"Now, are you sure you want me to stay the night?" Utha Mae asked. "I know you two just got married, and I don't want to get in the way of anything you might want to do together."

I tried very hard not to blush at Utha Mae's insinuation. Intellectually, I knew she understood Brand and I were having sex now, but the little girl who Utha Mae raised didn't want to admit it to her.

"You could never be in the way," I told her, putting one arm around her waist. "Come on. I want to know what you think about what we cooked."

As all nine of us sat down to eat, we joined hands and let Utha Mae make her annual prayer of thanks.

"Dear Lord above, we thank You for providing for us not only on this day but every day of our lives. Please give us Your blessing in the next year to come and watch over us to make sure we honor You in the things we do. Thank You for bestowing Your grace on my babies this year, especially Lilly. You have truly gifted her with a wonderful new family. Thank You, Lord. Amen."

"Let's eat!" Tara said, immediately helping herself to the beef tongue and caramelized onions Malik made especially for her.

Everyone laughed at her audacious behavior, and quickly joined her.

As I looked around the table, I realized what Utha Mae said was true. I did have a new family, and couldn't imagine my life without any of them in it.

"Where's your mother, Lilly?" Malcolm asked as he helped Brand and me clean the kitchen after the meal.

"She's in Las Vegas," I said. "Lucas surprised her with a trip there for Thanksgiving."

Malcolm lifted an eyebrow. "Is that wise?"

"No," I admitted, "but there really wasn't any way for me to stop her. I can't exactly tell her the truth. She'd think I'd lost my mind and try to have me committed to Whitfield. Lucas pretty much has her wrapped around his little finger."

"Yes," Malcolm agreed. "He was always very good at doing that, especially with women. Which reminds me, have you heard back from Samyaza yet?"

"No, not yet," Brand said. "I thought I would go see Isaiah tomorrow while the girls are out shopping, to see if he's heard anything. I also want to ask Isaiah if he thinks Lilly should ask for the gathering herself."

"Let me know what he says. The sooner we do the gathering, the more time we will have to discover what the plan is."

"Lilly, baby," Utha Mae called to me over the Walmart sales paper in her hands. "Could you bring me some of that chocolate bourbon pecan pie Brand made?"

"I'll get it for you," Brand told her, dazzling her with his smile.

"Thank you, hon. Just put a dollop of whip cream on it too. I'd sure appreciate it."

Brand leaned into me and whispered in my ear, "Is it just me or does Utha Mae look tired to you?"

I chanced a glance at Utha Mae, and did notice she didn't seem to be diving into the sales papers with her usual gusto.

"I think the wedding just took things out of her," I said, not willing to entertain any other thought. "She'll be all right once she gets a little rest."

Brand nodded, but I could tell he wasn't quite convinced of my assessment of Utha Mae's health.

I spent the rest of the day marveling at how large my family had become in such a short time. Will, Malcolm, and Brand seemed to have finally worked things out, and even enjoyed watching a college football game together on TV. Tara, Utha Mae, and I planned out our route for the next day, and Malik took studious notes for us so we wouldn't forget what it was we wanted to buy at each spot. It was one of the best Thanksgivings I could ever remember having. I made a fervent wish that it wouldn't be the last.

CHAPTER 10.

Later that evening, when it was just Utha Mae, Brand, and me in the house, I went to her bedroom to check on her. She was sitting in the chair by the window, reading her Bible, a familiar sight ever since I was a child.

"We're about to go to bed, Utha Mae. Do you need anything?" I asked.

She put her bookmark in her Bible and looked up at me. "If you could help me get out of this chair and into bed, I'd appreciate it, baby."

I went to her and held one of her arms as she slowly tried to stand up. I hadn't realized such a simple task had become something she needed help with. I began to wonder if maybe it wasn't time to hire Utha Mae a part-time nurse to help her out around her home. I knew Brand wouldn't mind paying for it if I asked.

I tucked Utha Mae in and kissed her on the cheek.

"Need anything else?" I asked.

"No, baby," she said, letting out a large exhalation of breath before closing her eyes. "I'll see you bright and early in the morning."

I turned off the light in the room and pulled the door gently closed. When I went back into the bedroom Brand and I now called ours, I told him my concerns for Utha Mae.

"I can arrange for someone to help take care of her," Brand said, "but you should probably ask if that's something she wants first. Some people don't like strangers in their home."

"I wish she lived closer."

"We could always build her a house on the property. That way, you and Tara can take turns checking on her."

"You would build her a house for me?"

"I would be doing it for all of us. Utha Mae's become important to me, too, you know. I care what happens to her, and I would feel better if she were closer to us. I'm just not sure how well we'll be able to keep our secrets from her if she lives beside us. Her body may be old, but she's still mentally sharp."

"We'll cross that bridge when we have to," I said, snuggling closer against his side as we lay together in bed.

I felt Brand's hands start to venture into dangerous territory, considering Utha Mae was in our home.

"What are you trying to do to me?" I moaned, unable to conjure up the will to ask him to stop.

"I thought it was quite obvious what I'm trying to do to you," he murmured, bringing his lips to mine in a breath-stealing kiss.

"We can't do this," I said, "not with Utha Mae in the house."

"Hmm, then I guess we need to go somewhere else for a few minutes."

Before I knew it, we were in our bedroom at our London home.

"Is this better?" Brand asked, nibbling the side of my neck.

"Much," I said, before rolling Brand over to have my way with him for the rest of the night.

The next morning, Utha Mae, Tara, and I ventured out early on our annual holiday shopping adventure. Malik let Tara borrow his SUV, because I wanted to buy a new Christmas tree and decorations for my home with Brand. It would be our first Christmas together, and I wanted everything to be perfect.

Top on Tara's list of wants was the latest Nintendo gaming system. It was the only thing Malik wanted for Christmas. So, naturally, Tara was hell bent on getting it for him. The problem was that our Walmart only had ten of them in stock on Black Friday. So, her chances of actually getting one were about a 100 to 1, considering the number of people waiting outside the store to rush in and start shopping.

While we stood in line with the other holiday shoppers, Tara began doing squats on the sidewalk.

"What are you doing?" I asked, eyeing her suspiciously.

"Gettin' ready," she said, standing to start pumping her arms in the air above her head with fisted hands.

"Getting ready for what? World War III?"

"Don't laugh at me, Lilly Rayne," Tara said in all seriousness, twisting at the waist to loosen her muscles. "You know how some of these people are. I'm not about to let anybody get between me and that new Nintendo gamepad. Not when my man asked for it in particular."

"Your man?" Utha Mae asked, as if to question when Malik had officially become Tara's man.

"He's mine, Grandma, and I plan to keep him for a long time," Tara declared as she began to whirl her arms around and around, like propellers on an airplane.

I noticed the people around us start to cautiously inch away. I felt sure they thought Tara had completely lost her mind, and would be sure to keep their distance from her once inside the store. And maybe that was Tara's strategy all along. When the front doors finally did open, everyone gave her a wide berth as she dashed inside, letting out a mighty war cry from the top of her lungs, like a banshee escaping out of the gates of Hell itself.

Utha Mae and I stood stock still as those around us cautiously followed behind Tara.

"Did my grandbaby just do what I think she did?" Utha Mae said to me discreetly out the side of her mouth, complete disbelief on her face.

"Let's never speak of this to anyone," I said, hoping to take what I had just witnessed to my grave. "And let's get our stuff and get out as quick as we can. Maybe she won't be able to find us if we hurry."

However, find us she did.

In the middle of the Christmas decoration aisle, Tara held up her Nintendo box and did what I can only call her touchdown dance, similar to the one football players do in the end zone when they've scored for their team. Utha Mae and I just stared at her silently as she gyrated and held up her prized possession, all the while saying, "Who's the best shopper in the world? Tara Jenkins is the best shopper in the world, that's who!"

Utha Mae and I looked at one another and couldn't prevent the laughter that followed. This only seemed to embolden Tara as she began to jerk her body even faster.

By the end of the day, we had all gotten pretty much everything we'd set our sights on the day before. As we drove Utha Mae back to Dalton, I asked her about moving to Lakewood to be closer to Tara and me.

"Brand wants to build me a house?" she questioned. "I haven't had a house since I was married to Harry."

"Will you let us do this for you?" I asked her. "We really want you to be closer to us."

"Normally, I wouldn't accept such generosity," she said. "But I can't say it wouldn't be nice to be closer to you girls. Do you think I could help design it?"

I smiled. "I know the perfect person to draw up the plans. Malcolm is a fantastic architect. I'm sure he would love to help you design your dream home."

"All right then, baby. I would be happy to accept your generous offer. Who knows, maybe I can pay you back by babysitting."

I heard Tara almost choke on the Coke she was drinking. I was just thankful she was able to keep the car on the road.

"We'll see," I told Utha Mae, not wanting to tell her why I would never be able to have children unless a small miracle occurred.

Who knew what the future might bring? On my last visit with God, He showed me my daughter again and called her a wedding gift. Could He possibly plan to allow Brand and me to have a child who wasn't cursed? And what of the dream I had in which I first met my daughter and found myself pregnant with a rather rambunctious baby boy? Had it just been a dream, conjured by my own desires for a real family, or had it been a possible glimpse into the future? Only time would give me the answers I needed. I just prayed I had enough of it to discover the answers for myself.

When Tara dropped me off, Brand wasn't home. After we got all my purchases inside, Tara left, saying she planned to have supper with Malik.

I decided to try to assemble the new Christmas tree I bought while I waited for Brand to come back home. I had just laid out all the tree limbs by their color-coding, when I suddenly felt the warm hands of my husband encircle my waist.

"Did you have fun today?" he asked, propping his chin on my shoulder as he surveyed the pile of artificial limbs lined up on the floor. "You know, we could have just bought a real tree."

"Oh, I didn't think about that. I've always just had artificial ones. Would you rather have a real one?"

"It doesn't matter to me. I already have my Christmas present, and I don't think she'll fit under a tree," he said, squeezing me tight.

I turned to face him within the circle of his arms, and wrapped my own around his neck.

"Were you able to speak with Samyaza today?"

"No, but Isaiah tracked him down and told me to expect a message from him tomorrow sometime."

"Did you tell Isaiah what we planned to ask him to do?"

"Yes."

"And?"

"He thinks it's a long-shot but certainly worth a try."

"Does he still feel guilty after all these years? He may have been your leader, but it's not like he forced you to follow him."

"I think he understands that intellectually, but those who are leaders, at least good ones, always feel like they're responsible for the ones placed under their command. He feels like he failed us and just can't seem to get rid of the guilt."

"Well, Isaiah's right; we have to try. There's no other choice."

"But that's not until tomorrow," Brand said, drawing me closer to him. "I say we spend the time in between in a more productive way."

And that we did…

Later, when we lay in bed, holding each other afterwards, Brand said, "I want you to take me somewhere."

I lifted my head off his chest. "Where do I know that you don't?"

"The house Malcolm built you. I only saw it that once in your dream. You've never actually taken me there. I would like to see it in person."

We got dressed and I phased us to my Colorado home.

Brand looked out the picture window at the snow-capped mountain and lake. When he turned around in the empty living room, he said, "Let me buy you some furniture for this place as a Christmas present."

I hugged him around the waist and asked, "What can I get you for Christmas?"

"Like I said earlier, you are my present."

"I have to get you something for under the Christmas tree."

"You really don't, my love. I have everything I want."

"Well, if I end up buying you a funny-looking Christmas sweater, just act like you love it and can't live without it."

Brand laughed. "All I will ever want, all I will ever need, is you, Lilly. Even if I lost every possession I own, I wouldn't care, as long as you were still by my side."

With words like those, how could I stop myself from phasing us back home and having my way with my husband?

CHAPTER 11.

The next afternoon, Isaiah phased into our living room as Brand and I were making out on the couch.

"Whoa, did *not* mean to see that," Isaiah said, lifting his hand to shield his eyes and turning away from us. "I guess I should have called first. I forgot you're still newlyweds."

Brand stood and I quickly began to button my shirt.

"Yes," Brand said, not bothering to put his t-shirt back on, "you should have."

"I promise I will next time. Are you decent, Lilly?" Isaiah asked.

"Yes, you can look now." I stood by Brand, eager to hear what Isaiah had to tell us.

Isaiah faced us with a sheepish grin on his face. "A thousand apologizes, truly. I only came to tell you Mason is ready to see you now."

"Who's Mason?" I asked.

"It's Samyaza's human name," Brand said. "Most of us adopted one when we had to live here on Earth."

"What was your angelic name?" I asked Brand.

"Tir."

"And Malcolm?"

"Raum."

"He'll meet with you at the stones," Isaiah said. "And he wants to speak with Lilly alone."

"Why alone?" Brand asked, immediately suspicious.

"He said he didn't want you there influencing his decision. He wants Lilly to plead her own case for his help. I'm to bring Lilly only."

"Right now?" I questioned, feeling as though I should change out of my simple white button-down shirt and blue jeans.

"If you want to speak with him, it will have to be now or never," Isaiah told me.

I quickly went upstairs to grab a coat and put some shoes on. When I came back downstairs, Brand pulled me into his arms.

"Can I have a kiss for good luck?" I said.

Brand kissed me tenderly on the lips. "You don't need luck. He won't be able to refuse you."

I placed my hand in Isaiah's, and soon found myself standing beside something I had only seen on TV and online: Stonehenge.

It was nighttime in England. The moon was full in the star-filled sky, illuminating the lone figure standing in the middle of the ancient ring of stones, his back turned to me. He wore a long dark coat with the collar standing stiffly around his neck.

"I have to leave you," Isaiah said reluctantly. I turned to him and saw how despondent his expression was. He, like most of the Watchers I knew, felt the calm I brought to their souls. I knew his craving for human blood would be almost nonexistent around me, and pitied him for having to endure such pain.

Isaiah phased, leaving me to do my best to convince the leader of the Watchers to help me in my quest.

When I stepped into the ring of stones, Mason didn't turn to face me. I heard him take a deep breath, and saw his shoulders shudder slightly.

"I see why they treasure you so," he said, still with his back to me. "I thought Brand was lying at first, and needed to know for myself what power you held over the fallen under your control."

"I don't control anyone," I said, slightly offended.

"You are the child of Michael, Lilly. Of course you control them. You control them without even having to consciously make an effort to bend them to your will. Your power is in your blood. It courses through your veins, like fire."

"I would never use my power to make them do anything they didn't want to do."

"Do you offer me the same courtesy?" Mason turned to face me. "Can you honestly stand there and tell me, if I refuse your request, you wouldn't use your power to make me do what you want anyway?"

I looked away from Mason's penetrating gaze. Even though I couldn't see him clearly, I felt the strength of his will, and understood why he had been chosen to lead the Watchers on Earth.

"No, I would not make you do what I want against your will. That isn't the type of person I am."

"Michael would use his power. Why not you, his only daughter?"

"Because I'm not my father."

Mason was silent for a while before saying, "No, I guess you're not."

"I came here to ask for your help. Brand seems to think if we bring the Watchers together, they can figure out Lucifer's plans for me. Whatever he does have planned, I can assure you it won't be good for any of us. Please, I'm asking for your help. Will you gather the Watchers together to help me?"

Mason sighed heavily. "What you ask me to do is something that hasn't been done since we were exiled here. Why are you so sure the Watchers will even listen to me after all these years?"

"Because you were their leader; I believe they want something to fight for again."

"You know our father sent us here to help humanity flourish. We were scholars, artists, craftsmen - everything the human race needed to learn, we provided. Then, we did the one thing He forbade us to do. We took human women as our wives and tried to have children with them. We tried to have families because we craved such a connection to other living souls. I stood silent as all of those under my command eventually succumbed to their desires, because that was what I wanted for myself too. Even though I knew it was wrong, I still let it happen."

"Did you have a child with your wife?"

"Yes. And now he is burdened with the curse of all Watcher children. He writhes in pain every night, because I was too weak, yet he still loves me. I can only assume it's his mother's half which can still love a monster."

"Has Brand told you about my dreams?"

Mason cocked his head. "What dreams?"

"God has visited me in my dreams. From what He's shown me and told me, I can tell He still loves all of you, and I believe He wants to give you a way to be forgiven for the sin you committed."

"Did He tell you this?"

"In a way; Malcolm says He speaks obtusely, that you have to make out his real meaning by what He provides you."

"I had hoped He would outgrow that annoying habit."

I smiled. "No, apparently He's still doing it. But from what we've been able to piece together, God has been watching all of you, and I believe He's allowing Lucifer's plan to play out, at least to a certain extent, in order to bring you all closer to Him. Don't you owe it to the others to give them a chance at redemption? If you say you regret not stopping them from falling from grace, then do something now to help them at least have a chance at forgiveness."

Mason was silent for a while. Then he walked up to me, completely revealing his face to my eyes in the moonlight.

He was handsome, like all Watchers are, but his beauty was marred by a scar over his left eye. The slash looked like it had been deep when made, stretching from right above his eye to just below his cheekbone. The pain he must have endured from such a wound had to have been great. I felt compelled to touch the old wound and raised my hand towards his face, only then realizing my hand once again flamed bright with the light of my power. When I touched the edge of the scar with the tips of my fingers, Mason took in a sharp breath. I knew my touch didn't hurt him because that wasn't my intention. I wanted to heal his wound.

"It can't be healed," Mason said in a tight voice, somehow knowing my true intention.

"Why?" I asked.

"It is a wound from my father, proof of His disappointment in me and a constant reminder of how I failed Him."

I let my hand fall back down to my side, the flames instantly extinguishing.

"Thank you," he said, bowing his head to me.

"For what?" I asked.

"I haven't felt the Touch in quite a while."

I remembered what my power had done to Robert. But when I touched Robert, I was angry, and my power destroyed him. Apparently, that wasn't all it did.

"I don't understand. What did you feel?"

"For just a second, I felt the love my father still holds for me."

"But my touch can kill the fallen."

"Your touch also acts as a conduit between Him and the person you're touching. It can bring a peace so great it negates any pain they may be feeling. Thank you for giving me hope He can forgive me. And I will do what you have requested. I will gather the Watchers."

"And King Solomon's ring? Have you been able to track it down yet?"

"Not exactly, but I found someone who knows where it can be found. I won't lie and say obtaining the ring will be easy for you. From what I was told, you will be judged by those who have no right to judge you. However, if you pass their test, you will be granted access to the ring."

"Who is this someone you found?"

"A jinn named Horace."

"He knows where it is?" I asked in disbelief, remembering the ragged pawnshop owner who told Malcolm and me the whereabouts of Faust not long ago.

"From your tone, I take it you know him."

"Yes, we've met."

"Go to him and tell him I sent you. He will tell you what you need to know. Make sure Brand and Malcolm are with you, though. I trust Horace about as far as I can throw him. Brand will make sure he is telling the truth, and Malcolm isn't someone Horace wants to intentionally anger."

"Thank you," I touched Mason on the arm, and instantly felt his tenseness fade. "Thank you for your help."

"There's no need for you to thank me. You've given me more than you ask of me. I will contact you when it's time for the gathering. It will take me a while to track down all of the Watchers, but I will do it as quickly as I can. Farewell, Lilly. I will see you soon."

When I returned home, I told Brand everything that happened. We phased to Malcolm's house, and filled him in on what I'd learned from Mason.

"Of course," Malcolm said. "Why didn't I think about Horace? Considering he's spent the greater part of his life searching for his own ring, it makes sense he would know the whereabouts of other relics."

"I say we go now and find out what he knows," Brand said. "The sooner we get the ring for Lilly, the better."

When we entered Horace's pawnshop, the dirty little jinn was sitting behind his counter, stuffing his face with a Twinkie. His eyes widened when we entered, and he spat out the Twinkie into a trash can before he choked on it.

"To what do I owe the pleasure of this little visit?" Horace asked, wiping crumbs from his beard.

"Mason sent me," I told him.

"So you're the one? He didn't tell me it was you."

"What do you know about King Solomon's ring?" Malcolm asked, making it clear we weren't there to make small talk.

"I know *you* can't get it, Malcolm," Horace said, a self-satisfied grin on his face. "Only someone with a pure soul can reach it."

"What do you mean? Where is it?" I asked.

"The old bastard took it to his grave. But it wasn't the only thing buried with him. All of the demons he commanded with it are there protecting it. They won't let a fallen come near it. I've tried; our souls are too tainted."

"But someone with a pure soul can go in and get it?" I asked. "The demons won't harm that person?"

"So goes the legend," Horace said, eyeing me curiously. "But if you have the slightest thing to feel guilty about, or if you have doubt in yourself, they'll use it to drive you insane. You may never recover and end up being trapped with them"

I looked at Brand beside me. "Is he telling the truth?"

Brand nodded. "Yes, he's telling the truth as he knows it."

I looked back at Horace. "Do you know where the king's tomb is?"

"Sure, I can even take you there….for a price."

"Everyone knows where the tomb is, Horace" Brand said. "We don't need you to take us there."

"Ah," Horace said, pointing his index finger in the air. "You all *think* you do, but you don't. Solomon wasn't a fool. He made sure everyone knew where he was *supposed* to be buried, but he's not actually there. He left instructions with those he trusted to place his body somewhere no one would think to look for it."

I looked at Brand and saw him nod his head. Horace was telling the truth.

"What's your price?" Malcolm asked, daring Horace to ask for something that would be impossible for us to grant.

"Once you have the ring, I want a favor. Let's just say you would owe me one."

"What type of favor?"

"I won't tell you, because you might not do it if you know what it is."

"Would it hurt anyone?" I asked.

"Not really," Horace said, with a small shrug of his shoulders, his voice not completely certain. "It all depends on how you look at it, I guess."

Time was a precious commodity. The faster we got the ring, the better.

"Can you at least promise me no one will die because of the favor you wish to ask?" I said.

Horace raised his right hand. "You have my oath, as a jinn, that no one will die if you do as I ask."

I looked to Brand for confirmation that Horace was telling the truth. Brand nodded his head.

"Then take us," I told Horace, praying I hadn't just made a deal I would later come to regret.

CHAPTER 12.

Before we left, Horace scavenged around in his horde of stuff in the pawnshop, and handed us all flashlights.

"It's going to be dark where we're going," Horace said, by way of explanation.

We all held on to Horace as he phased us to the location of King Solomon's tomb.

A cold wind swirled the air around us. My eyes were drawn to the lights of a city not that far in the distance. A multitude of light-colored buildings with red-tiled roofs dotted the landscape. I turned my flashlight on and saw that we were standing on hard- packed sand with clumps of dried grass a foot high scattered in a random pattern. A small broken stone wall stood on one side of me, while a scattering of mostly-buried structures made of the same stone jutted up from the ground.

"Tel Beit Shemesh?" Malcolm questioned. "Why would he bury himself here?"

"Exactly; who would think to look for him in this dump?" Horace said, like the answer was self-evident.

"Where is the tomb?" Brand asked, obviously wanting to get down to business and get out.

"I'll have to take her down myself," Horace said, pointing to the ground at his feet.

"Down where?" I asked.

"Down to the tomb, of course; you don't think he would bury himself where just anyone could find him, do you?"

"If you take her, you take us all," Malcolm told Horace.

"Did you not hear a word I said back at the shop?" Horace huffed in irritation. "They won't let you in there. Only she can go in and get it. Trust me; you being there would just make things worse for her. I'm going to phase her down and come right back up before they sense me. She'll be fine."

"It's ok," I told Brand and Malcolm. "I'm not scared."

Brand took me in his arms. "At the first sign of danger, come back up. Don't risk your life."

"Everything's going to be all right," I said, giving Brand a kiss before I took Horace's hand.

"Now when you get down there, just walk to the other end of the hallway," Horace instructed. "The tomb is there."

Horace was true to his word. He phased me down to a dark corridor and immediately left.

Living in the modern world, you become used to small noises always being in the background and you don't even realize it. The hallway I stood in was cut out of rock, and complete, undisturbed silence surrounded me.

I cautiously made my way down the corridor, scanning the walls with my flashlight for any signs of trouble, but seeing none. I began to wonder if Horace had made his ghost story up to frighten me, until I saw a white apparition appear at the end of the hallway. The ghostly form slowly floated towards me. I felt the temperature in the room drop by about ten degrees, and pulled the lapels of my coat closer around my neck to ward off the chill. I stood stock-still until the spirit stood before me, shimmering in its otherworldly beauty. It didn't really have a true form. Its misty shape held a glowing orb of incandescent light at its center.

"Why are you here?" it asked, its voice sounding like wind passing over metal chimes.

"I've come for King Solomon's ring."

"Why do you wish to have it?"

"To prevent Lucifer from using me in his plans."

The mist floated around me, as if it were judging me. Finally, it said, "To pass through them, you must show no fear. They derive their power from the fear of others."

"I'm not afraid of them," I said, knowing he was talking about the demon souls.

"We shall see," the spirit said before fading away.

I continued down the hallway, until I reached a room with a stone box sitting in the middle of the room. As soon as I stepped over the threshold, I felt them. They whirled around me like a hot wind on a summer day. One of them passed through my body, sending a cold shiver of dread down my spine. One by one, the souls of the damned demons buried inside King Solomon's tomb battered my body, like they were searching out my weaknesses.

All of a sudden, I found myself standing on the old wooden half-bridge back in Dalton.

I saw the Will of my childhood sitting with his feet dangling off the edge of the bridge. He turned when he heard my younger version walk up behind him.

"Where's Tara?" he asked.

"She fell asleep," I told him.

"Oh, well," he said, his eyes filled with mischief.

"What are you planning, Will Allen?"

I watched as my younger self stood up, and Will began to chase me around with his stupid garter snake. My young counterpart tripped, hit her head on an old wooden post, and fell into the water.

"Lilly!" Will yelled before diving in after me.

"You feel guilt over this one's death," one of the demons accused.

"It was an accident," I said. "It wasn't anyone's fault."

"Yet, you feel as though you should have done something to prevent it."

"There wasn't anything I could have done," I said, truly realizing for the first time that it was the truth. Will had died because of me, but what had happened hadn't been planned. It was an accident, nothing more.

The scene melted away and changed to the moment I found Tara and Malik, in the forest Robert had taken them to. Tara lay on the ground with Malik transformed into his panther form, licking the torn flesh of her wound. Robert had ripped open her throat, almost killing her because of me.

"Proof that you are a danger to your friends," another demon accused.

"Robert is the one who put them in danger. I did what I had to do to save them."

The dark forest faded and was replaced by a bright, sunny day. I saw Malcolm about to kiss me on our day together. I didn't try to stop him, and felt guilt over the small indiscretion. I shouldn't have let him do it, but I wanted to know what it would feel like, so I let it happen. I watched as we had our talk, and relived the question that broke my heart the first time he asked me.

"May I have one last kiss, dearest Lilly, before I make my heart let you go?"

"You allowed this man to kiss you, even though you had pledged your heart to another," another demon mocked.

"I had a moment of weakness," I confessed. "But I never let Malcolm think I loved him more than Brand. I did what I had to do to make him finally realize we couldn't be anything more than friends after that."

A vision of Robert and me struggling against one another materialized, and I was forced to watch myself discover my true power and reduce him to a pile of ash.

"He tried to harm you, yet you still feel guilt over his death. Why?"

"You should never take joy in the death of someone else," I said, remembering God's words to me. "I don't believe what I did was wrong, but it brought me no joy either."

The scene melted away, as did my guilt over the events in my life that the demons tried to use against me to weaken me. Now I knew why Horace had said only someone with a pure heart could get close to the ring. No human can have a completely pure heart. We all have things we regret. We all have something in our pasts that we feel guilty about, but you can't let regret and guilt rule your life. You have to find the strength within to forgive yourself. I let go of my guilt and regrets, realizing some had been out of my control and some had been simple human mistakes.

The spirits ceased their bombardment of my soul, fading into nothingness.

S.J. WEST

I stood and walked over to the tomb, sliding the stone cover with more ease than I had expected. Lying within were the bones of King Solomon, still wearing his crown around his skull and the ring on his finger.

I pulled the simple silver ring off his skeletal finger, and looked at it in the light of my flashlight.

The ring was embossed with a pentagram and six colorful jewels, which twinkled against the light to illuminate the stone walls with their brilliance.

"Be careful with the power it possesses," the misty white spirit said as it floated into the room.

"I'll bring it back to you when I'm done with it," I promised, now knowing the spirit was that of King Solomon.

"I will be waiting," he said, fading once again.

I phased back to the surface.

Brand and Malcolm immediately made me put the ring on. It was large, so I had to place it on my thumb.

"Try it out," Malcolm encouraged.

"On what?" I asked.

"Horace, of course," Malcolm replied, gesturing to the jinn with his hand.

"Now wait just a damn minute," Horace said, filled with righteous indignation. "I didn't say you could do that."

"How do I control him?" I asked, having my own reasons for wanting to control Horace.

"Just tell him to do something," Brand said.

I looked at Horace and said, "Sit down."

Horace sat down on the packed sand without argument.

"Tell me what favor you want me to do for you," I said, still wanting to know what type of bargain I had struck with the jinn.

132

"I want you to make Faust give me my ring." Horace clamped both of his hands over his mouth, but it was too late. I knew what I wanted to know now.

"How do you know he has it?" I asked.

"Because another jinn saw him with it," Horace said, then quickly covered his mouth again, as if that would stop him from answering any more of my questions.

"We did promise to do his favor, dearest," Malcolm reminded me.

"But if he gets his ring back, he'll start making bargains with people and ruining their lives. You saw the actor Faust was using. He lost everything when Faust left, but he didn't care, because he finally had his freedom back. How can I let Horace do that to people?"

"Anyone Horace tries to trick is looking for an easy way to obtain something," Brand said. "You shouldn't pity people like that."

I knew both Brand and Malcolm were right. We had struck a bargain with Horace. He'd kept his end of the deal. Now I had to keep mine.

"Where is Faust?" I asked.

"I don't know just yet, but I'll find him," Horace said fervently. "Can I get up now? This ground is cold."

"Get up," I said in irritation. "Go back to your shop and don't contact me until you know where Faust is."

"Got a phone number?" Horace asked.

Brand gave him his cell phone number. Horace memorized it and quickly phased back to his shop.

I looked at the ring on my hand and asked, "Now how do we test it out on Lucifer?"

"Are he and your mother back from Vegas yet?" Brand asked.

"I'm not sure."

"Call her and try to arrange a night where we can take them out to dinner. It'll give us a good excuse to meet with them, without him being too suspicious of our motives. We need to catch him off-guard to truly test the ring's effect on him."

CHAPTER 13.

My mom wasn't back from Vegas yet, but we did arrange to have dinner with them the following Monday.

"I have some wonderful news for you," my mother said to me over the phone, sounding happier than I had ever heard her before, "but I'll wait until I see you to tell you what's happened."

When I got off the phone with my mom, I told Brand what she had said.

"I'm worried," I confessed. "What do you think he's done to her? Can he brainwash people? She's never sounded that happy before."

"I know you haven't had the best relationship with your mother in the past, but, just because she's acting happy, doesn't mean Lucifer is influencing her more than he would any other human. He can't make people do what he wants unless he's possessed them. Whatever he's doing is genuinely making her happy."

"But isn't that reason enough to be worried?" I felt on the edge of hysterics. "You and I both know this won't end well for her. She's going to get her heart broken one way or the other."

"Then let her enjoy the happiness she thinks she has, for however long it lasts. All you can do is help her pick up the pieces afterwards."

I pulled Brand close to me. "I don't know what I would do without you."

"Well, that's something you will never have to worry about. I will always be with you."

As I stood close to Brand, feeling his love like a physical bond between the two of us, I decided it was time to tell him about my touch.

"I learned something about my power when I was with Mason," I said, pulling away from Brand slightly.

"What was that, my love?"

I raised my hand, now lit with the fire of my power.

"He called it the Touch," I said. "He said I was a conduit between God and whoever I touched, that you could feel what God feels for you from it."

Brand looked at my hand and took a step back. The cautious way he stared at it told me he wasn't sure he wanted to know exactly what God thought of him. Like all the Watchers, Brand still held the guilt of his sin in his heart. Even though he had spent his life here on Earth trying to be the best person he could, Brand wasn't sure it was enough to atone for going against God's law.

Taking a deep breath, Brand nodded his head, giving me permission to touch him, to finally let him know where he stood with his father.

I reached out and cupped the side of his face with my hand. Brand closed his eyes as he took in a sharp breath, and fell to his knees in front of me. When he looked back up at me, I saw the shimmer of tears in his eyes.

"How could He..." he started to say.

I let the fire fade and knelt in front of Brand.

"How could He what?"

"How could He still love me?"

136

"How could He not?" I asked in return.

Brand pulled me into his arms. "Thank you, my love. Thank you for sharing that with me."

I felt Brand's shoulders shake slightly, and knew he was crying. I held my husband close and, for the first time, felt thankful for the power my father had passed down to me.

The next day, I asked Malcolm to go to Utha Mae's with me. When I told him about our plans to build her a house next to ours, he was like a kid given carte blanche to a candy store.

Brand wasn't able to go with us, because Isaiah called on him to help give Mason's message about the gathering to all the Watchers he knew.

"So you're ok with me being alone with Malcolm?" I said.

"Of course I am; he won't do anything you don't allow him to."

The gnawing guilt of Brand not knowing everything that had happened on the day I spent with Malcolm felt like it would literally split me in two.

"I have to tell you something," I finally said, gaining Brand's full attention.

"You know you can tell me anything," he replied, leaning against the kitchen island as he waited patiently for me to continue.

"I know you said you didn't need to know the details about that day I spent with Malcolm, but I need you to know. I need you to know what I did."

Brand crossed his arms over his chest, as if preparing himself for what I was about to say. "If you feel like you need to tell me, and if it would make you feel better, I'll try to listen with an open mind."

"I let Malcolm kiss me," I confessed.

Brand's eyebrows lowered. He was silent for a while, as if measuring his next words to me carefully.

"Did you enjoy it?" he asked.

I wanted to deny my true feeling to Brand, but knew he would see right through a lie. If I was going to finally purge myself of guilt, I had to be completely honest, even if it hurt us both.

"Yes," I admitted, without trying to make excuses for myself.

"And was this just one kiss?"

If at all possible, I felt my heart sink even lower with his question.

"Two," I said, "but the last one was more of a way to say goodbye to his feelings for me."

Brand's chin lowered closer to his chest as he thought about what I told him.

"Do you plan to let it happen again?" he questioned tersely.

"No, of course not." I shook my head to emphasize the point. "I shouldn't have let it happen the first time."

"Then why did you?" Brand asked, finally looking back up at me. The hurt I saw in his eyes from my betrayal cut me to the quick.

"I wanted to know what it would feel like," I replied, knowing how lame my reasoning sounded, even to my own ears, but not having a better answer to give him.

"And what did you think? Was it as good as you dreamt it would be?"

I could see Brand's hurt quickly turn to anger, and felt helpless to stop it.

"Please," I begged, "don't make me regret telling you the truth. You have to know how much I love you. There's no one else in the world for me but you. I made a stupid mistake, and I'm sorry for it. Please don't let this come between us. I don't think I could go on if you stayed mad at me."

Brand's pose relaxed a bit. "I'm not exactly angry at you, more like disappointed, Lilly. I never thought you would let him do something like that, but I can't let you take all the blame. I pushed you to spend the day with him, because I needed to know whether or not you would return to me. I needed to know you loved me more than you do him."

"You have to know, after all the time we've spent together, that you are the only man I love, the only man I have ever completely shared myself with, body and soul. I can't live with you being disappointed with me. You have to find it in your heart to forgive me, or I'll never be able to forgive myself for hurting you."

Brand let his arms fall to his side.

"I am hurt," he admitted, "but I'm the last person who you should be begging forgiveness from, considering my past."

I walked up to Brand and leaned into him. He didn't immediately put his arms around me like he usually did, but, after a few seconds, I felt them encircle me.

"I'm sorry," I said, tentatively pressing my lips against his, trying to coax him into thinking about our future together, not my past transgressions. "I'm so sorry."

I continued to kiss him lightly, until he pulled himself out of his sad reverie and held my head in between his hands, deepening the kiss with an urgency and forcefulness he'd never displayed before. I felt him try to undo the buttons of my shirt, and heard him groan in frustration as he finally yanked the shirt open, tearing the buttons loose from their thin threads to allow him free access to my flesh.

Our lovemaking was filled with a desperate need on both our parts. My desperation stemmed from a need to erase Brand's mental picture of me allowing Malcolm to kiss me. I wanted him to know, without any doubt, that he was the only man I wanted to share all of me with. Brand seemed intent on wiping any trace of desire I might have had for Malcolm from my mind and every inch of my body. He was slightly rougher than usual, but it only added to the fuel of our passion for one another. When we reached that point where our world shattered, we met it together, with our thoughts only for one another.

We lay on the kitchen floor, trying to calm our beating hearts afterward. Suddenly, Brand sat up, looking down at me in alarm.

"What?" I asked, still basking in the glow of our heated lovemaking, wondering why we hadn't done it that way sooner.

Brand watched me, his breathing heavy.

When he didn't say anything, I sat up too. "What's wrong?"

"How do you feel?" he whispered, almost like he was scared to hear my answer.

"I feel wonderful," I said, not understanding why he was looking at me so strangely. "What's wrong, Brand?"

Brand drew me into his arms, and I felt him breathe a sigh of relief.

"I didn't use anything," he said. "I was worried…" he couldn't finish the rest of his statement, but I knew what he was thinking.

"Would we know instantly?" I asked.

"If you were pregnant, we would know by now. That's the way it happened with Abby's mother."

I hugged Brand tightly, needing him to feel my strength, a reassurance that I wasn't pregnant.

"I won't let that happen again," he promised fervently.

I pulled back slightly, holding his head in my hands, forcing him to look into my eyes.

"Please don't keep that promise," I said to him in earnest, "because I want that to happen again and again and again, and as many times as we can possibly do it in my lifetime."

Brand's mouth finally twitched into a smile, and the light of happiness I loved to see in his eyes when he looked at me reappeared. He phased us to our bed and proved to me that my worry was completely unfounded.

A couple of hours later, Brand and I decided we needed to meet our obligations for the day. Malcolm came to the house and picked me up in his Bugatti, saying he didn't get to drive it much and the trip gave him a good excuse to stretch its legs.

Brand answered the door when Malcolm knocked on it. I suppose, in hindsight, I should have made sure I was the one who greeted Malcolm, but what followed probably would have happened one way or the other.

As soon as Brand opened the door to a grinning Malcolm, he pulled back his fist and hit Malcolm so hard across the chin the force of the blow sent Malcolm flying over his car and into the dirt road in front of the house.

I ran to the front porch to make sure my friend was still in one piece, and breathed a sigh of relief when I saw him stand up, rubbing his chin.

"What the hell was that for?" Malcolm grumbled, walking back up to the house.

"That," Brand yelled back, pointing his index finger at Malcolm, "was for kissing my wife!"

Malcolm looked at me. I shrugged lamely.

"Well, at least you didn't take my head off this time. I guess that's an improvement."

"Take your head off?" I asked, assuming I had heard him wrong. "When did he take your head off?"

Brand crossed his arms over his chest and said, "After he saw you naked in the shower."

I looked at Malcolm for confirmation, and saw him nod his head as he walked up the steps to the front porch.

I felt myself start to smile, and then found myself completely amused by such an absurd vision as Malcolm without a head. Will had told me Watchers could tear each other apart and still survive, but I guess I'd never thought Brand would go that far to avenge my honor.

I was still giggling when Malcolm drove us away from Lakewood, towards Dalton.

"Why on Earth would you tell your overprotective husband about our innocent little interlude, dearest?"

"Because I don't want to keep any secrets from him; he deserved to know the truth, and I needed to get rid of the guilt."

"Could you possibly warn me the next time you tell Brand something which might result in me having to reattach a part of my body?"

I smiled. "Just keep your hands to yourself, and we won't have anything to worry about."

Malcolm sighed heavily, clearly disappointed by my suggestion.

"I'll try," he said, "but don't hate me if I take advantage of an opportunity. The loss of a limb might be worth it."

I hit Malcolm on the arm, which just made him chuckle.

That afternoon, Utha Mae described to Malcolm the home she wanted us to build for her.

"Nothing too big," she said. "I just want a little yellow-painted house with a wraparound porch. I don't want an upstairs. These poor old legs aren't what they used to be anymore. I need a good sized kitchen, a couple of bedrooms, and a living room."

Malcolm jotted down the details in his notebook. "What about a nice sunroom to watch the lake from?" Malcolm suggested.

"Oh, do you think I could have that?" Utha Mae asked, her eyes lit like a kid at Christmas.

"You can have anything you want," I told her. "All you have to do is tell us."

"I just don't want you and Brand spending too much money on me," Utha Mae said.

I knew Utha Mae wasn't one to spend money on herself very often. All her life, she struggled to keep a roof over her and Tara's heads. Letting herself indulge in something she really wanted by using other people's money just wasn't something she did. I was thankful she was allowing Brand and me to gift her with a new home of her own, but, honestly, it felt like we were being given the gift. Her willingness to abandon a home she owned, and allowing us to spend whatever time she had near us, was priceless.

Malcolm quickly drew up a picture of what he thought Utha Mae wanted, and got her input on what needed to be added. By the time we got ready to leave, they had pretty much decided on a plan.

While Malcolm was gathering up his drawing supplies, Utha Mae asked him, "You think you could give me a ride in that fancy car of yours?"

Malcolm smiled with genuine happiness.

"I was just waiting for you to ask," he told her, taking Utha Mae by the arm, and giving me a wink as they walked out the door.

Malcolm helped Utha Mae into his car, and spun his tires as he raced out of the trailer park. I made the sign of the cross on my body, even though I wasn't Catholic. I sent up a silent prayer ensuring Utha Mae didn't have a heart attack on her little excursion with Malcolm. The way he drove almost always gave my heart palpitations.

When they made it back half an hour later, I could hear Utha Mae's joyful laughter through the open window of the car as they pulled back up to her trailer. She sounded like a teenage girl who had just been taken on her first joyride.

"Have fun?" I asked her while Malcolm helped her exit the passenger side.

"Oh, Lordy," she said, a smile so large on her face it dimpled her cheeks, "I don't think I've ever been driven that fast in my whole entire life. I'll never forget it, that's for sure."

On our way back to Lakewood, I decided to tell Malcolm about the Touch I possessed. Brand had been so deeply affected by it, and I wanted to give my best friend a chance to experience it for himself.

"No, thank you, dearest."

"Why not?"

"I have a good idea what He thinks of me, and I would rather not have it confirmed."

"I think He still loves you, Malcolm."

"That's because I've only let you see the good side of me. If you knew the culmination of things I've done in my past, you wouldn't so readily offer to share what He thinks of me. I have a lot to atone for, far more than Brand and Mason put together."

"I think you might be surprised by what you find out," I told him. "When you change your mind, just let me know."

"Maybe one day," Malcolm half-promised, even though I felt sure that one day might never come.

CHAPTER 14.

The next day, Brand and I attended our classes, trying our best to keep things as normal as possible. I still kept my job as Dr. Barry's teacher's aide, but I told her I wouldn't be able to help her the following semester; partly because I wasn't a hundred percent sure I would still be alive. She took my resignation in stride, and said she had already assumed I would probably be quitting, since I married Brand. She didn't say it in so many words, but I could tell she knew Brand wasn't exactly hurting for money.

That night, as Brand and I prepared to meet my mom and Lucifer at a restaurant in Lakewood, I asked Brand, "How do I test the ring on Lucifer without it looking like I am?"

"You'll have to wait for an opportunity to present itself. The most important thing is to find a way to make sure he sees the ring. His reaction to it might be a dead giveaway to how it affects him."

We were the first to arrive at the Purple Parrot restaurant. It was one of the more upscale establishments in Lakewood, with a master chef who had been trained at the Cordon Bleu in Paris. The cuisine was touted as being the best in the state. The maître d' sat us at a private table in the far corner of the room. It was tastefully decorated with the restaurant's signature purple tablecloth and candle-lit centerpiece.

We had just ordered our drinks when I saw my mom and Lucifer walk in.

"Hey, sweetie," my mom said, when she got to the table, bending down to kiss me on the cheek.

Lucifer pulled out my mother's chair for her, like it was the most natural thing in the world for him to do.

"How was your trip to Vegas?" I asked, trying to force a pleasant smile, even though I felt Lucifer's eyes on me.

Cora looked over at Lucifer and said, "Do you think I should tell her now?"

Lucifer smiled, sending a shiver down my spine.

"I don't see why not. She'll need to know sooner or later, and I would rather not keep it a secret from anyone."

My mother held out her left hand to me. Wrapped around her ring finger was a beautiful diamond solitaire.

"You're not the only one who just got married!" she said, giddy with happiness.

I sat there, stunned into silence. I distantly heard Brand make the perfunctory congratulations, but I couldn't bring myself to say anything. I just stared at the ring in disbelief. My heart began to pound so hard inside my chest all I could hear was the rush of blood inside my head. I suddenly felt as though I might hyperventilate.

"Lilly?" my mom asked in a worried voice. "Are you all right, sweetie?"

"I have to go to the bathroom," I said, quickly getting up and making my way to the ladies' room. Once there, I locked myself into a stall and leaned up against the door, taking deep breaths to steady myself.

I heard someone come in.

"Lilly?" I heard my mom call.

I silently cursed to myself.

"Be right out, Mom."

I flushed the toilet to make it at least appear that I actually did need to use the bathroom, and took a deep breath before I walked out of the stall.

I found my mother leaned against the counter by the sinks, waiting for me.

"Are you sure you're all right?" she asked.

"Yeah, I'm fine," I said, grinning for all I was worth as I walked up to one of the sinks to wash my hands. "You just took me by surprise is all. Really, I'm happy for you."

"I know it must be a shock," my mother admitted. "And I wanted to tell you sooner, but it just didn't feel right saying it over the phone. You know how hard it's been for me to find a good man. When Lucas asked me to marry him in Vegas, I couldn't think of one reason I shouldn't. You're married now, and will have a family of your own soon, and I still have a long life ahead of me. Plus, I'm still young enough to have another child, if Lucas wants to have one."

I felt grateful that would never have a chance of happening. All I needed was the spawn of Lucifer as a new sibling.

"In fact,, I thought maybe you were experiencing some sort of sickness," she hinted in an insinuating voice.

"Mom, I wasn't sick to my stomach, and we've only been married a couple of weeks. That's not really enough time to get pregnant."

"It only took a few days with your father for me to get pregnant," my mother reminded me.

"Could we please stop talking about either of our sex lives?" I pleaded. "Or I might actually become sick."

My mother laughed. "All right. Let's get back to the men before they think we've run away from them."

When we got back to the table, Brand and Lucifer stood like gentlemen should when their ladies return. We placed our orders with the waiter, and I decided to show my mother my own newly-acquired ring.

"Brand gave me a family heirloom the other day," I told my mom, showing her King Solomon's ring still on my thumb. I carefully watched Lucifer's reaction as my mother examined the ring. When he saw it, he looked slightly alarmed. I took it as a good sign.

"It looks really old," my mother said. "I can't say it's very attractive."

"It's meant to ward off bad spirits," Brand explained. "It's an old family tradition to have the wife wear it the first year of marriage; like a good luck charm."

"Oh," my mother said knowingly, "is it supposed to make the woman more fertile?"

"*Mom,*" I said, completely embarrassed.

"Well, a grandbaby wouldn't be so bad," she said. "Everyone said you were the most beautiful baby they ever saw. I can only imagine what a gorgeous baby the two of you will have one day."

"Some people shouldn't have children," Lucifer commented, looking pointedly at Brand while taking a sip from his wine glass.

The rudeness of his statement wasn't missed by my mother, but she still didn't comment on it. She simply let it slide by, as if he hadn't said anything at all. I'm not sure why I expected more from her.

"Perhaps you should leave," I said to Lucifer.

He stared at me for the space of five seconds before standing up and heading out of the restaurant without saying another word. My mother mumbled some sort of excuse about jet lag, and hurriedly walked out of the restaurant with her new husband.

"Was that me, or did he just get up and leave on his own?" I asked Brand.

Brand sat back in his chair and sighed. "I wish I knew."

My mother called me the next day to apologize for Lucifer's behavior the night before. I told her not to worry about it. I didn't want her to feel guilt over something she had no control over. As it was, I felt enough guilt for the both of us. I was allowing my mother to live with the devil himself. If I'd been a better daughter, I would have made her leave him, yet fear of giving her an ultimatum about it being him or me made me realize I felt sure she would choose him.

The next day, Brand got a phone call from Horace. He was finally able to track down the whereabouts of Faust. We were to pick Horace up at his pawnshop, and he would direct us where to go from there.

The sight of Horace as we entered his establishment threw me for a loop. It looked like he had actually taken a bath, his face clean-shaven and hair slicked back. He wore a tailored black suit, pristine white shirt, and black bow tie.

"So where is he?" Brand asked, wanting to get our business with Horace over with as quickly as I did.

"Here in New York, actually," Horace said. I saw him glance down at my hand, as if to make sure I was wearing the ring.

"Ready?" he asked me.

"Yeah," I answered. "Let's get this over with. After today, I don't ever want to see or hear from you again. Is that understood?"

"Absolutely," Horace said nodding his head. "I wouldn't have it any other way."

Horace phased us to the balcony of a penthouse apartment. The outer glass wall in front of us revealed a modern-looking living room with sparse, minimalist furnishings. A well-stocked bar lined one of the interior walls, and we saw Faust there, mixing a pitcher of some sort of pink drink. When he noticed us, he looked surprised, but not stunned by our appearance.

We walked into the apartment. The sound of ice being stirred in the glass pitcher in front of Faust was the only sound in the room.

"Well, to what do I owe this pleasure?" Faust asked tritely.

"Give Horace his ring," I ordered Faust.

Without questioning my order, Faust went to the back of the apartment, only to return a minute later with Horace's ring. Horace snatched the ring from Faust, immediately placing it on the middle finger of his right hand, and phased, having gotten what he came for.

After completing the order I gave him, Faust looked down at me and saw the glint of King Solomon's ring on my hand.

"I guess I should have known," he said before returning to the bar to pour a drink from the pitcher. "Are you going to make me do anything else for you?"

I walked up to him. "Do you know what Lucifer has planned for me?"

Faust had already admitted he wanted Lucifer's plan to succeed, indicating he at least knew what the end result of it would be.

"He plans to tear a whole in the fabric of space and time. There won't be a Heaven or a Hell or an Earth the way you know it."

"How does he plan to do that?" I asked. "How is he going to use me to make it happen?"

Faust stared at me and said nothing.

"I don't think he knows," Brand said, coming to stand behind me. "If he did, the ring would compel him to tell you."

I felt my heart drop. I felt sure Faust would be able to answer my questions, but apparently Lucifer was keeping the details of his plan close to the vest. If Faust didn't know, I wasn't sure who else would.

"Why were you hiding Horace's ring from him?" I asked out of curiosity.

"Because he was becoming an uppity little jinn. I thought he needed to realize he was nothing without his powers."

"That's the only reason?"

"It was enough for me."

I heard the jangle of keys in the door to the apartment and watched as a person I faintly recognized walked inside.

"Heath, dear boy," Faust said, "come in and meet our visitors."

The man was tall, blond, and quite nice to look at. A picture of him surfaced in my mind, and I remembered seeing an article about him writing some best-selling book that was sweeping the nation right now. Everyone was reading the erotic novel he just wrote.

"Your new patron?" I asked Faust.

"Partner is the term I like better," Faust said.

Heath Knowles closed the door behind him and joined us.

"Everything all right here, Faust?" he asked, eyeing Brand and me curiously.

"Just speaking with some old friends; they were just about to leave, I believe."

I turned to Heath. "You realize what he is, right?"

Heath shrugged. "Of course I do. He's like a genie. He made my wishes come true. I was living in a tiny little apartment, trying to make it as a writer when he found me. Now look at where I am," he said, indicating his penthouse, with arms outstretched. "I owe it all to him."

"And you're all right with what you had to give up in order to get it?"

"What, my family? My friends? What did they ever give me but grief? I have what I want now. I don't need them anymore."

Brand had been right. Some people didn't care who got hurt in the bargains with the jinn. Sometimes they just wanted an easy way to get what they most desired.

Heath walked up to Faust and gave him a kiss on the lips, making me realize the apartment wasn't the only thing they were sharing with one another. I had thought perhaps Faust's new patron would be like the actor, but I was apparently wrong. Heath seemed to be enjoying Faust in more ways than one.

I grabbed Brand's hand and phased us back home, not willingly wanting to subject myself to a public display of their amorous feelings for one another.

"Well, that was disturbing to watch," I said, shivering slightly. Thinking of Faust as a sexual being just seemed wrong on so many levels.

"Let's concentrate on what he told us," Brand suggested instead.

"Do you know what he was talking about? How can Lucifer tear a hole in space?"

"Space and time," Brand said. "And how he can do that, I'm not sure. It would take a lot more energy than he possesses."

"How do I factor into it, though?"

"The only thing I can think of is that he intends to combine your archangel powers with his."

"So, he would have to possess me in order to do that, right?"

"Yes." Brand began to pace in front of me, trying to piece together what we knew. "If he truly does plan to connect everything together, he would have to produce a vortex of power here on Earth and in Heaven, at almost the same time."

"Lillith," I said. "You said she could phase into Heaven whenever she wanted. If he can use my archangel power and the power Lillith may have passed down, then I'm the key to it all."

"But it still doesn't explain how he intends to produce that much energy. It would take something far more powerful than just the power of two archangels. We're still missing something important. It's virtually impossible."

"Maybe Uriel was right," I said, feeling as though maybe the angel in charge of protecting Heaven had been correct. Maybe it would be better if I were dead. How could I be so selfish and put the world, the whole universe, in jeopardy?

Brand put his hands on my shoulders. "Look at me."

I forced myself to look at his face, and saw the answer to my own question written there. I had everything to live for standing in front of me. If God thought I could stop what Lucifer had planned, then I had to have faith that, with Brand's help, we would find a way to stop him. What was that phrase? Oh, yes, 'love conquerors all'. If that phrase could be proven, I knew Brand and I would find a way to do it.

"We will find a way to stop him," he said to me, each word filled with conviction. "Trust me."

I pulled him closer, needing to feel his warmth.

"I do trust you," I said. "I trust you more than I've ever trusted anyone. And I need you to make me a promise."

Brand pulled away and asked, "What promise?"

"When the time comes, and if we haven't found a way to stop Lucifer…"

"We will," Brand insisted.

"If we don't," I said, refusing to let him view everything through rose-colored glasses, "don't let me become the reason he succeeds."

Brand looked confused. "What exactly are you asking me to do, Lilly?"

"If there's no hope left, I need you to kill me."

Brand staggered away from me, as if I had just stabbed a knife directly into his heart.

"You can't ask me to do that," he whispered.

"I can," I said. "You have to promise me that you'll do it. I might not be in control of myself when it happens, and I won't be able to kill myself."

"Lilly, please," Brand begged, on the verge of tears, "I can't make that promise. I can't kill you."

"If the ring fails, and Lucifer possesses me, I'll already be dead," I told him. "You would only be killing my body, because my soul wouldn't be there anymore. I have to know Lucifer won't be able to win, Brand. Don't let me be the cause of so much pain. If you love me, be strong enough to let me go when the time comes."

Brand swallowed hard and closed his eyes, so I wouldn't see his pain. I knew what I was asking was a lot. I'm not sure I would have the strength to do what I asked if the tables were turned. But if I was going to die, I needed to know it was because I did the right thing.

"Ok," Brand said so low I had to strain to hear him. "I'll do what you ask if it comes to that. But it won't. I won't let it."

I went up to Brand and hugged him close. I knew how much it took for him to agree to my plan, and I knew he would keep his word to me if it came down to it.

"Thank you," I said to him. "Thank you."

CHAPTER 15.

The following Saturday, the contractors began work on Utha Mae's house. They brought in a large crew to set the pipes and pour the concrete foundation. Malcolm came to watch over the construction. As she did to almost everyone she met, Utha Mae had made Malcolm completely devoted to her, and he wasn't about to let anyone make a mistake in the construction of her new home.

Brand and I chose a spot on the other side of the tree line around our own house. For the past two days, crews had worked to cut down some of the pine trees, to make a clearing big enough for the construction crew. We wanted to make sure she felt close, but not so close that we would completely take away her privacy.

Will brought Utha Mae and my mom over that afternoon so they could see for themselves exactly where we were building Utha Mae's new home. My mother was in unusually high spirits, and seemed to have completely expunged the incident at the restaurant from her mind, like it had never happened. I didn't bring it up to her because, in the grand scheme of things, it really didn't matter. I didn't want my last days with my mom to be filled with strife. It just wasn't worth it, and I felt like if I did keep a grudge against my mom, it would be like giving Lucifer a victory over me. If anything, that thought made me decide to forgive my mother for not being a stronger person. Her life had been manipulated by powers well beyond her control or even comprehension. I couldn't fault her for being human. She had been played like a pawn in a chess game, from all sides; a true victim of circumstance.

I gave my mother a big hug when they all came to the construction site.

"Wow, what was that for?" she asked, pleasantly surprised.

"Just for being my mom," I said. "I love you."

When I pulled away, I saw tears in her eyes.

"You haven't said that since you were a little girl," she told me, only then making me realize how long it had been. It was amazing how three little words could completely change the dynamics of a relationship. She hugged me tightly to her, something she hadn't done in years, and said, "I love you, too, sweetie."

My mom looked at the house construction and said, "I'm so glad you and Brand are doing this for her. I was concerned about leaving her in that trailer park alone. She hasn't been getting around very well lately, but ever since she learned you two were building her this house, it's like she's grown ten years younger."

"So have you moved in with Lucas already?"

"Oh, we moved my stuff right when we got back from Vegas. He has a large house, and I didn't really need to take anything but my clothes and sentimental things, like pictures."

"Does he make you happy?" I asked, not understanding how Lucifer could make any woman happy without hypnotizing them, or some other type of mind control.

"He really does, sweetie. I can't imagine my life without him now. I'm such a better person with him in my life. I always felt like the biggest failure, and now look at me. I'm a doctor's wife. I couldn't be happier. And I'm sorry about what he said to you two the other night; I don't know what got into him. He's usually so loving."

"We all have bad days," I said. "Don't blame yourself."

Will took Utha Mae and my mom home early that evening. Utha Mae said she was tired and needed a little rest. We offered to let her stay at our house for the night, but she said she wanted to be in her own bed. I didn't push the matter. She would be living near us soon enough. I would have plenty of time then to take care of her.

The next day was the day we had been waiting for: the Watcher gathering. Brand had already told me it was to take place in a spot within the Sahara Desert.

I was sitting on our bed as Brand searched in the walk-in closet for something.

"Isn't the Sahara Desert, like, huge?" I said, loud enough for him to hear. "How will everyone know where to go?"

"It's the one place every Watcher knows," he called back, the sound of boxes being moved on a shelf, reached me. "It's where we were sent when we first came to Earth."

Brand walked out of the closet with a large white cardboard box, like something you would store a coat in.

He set it down beside me on the bed and took the lid off.

My breath caught in my throat when I saw what lay within.

"Why do you have one of those?" I asked, as he pulled out the black feathered cloak. It looked identical to the one the Watchers who gave into their bloodlust wore when they were on a hunt.

"It's our formal wear," Brand explained. "I know you've only seen the Watchers on Malcolm's side wear them, but we all wore them at one time. We will all wear them at the gathering, so don't be afraid. No one there will be allowed to harm you."

"How many Watchers are there?"

"Originally there were 200 of us. Now that Justin can't seem to be found and, well, Robert is gone, of course, there should be 198 of us left."

"Is Allan coming?" I asked.

"He said he would be there, but I think it's only because he wants to make sure nothing happens to you."

"Didn't you just say no one would be allowed to hurt me?"

"Yes, but you can't always prepare for everything."

"Do you think Lucifer will try to do something?"

"It's a possibility," Brand admitted. "I doubt he wants us to form a united front against him. We would be too powerful. He would never be able to defeat us all at one time."

"Do you think the others will help me?"

"I'm not sure they all will," Brand admitted, "especially the ones who have given into their craving for human blood. Those Watchers sometimes go insane because of the blood lust. It takes a disciplined Watcher to drink only enough to not kill a human. Most just rampage through their lives, not caring how many humans they kill."

"Did Malcolm kill many people?"

"I'm sure he did a few, especially in the beginning," Brand said, taking off his shirt and placing the cloak over his shoulders, as if he wanted to make sure it still fit. "But Malcolm was able to control his blood lust by being sexually active."

Brand walked to the full-length mirror in the room to look at himself wearing the cloak.

"I haven't worn this in a long time," he told me, staring at his reflection, as if he wasn't quite sure who the man in the mirror was.

On Brand, the cloak didn't look menacing at all. It looked like he had been born to wear it across his broad shoulders, allowing his pale bare chest to stand out against the ebony. I stood from the bed and walked to him, letting my fingers glide over the glossy black feathers. When I looked at his reflection in the mirror, I found him watching me.

"What are you thinking?" he asked.

"I was just thinking that I can't help but find you sexy in whatever it is you put on."

I let my hand drop to my side as Brand turned to face me, a roguish grin on his face. "Was that an invitation to ravish you until we have to leave, Mrs. Cole?"

"Hmm," I said, lowering my eyelashes as coquettishly as I could, "that depends, Mr. Cole."

Brand smile widened. "Depends on what, exactly?"

"Depends on whether or not you can catch me." I phased to the kitchen and Brand quickly followed. Just as he was about to grab me with both arms, I phased to the spare bedroom, where he almost phased in on top of me before I phased to the living room. I waited a full minute, but he didn't phase in after me. Worried something might have happened to him, I phased back to our bedroom, to find him lying on his side with his head propped up in one hand on our bed, completely naked.

"That's so unfair," I said, quickly stripping my clothes off and phasing in on top of my husband to straddle his hips.

"You weren't playing fair either," he reminded me, sliding his hands up my naked thighs to my hips.

"How long did you say we have until we need to go?" I asked, letting his hands guide me into a better position.

"Couple of hours," Brand said in a hoarse voice as I began to move against him.

"Not as long as I would like," I said, leaning down to kiss his mouth, "but I think we can get the job done by then."

Brand smiled against my lips, and proved to me two hours was plenty of time.

CHAPTER 16.

Brand insisted we wait until the exact second we were supposed to meet the others.

"How in the world can you have it timed out to the last second?" I asked.

"It's how we're built," he shrugged. "I guess you could say we have our own internal clocks. It makes us very punctual."

I smiled. Finally, I knew the secret to Brand's extreme sense of punctuality.

I talked him into being a minute early to the gathering. It went against his grain, but he did it for me. I had to assume the experience of watching all the Watchers phase in at the exact same second was something no one on Earth could ever claim to witness.

The sun was setting on the horizon of the vast desert, casting a glow with shades of orange and red, making it look like the sky had been set on fire. We stood at the top of a dune, surrounded by waves of sand mimicking the waves of an ocean in the last heat of day. We waited silently, holding each other's hand.

"Keep your eyes straight ahead of you," Brand told me. "They're coming."

I was scared to blink, in fear that I might miss their arrival. When they all phased in, I felt my heart jump in my throat. The Watchers stood dressed proudly in their ceremonial cloaks, blowing against the desert wind. Instantly, Brand and I were surrounded by Malcolm, Isaiah, Allan and Mason. I felt protected in their circle, shielding me from the others.

Brand held out his hand to Mason. "Thank you for doing this. We owe you everything."

"Don't thank me too soon," Mason said with a wry grin. "They haven't said they will help yet."

Mason looked down at me. A faint smile played across his lips, and I knew he was remembering the moment I touched him, granting him the peace of knowing his father still cared about him.

Mason turned to face the other Watchers.

"Brothers," he said, his voice carried by the desert wind, "thank you all for coming."

A Watcher who looked like he was of Egyptian descent stepped forward. "Why have you ordered us here, Samyaza? Why now after all these years?"

"When we were first sent here by our father," Mason said, "we were eager to help the humans like He wanted. We were their teachers and counselors. They trusted us to lead them in the ways of the world. Then, when we became filled with our own self-importance, we began to think of ourselves as gods among the mortals. We even thought we deserved to live normal lives, and stopped doing what we were sent here to do. We turned our backs on our father to satisfy our own needs. As your leader, I should have stopped what happened, but I didn't. I wanted what you all wanted - a family to call my own, no matter the cost. For that, we all paid a high price for our arrogance. Even our most beloved, our children, had to pay a price for our treachery. Now, I believe our father has presented us with the opportunity to begin the process of atonement for our sins."

"How?" the Watcher who seemed to be the spokesman for the group asked.

"I believe He sent this woman," Mason said, stepping to the side, so the others could get a clear view of me, "to provide us a way to atone for what we did and lead us back to Him."

I felt the eyes of all the Watchers suddenly fasten on me. It made me wish I had written down what I wanted to say to them, because the speech I had prepared in my head was chased away by nervousness.

"She is a descendant of Lillith," Mason told them, causing a disturbance among the Watchers, "and she is the daughter of Michael."

The Watchers went completely silent; only the whistling of the wind could be heard.

"How do you know this?" the Watcher asked.

"Because, Baruch, she has the Touch."

A collective gasp could be heard.

"Prove it," Baruch challenged.

Now it was my turn to prove I deserved their help. I took a few steps forward. Baruch walked to me, his eyes daring me to prove I was the child of an archangel. I physically felt my power awaken, yearning to show Baruch what I was.

I saw Baruch flinch slightly at the sight of my hands blazing with the blue fire of my gift. I laid my hands against his shoulders, instantly allowing him to feel whatever it was God felt for him. Baruch trembled under my touch, but didn't step away. I watched as myriad emotions passed over his face. First, there was disbelief, then sadness, and finally relief.

Baruch staggered back from me. He silently watched me before turning to face the other Watchers.

"She is the child of Michael," he announced, his voice filled with awe. "And I, for one," he said turning back to me, "will do whatever she might ask of me."

Baruch knelt down on one knee in front of me. Before I knew it, all of the Watchers knelt before me, even those I considered my friends. Brand was the only one who didn't kneel. He stood by my side and took my hand.

When I looked up at him to ask him what I should do now, he said, "Tell them why we need their help."

"Please," I said to them, "please stand. There's no reason for you to kneel in front of me."

"You are the first and only child of an archangel," Baruch said to me. "That is reason enough."

I looked to Brand for help.

"Baruch, you're making my wife uncomfortable. Please, stand up brothers."

Almost reluctantly, the Watchers stood. They watched me carefully, as if they were planning to etch my next words into their memory, which simply made me more nervous.

"We've called you all here to ask for your help. We've been told Lucifer plans to tear a hole in space and time to somehow rip our world, Heaven, and Hell apart. We know he will try to possess me and use the powers I inherited from my father and the power Lillith passed down to enter Heaven. We need you to help us figure out when he plans to do this, and how he intends to harness enough energy to accomplish his goal. Brand's told me my powers aren't enough to achieve what he plans to do. We hope, with your combined knowledge, at least one of you can figure out what else he needs and from where he intends to draw the power. We're missing a piece of the puzzle, and desperately need it to know how to stop him. Please, if any of you can help, I beg you to help me."

"If you are willing to help Lilly," Mason said, "take a step forward and be counted."

I took a deep breath, waiting to see how many of the Watchers would help us. As one, they all stepped forward, bringing tears of relief to my eyes.

"Thank you," I told them, my voice quavering with emotion. "Thank you all."

Before we could leave, some of the Watchers came up to me, asking that I use my touch on them, like I had Baruch. Almost all of them had the same reaction as Baruch. I was told by some that they felt their father's disappointment in them, but they also felt His love and that He wanted to have them back by His side. It seemed to be enough for most of them to know that even they could be forgiven in time, and that Heaven wasn't completely lost to them.

I looked to Malcolm, offering him once again the opportunity to feel what I had to offer, but he simply shook his head, refusing to allow me to touch him.

It was decided that anyone who found out something which might be of use to us would contact Isaiah, who would, in turn, contact Brand and me if he thought it was worth investigating further.

The last of the Watchers to ask for the Touch was Allan.

He seemed uncertain when he came to stand in front of me, like he wasn't sure if he really wanted to know what God thought of him.

I smiled to encourage him to accept the Touch.

"I don't know, Lilly," he said. "It's been so long; maybe He's forgotten about me."

"No," I said, "I don't think He has Allan, but there is only one way to know for sure."

I held my blazing hands out to him. Finally, he placed his hands in mine. I felt him automatically tighten his hold. Overcome with emotion, he fell to his knees as silent tears coursed down his cheeks. When he let go of me, he stayed knelt in front of me before saying, "Thank you, Lilly. Thank you."

He phased then. I could only assume he needed some time alone to deal with what I had just shared. I hoped being able to let the Watchers feel their father's love again, after all these years, gave them a new-found sense of hope and purpose. They had all been living with the guilt of their sins for a very long time. I couldn't imagine what it was like for them to know He still loved them. I only wished Malcolm would let me open his heart to his father's love. I felt like it would be good for him, somehow cathartic.

I also knew he needed to deal with his demons first. Malcolm didn't believe he had the right to ask for forgiveness. I had a feeling he would have to prove to himself that he was a different person before he allowed me to show him God's true feelings for him.

I only hoped I lived long enough to help him through his self-doubt. I knew he had a good heart. It had just been a long time since he thought that way about himself too.

CHAPTER 17.

While we waited for new information to be collected by the Watchers, Brand and I tried to act normally for the next week. We had finals at school during that time, which helped me take my mind off some of the stress we were under. I knew time was running out, and I tried to spend as much of it with Brand as I possibly could, without him becoming suspicious of my motives. I didn't want him to worry that I had lost faith in us finding the answers we needed, because I hadn't. However, I was also a realist, and knew the future wasn't something any of us could control. Whatever was meant to happen, would, and I was always one to prepare for any eventuality.

Tara finally talked me into going shopping with her that Friday afternoon, by embarrassing the heck out of me, as usual.

"Lilly Rayne, you've been with Brand so much, you're starting to walk funny," she said to me, making me want to hide from her knowing eyes. "We haven't been able to spend a lot of time together since you got married, and, well, girl, I'm feeling a little neglected."

The last thing I wanted was for Tara to feel like my marrying Brand meant he had a monopoly on me. If things ended badly with Lucifer's plan, I didn't want my best friend to feel like I hadn't cared enough to share my last remaining days with her. She was one of the rocks in the foundation of my life, and I knew she deserved better. So, we made plans to go shopping and eat somewhere for lunch. I wish I could say those plans happened. I wish I could say we were able to spend the day together, just acting like any other young adults our age, but I can't do that, because the world as we knew it began to fall apart instead.

Right before I was supposed to leave to pick up Tara, I received a frantic phone call from my mother.

"Lilly, you have to come home right now," she said, sobbing hysterically.

"Mom, what's wrong?" I asked, praying Lucifer hadn't harmed her in some way. "Are you all right? Are you hurt?"

"It's not me, Lilly," my mother cried. "It's Utha Mae. I think she's had a heart attack. Lucas called the ambulance as soon as he found her in her trailer. Come home, Lilly, and bring Tara with you. I don't know how long she might have left."

When I hung up the phone, I yelled for Brand.

"What's wrong?" he asked, phasing in next to me.

I felt tears burn my eyes and found it hard to see, much less speak.

"Utha Mae's had a heart attack," I was finally able to get out. "We have to get Tara."

When we phased into Tara's house, we found her just grabbing her coat, expecting me to come pick her up for our day of shopping.

"Good grief," she complained, putting a hand to her heart. "You two know I hate that!"

When she saw my tear-streaked face, her anger immediately faded.

"What's wrong? What's happened?"

I held my hand out to her and drew her into my arms, crying uncontrollably.

"Lilly, girl, you're scaring me. Tell me what's wrong."

"Utha Mae's had a heart attack," Brand said for me, since I was a complete basket case.

"Then get us to the hospital," Tara said in a calm voice.

Not caring what it would look like, we phased to the hospital in Dalton. We were there before Utha Mae's ambulance arrived. When my mother and Lucifer entered, my mom looked stunned that we were there already.

"How did you get here so fast?" she questioned, giving me a hug.

Thankfully, we didn't have to come up with a lie, because the gurney with Utha Mae came barreling through the ER entrance. She lay dead-still on the mobile bed, making me wonder if we were already too late to say goodbye. The EMTs wheeled her quickly past us into a glass-enclosed room. Doctors came at a run and quickly examined the situation. The curtain was drawn around her bed, completely blocking our view of what was happening.

Brand held me as I tried to stem the flow of my grief. Tara had the presence of mind to call Will and ask him to bring Malik. I marveled at my best friend in those moments. She bore strength inside her that I had never seen before. She reminded me so much of Utha Mae then. Whenever the world around her was in chaos, Utha Mae was always there to keep everyone calm until the trouble passed. I knew then that Tara had inherited the same ability as her grandmother to weather any storm placed in her path.

An hour later a doctor came to tell us Utha Mae had survived the initial heart attack, but that it had weakened her heart to a point that it would eventually give out.

"Given her age, we can't risk doing surgery, because that would surely kill her," he told us. "All we can do is wait to see how she progresses in the next few days."

"Tell us the truth," Tara said. "Is she about to die? Do you see her walking out of this hospital?"

"Any number of things could happen," the doctor said, but even I could hear the doubt in his voice, "but if you want my professional opinion, I would say she only has a few more days to live before her heart completely gives out. If you have anything you want to say to her, I wouldn't put it off. Let her know how much you love her while she's still with us."

"Thanks, doc," Tara said, lifting her chin a little higher. "I appreciate your honesty."

They moved Utha Mae to a private suite. Brand arranged it so we had the best room the hospital had to offer. It was much like a regular bedroom, with a normal bed, a comfortable couch which folded out into a bed, and a couple of comfortable chairs. I was thankful Utha Mae's last days wouldn't be lived in a stark hospital room.

Tara and I insisted on staying with Utha Mae the first night. Will refused to leave her bedside, saying he didn't have anywhere else he needed to be. All three of us felt like Utha Mae was our mother, and none of us wanted to leave her. If the situation were reversed, we knew she wouldn't leave us, and we weren't about to let her down. She'd raised us too well.

Around suppertime, Lucifer offered to go to the cafeteria and bring us all something to eat. As soon as he left the room, I made my own excuse, intent on following him, but Brand held me back.

"What are you going to do?" he questioned quietly, so the others wouldn't hear.

I jerked my arm free of his grasp. "I just have one question," I told him. "He won't hurt me. I'm too important to him."

"Then let me go with you."

"No, I need to do this myself. You stay here. If anything happens to Utha Mae while I'm gone, come and get me."

With that, I left the room, and saw Lucifer strolling down the hallway, whistling like he was on a pleasant walk through a field of daisies, instead of inside a hospital where people lay dying all around him.

I phased in front of him, bringing him up short in the empty hallway.

"What did you do to her?" I demanded, daring him to try to lie to me.

"Nothing time hadn't already prepared her for," he said, smirking.

I grabbed him by the throat suddenly, igniting my power, forcing him to feel the *Touch*.

He grimaced for a moment, but then started to laugh. Angry, I flung him away from me, letting the fire of my power ebb.

He held a hand to his throat.

"Did you really think that was going to hurt me?" he asked. "You're not dealing with some Watcher, Lilly. You're only half-archangel. I'm the real deal. I feel what He thinks of me every day of my existence."

"How do you live with yourself," I spat, "knowing what a disappointment you are to Him?"

"Well, if He hadn't disappointed me first," Lucifer spat, "it might affect me more."

"You haven't learned anything while you've been on Earth. You still hate humans as much as you did when you first gave God your ultimatum."

"If it's possible, I hate you more than I did then."

"Why?" I asked. "Why do you hate us so much?"

"Because you have *everything*," he stormed, "yet you do nothing with it. He handed you the universe on a silver platter, and still some of you spit in His face. He touted your free will in front of us, like it was some grand design, but all I see are your flaws. He should have let us destroy you when we had the chance. You're nothing but a virus on this planet, spoiling the gifts He gave you, for your own selfish wants. How can He love you more than His firstborn? How can He still love you more than me?"

"How can you think He loves us more? He showed me the day you gave Him your ultimatum in the Hall of Angels. If you hadn't been so blinded by your hatred for humanity, maybe you would have seen how much it pained Him to exile you here. For some reason, He thought living among us would show you how wrong you were. He wanted you to share in His joy at his creation, but all you wanted to do was destroy us and force Him to admit He made a mistake when He made humanity. You let your jealousy get the better of you, Lucifer. Don't you think it's time to let go of the pain? Why can't you just admit you made a mistake?"

"Because I didn't," Lucifer hissed, making me scared for my safety for the first time. The hatred and anger he felt seemed to be blinding him. I wasn't sure if he intended to take it out on me or not. "I didn't make a mistake. He's just too stubborn to admit He shouldn't have made you things at all. But I'll have the last laugh, because I'll destroy everything He loves, and He'll be helpless to stop me."

"Faust told us what you have planned," I said, hoping the little bit of information I had might make Lucifer slip up and tell me more.

Unfortunately, Lucifer didn't look surprised. "I know what he told you, but you don't have the whole truth of it, and don't stand there and think a mere human can outwit me. I've lived longer than this universe has been in existence. Do you really want to try to have a battle of wits with me?"

"Then tell me how you plan to do it. If you don't think we can figure out a way to stop you, what will it hurt to tell me what I want to know?"

Lucifer shook his head. "Do you really believe I'm that stupid?"

"No, I don't believe you're stupid at all, but I think your vanity is begging you to tell me everything, just to prove how smart you are."

Lucifer walked so close to me I could feel his hot breath on my face. "You'll know soon enough, dear Lilly. It's almost time for you to serve the purpose you were born for."

Lucifer turned away from me, intent on continuing to walk down to the cafeteria.

"Stop," I ordered in a soft voice.

Lucifer stopped dead in his tracks, like he'd hit a brick wall.

"Turn to face me," I said.

Lucifer turned on his heels and looked directly at me, defiantly.

"Your plan will fail," I told him. "Or did you forget I have King Solomon's ring?"

"No, I didn't forget," Lucifer said. "But when the time comes, even that little trinket won't be able to protect you from me."

"Tell me what you did to Utha Mae," I demanded.

Lucifer smiled. "I showed her what I truly am."

"A monster?"

"Among other things; poor thing just couldn't take knowing the truth about angels and demons. Even for all her Bible-thumping, she wasn't able to face the truth, even when it was standing in front of her; such a shame, too. I had planned to make her watch what I do to you, but, for some reason, I just couldn't control myself. I guess I wanted to hurt you more than I wanted to hurt her."

"Leave this hospital and don't come back. Don't contact my mother. Don't even look in her general direction again. Now leave," I ordered, causing Lucifer to instantly phase from the hallway. I turned back towards Utha Mae's room, now knowing Utha Mae's final moments had been filled with terror. I was filled with a new determination to find a way to show her peace.

CHAPTER 18.

For the next five days, Tara, Will, and I took turns watching over Utha Mae. We only left when we needed to go home to change clothes. Brand stayed by me, never leaving my side. I forced myself not to cry, because all that did was cloud my thoughts and make it more difficult to do what needed to be done.

Malcolm came to the hospital. He told us not to worry about anything concerning the Watchers. He would be our eyes and ears while we spent time with Utha Mae. Brand and I thanked him. He gave me a hug and kissed my cheek before he left, telling me to be strong, and that if I needed him for anything to just call.

I attempted to bring Utha Mae into my dream world, but nothing I did worked. I had almost given up hope, until I was finally visited by the one person I knew could help me.

I dreamt of sitting on the porch of my Colorado home, swaying back and forth on my swing when He finally arrived.

"Where have you been?" I asked.

"Watching and waiting," He answered.

"Waiting for what?"

"Waiting for you to ask for My help."

"I thought my power was strong enough to bring her here," I said, looking over at Him next to me on the swing. "But I can't. Can you do it?"

"Yes." He sat there, silently looking out at the snow-capped mountain. "But maybe you should allow her to show you what she is thinking instead. She is at peace with her coming death, but you aren't"

"How do I do that? How do I go into her mind?"

"You can't," God answered, taking my hand, "but I can."

I suddenly found myself standing in the trailer park, in front of the old trailer my mom and I had when we first moved to Dalton. I watched as my mother drove up to it, so young and innocent-looking. When she got out of the old red and white Dodge Plymouth, her first car, she opened up the back door of the driver's side and pulled out a crying baby.

"Oh, come on, Lilly Rayne, don't cry. This is our new home. It's a happy day, not a sad one."

My mother tried her best to sooth my tears, but nothing she did seemed to be working.

"Can I hold her?"

My mom looked up, and found Utha Mae smiling brightly at her from the front porch of her trailer.

"I don't know why she's so upset," my mother said, walking up to the porch. "She's usually such a quiet baby." My mother held her hand out to Utha Mae. "Hi, my name is Cora Nightingale. I guess I'm your new neighbor."

"I'm Utha Mae Jenkins. Welcome to Dalton, Cora Nightingale. Now, who is this little bit of preciousness you have in your hands?" Utha Mae asked, stretching her arms out to take me.

"Lilly Rayne," my mother said, handing me over to Utha Mae.

Utha Mae held me in the crook of her arm, like it was the most natural thing in the world for her to do, and began to rock me. I instantly stopped crying as I stared up at her.

"How did you do that?" my mother asked in amazement.

"Oh, I've had a lot of practice with babies," Utha Mae answered. "Now, why don't you just go ahead and get your stuff settled inside your home? Lilly Rayne and I will be just fine. I'll take good care of her."

"Are you sure?" my mother asked. "I don't want to impose on your hospitality on my first day as your new neighbor."

"Lord, child, this little baby is a gift directly from God. I can see it in her eyes. You go on now. Lilly and I will be just fine. And come on over when you're done; I'll have us a nice lunch prepared, and you can tell me what's brought you here to Dalton. We don't get a lot of new people around here."

My mother walked off, smiling, and I could tell she was happy she'd found someone who was willing to help her out when she needed it the most.

"Now," Utha Mae said, looking down at a now-gurgling baby in her arms, "let's me and you go make your poor momma some lunch. I have a feeling we'll be seeing a lot of one another, little Miss Lilly Rayne Nightingale."

The scene changed to one I remembered well. I was seven years old. Tara and I were chasing each other around Utha Mae's trailer when I saw my mother step out of our trailer, all dolled up to go out with her latest boyfriend.

"Now you be good for Utha Mae tonight," my mother called to me as she slipped into the driver's seat.

I ran up to her window, staring at her until she lowered it to speak with me.

"What, Lilly?" my mother asked, clearly agitated at my delaying her.

"I thought you would stay with me tonight," I said, not understanding why, on this of all nights, she would decide to abandon me again.

"Lilly, I have a date. I need some alone time every once in a while, you know. You'll be fine with Utha Mae. She always takes good care of you."

"But…"

"No buts; now move away from the car, sweetie. I'll see you tomorrow."

I watched as my mother drove away.

"Where is she going?" Tara asked. "She doesn't remember what today is?"

I shook my head, tears of sorrow streaming down my face. Tara put her arms around me. "I swear, Lilly. I really hate your mom sometimes."

"Lilly! Tara! Y'all come on in now. It's going to be getting dark soon."

"Come on, Lilly Rayne. Grandma needs us inside."

I followed Tara into Utha Mae's trailer, wiping the tears from my face, refusing to let Utha Mae see me cry yet again because of something my mother did.

When I stepped inside, Utha Mae and Will sprang out from behind her couch and yelled, "Surprise!"

They had spent the time while Tara and I were outside to decorate Utha Mae's trailer with streamers and balloons. A chocolate birthday cake lit with seven pink candles was sitting on the kitchen table. I burst into tears.

"What's she crying for?" Will asked, completely confused by my reaction.

I felt Utha Mae come pick me up and hold me in her arms. "Baby, don't cry," she begged, which made me cry even harder.

"Do you know what she's crying about?" I heard Will ask Tara as he came to stand beside her.

"Her good-for-nothing momma just left to go on a date."

"Tara Jenkins," Utha Mae said, a warning in her voice, "I've told you not to talk about Lilly's mom like that."

"But she just left!" Tara protested hotly. "I don't even think she remembered it was Lilly's birthday!"

"We don't know what other people go through in their lives," Utha Mae said. "Don't judge until you have all the facts."

"I agree with Tara," Will said, anger in his voice. "Mothers aren't supposed to forget your birthday. That's just not right."

Utha Mae rubbed my back, and hummed a hymn until my tears stopped flowing.

When I finally lifted my head from her shoulder, she looked at me with more love in her eyes than I had ever seen in my own mother's.

"Why doesn't she love me?" I asked, my voice breaking over the question.

"Oh, baby, she loves you. She just has a hard time showing it, I think. Now you dry those tears up. I made you my special double chocolate cake, and you have to blow the candles out and make a wish."

After I blew the candles out, I twitched my little finger to make Utha Mae lean down so I could whisper in her ear.

"I wished that you were my real momma," I said to her.

Utha Mae hugged me, and I knew then she would do everything in her power to make my wish come true.

The scene changed to my wedding day to Brand. Utha Mae was welcoming guests, which were mostly all of her friends.

"I can't believe she's all grown up," Ms. Ida, one of Utha Mae's closest friends, said as she entered the church.

Utha Mae smiled. "Me neither Ida; time sure does fly. My baby will be having babies of her own soon."

Ida laughed. "I swear you've been more of a mother to that child than her own."

"She's been like the daughter I never had. Both she and Tara have. I'm not sure I would have made it without them all these years. You know how hard it was for me when Harry died. Those babies gave me the will to go on. If it hadn't been for them, I'm not sure what would have happened to me."

"Well, good luck marrying off that hell-raiser you have for a granddaughter," Ida snorted. "It'll take a strong man to tame her heart."

Utha Mae smiled. "Oh, I don't know. I think she's closer to finding Mr. Right than even she realizes."

"Well, I hope you're right," Ida said. "Ain't neither one of us getting any younger, Utha Mae. It would be nice to leave them knowing they're taken care of."

Utha Mae nodded. "Yes it would, Ida. Yes, it would."

I found myself back on the swing with God.

"That's what she's thinking about right now?" I asked, wiping the tears from my cheeks.

"Yes. She's reliving a lot of memories from her past, like most people do during this time. Almost all of them center on you, Tara, and Will. In her heart, she always felt like your mother. She loves you that much."

"Will I be able to say goodbye to her before she dies?"

"There will be a time when you can all make your goodbyes. She won't leave this world without seeing you all one last time."

"Can't you heal her?" I asked, knowing what I was asking wasn't a fair question. "She's been a good person. She's always had faith in you."

"It's her time to go, Lilly. Don't ask me to take that away from her. She's waited a long time for this moment."

"When will it happen?"

"Soon."

The next day, Utha Mae finally woke up. She was smiling and talking with us, like nothing was wrong. She even asked Malik to sneak her in some of his chicken and dumplings. It made me wonder if God had changed His mind and decided it wasn't time for Utha Mae to leave us just yet. Maybe He realized I still needed her help to see me through the next few days.

At one point, she asked Brand and me to sit on either side of her. She placed one of her hands on Brand's arm and the other on mine.

"Now, I want you two to promise me that you will never let the sun set on your anger. There will come times when you get angry with each other, because that's just what happens when you care about someone more than you do yourself, but don't let that anger sit too long. When I look down at the two of you, I want to see happy faces."

"You're not going anywhere," I told her, squeezing her hand.

"Oh, baby, we're all going at some point. I think my time is coming sooner rather than later, and I'm just fine with that. I've lived a long, full life. That's more than a lot of people can say. I don't have any regrets to take with me. But promise me one thing: get your mom away from that devil."

"What did he show you?" I asked, needing to know what Lucifer had done to Utha Mae.

"I know what he is," she said, and I could see in her eyes that she fully understood the truth of things. "And I know what you are, child." She lifted her hand and cradled my face. "I knew you were an angel the moment I saw you as a baby."

"I don't know if I can make it without you," I said, tears writing the depth of my sorrow on my face.

"Baby, you are stronger than you know. That's how I raised you. So don't you dare disappoint me. You'll find a way to stop him. I know it." Utha Mae looked at Brand. "You have a good man by your side and, as long as the two of you stick together, there's nothing you won't be able to do."

When Malik came back with the dumplings later that afternoon, Utha Mae made him and Tara sit with her too.

She took one of Tara's hands and placed it in one of Malik's.

"You finally found your Prince Charming," Utha Mae said to Tara. "And I want you both to know you have my blessing when you decide to marry."

"Grandma…" Tara said, like what Utha Mae was saying didn't have a chance in Hell of happening anytime soon.

"You know your Grandpa Harry was a lot like Malik. I see the same love in his eyes for you that my Harry had for me when we were together. And you," Utha Mae said, looking at Malik, "I want you to promise me you'll look after my grandbaby when I'm gone. Can I trust you to do that?"

"Yes, ma'am," Malik was quick to promise. "I'll look after her as far as she will let me. But you know how stubborn she can be sometimes."

"You'll find a way to get past that part of her. She's built her wall so high, only a man who truly loves her can find a way through it, but I know you will."

"You two do realize I'm still sitting here, right?" Tara said, laughing through her tears.

"Baby, you let this man help you when you need it. He's a good man. And I'm just thankful he's here for you now. I'm glad I got to meet the love of your life before I have to go."

The last person Utha Mae wanted to speak with was Will. She asked that we all leave the room then, not wanting us to hear their conversation. When we were called back in, Will had tears in his eyes and left the room, saying he needed some time alone and would be back later.

"Is he alright?" I asked Utha Mae. "Do I need to go after him?"

"No, baby. I think he's just relieved he doesn't have to lie to me anymore."

"Lie about what?"

"Lie about who he really is. I think we all knew our Will died the night he rescued you out of that lake. I'm just glad I could tell the Will we know now that I forgive him. If he hadn't taken over, both you and Will would have been lost to me forever. He did what he had to do, even if it was for the devil. However, I think the devil is going to regret sending Will in the end. He's not the same person he used to be, and I think me, you, and Tara had a hand in changing him."

"Did Lucifer tell you everything?" I asked, not seeing that there was anything left secret to Utha Mae.

"No, not everything; I know he plans to try to use you in some way, but he didn't reveal how exactly, baby. I'm just glad I know what I do, so I can bring you peace of mind before it's time for me to go."

"I wish you would stop saying that," I said, selfishly wanting to keep Utha Mae with me forever. She had been a part of my life ever since I could remember.

"You know it's true, just like I do, child. And don't be sad for me when I'm gone. I'll finally be with my Harry. You just don't know how long I've waited for that."

Utha Mae's health deteriorated quickly after that. The doctors called the time she was awake and talking *the surge*, a time when a patient has one last bit of energy left to say their goodbyes and make their peace with death.

That night, Utha Mae's breathing became shallow, and we were told there wasn't anything to do but try to make her as comfortable as possible. Not caring that my mother was in the room, I let my power burn freely, holding on to Utha Mae's hand, hoping she could feel the peace I knew my touch would bring to her. If God loved anyone on Earth, I knew He had to love Utha Mae. A faint smile graced her lips as she took her last breath.

On the other side of the bed from me, I saw two shadows appear. As they became more distinct, I saw the ghost of eight-year-old Will, and a handsome man I had only seen in photographs, but knew instantly to be Utha Mae's Harry. They looked down at Utha Mae before looking over at me.

"We have her from here," Harry said to me, reaching down to take Utha Mae's hand and raising up a younger version of the woman I knew. She was as pretty as I always knew she probably was in her youth. She smiled at us all.

"Don't be sad for me," she said, taking her husband's arm. "I'm finally going home."

The ghost of our loved ones faded as they walked away from us, leaving us to deal with our sorrow.

Brand took me home after that. I cried until I had no tears left, and fell asleep in his arms.

The next morning, I walked over to the house we had been building for Utha Mae. The construction crew wasn't there, because there was no longer a need to keep building it. I knelt on the cold concrete, staring up at the two-by-fours that had just been erected to frame out the walls of the house. A sense of loss overwhelmed me as my heart felt like it would explode with grief. Before I knew it, the power of my grief ignited what remained of Utha Mae's home, sending whirls of flames and smoke in every direction around me. The fire didn't burn me, but I felt my clothes melt away, making me feel even more naked and vulnerable to my sorrow.

I distantly heard Brand yelling my name, but didn't have the strength to open my eyes and answer him. I felt him cradle me to his chest and phase us back home. He kissed my tear-swollen eyes, desperately asking what he could do to help me. I didn't have an answer for him. I just clung to him until I cried myself to sleep once more.

When I dreamt, I didn't find myself in my Colorado home like I usually did. I was standing in front of someone else's house. It was a small white clapboard house in the middle of Dalton, but it wasn't the Dalton I had grown up in. Cars you see in old movies set in the 1950s dotted the street, and the air smelled a little cleaner than usual.

"She wanted to see you one last time," I heard God say beside me. "She doesn't like to see your suffering, so she thought it might help if you saw where she was now."

He pointed to the front of the house.

"I'll be right back, Harry," I heard Utha Mae say as she walked out the front door, dressed in only a white silk robe.

"Well, hurry back here, woman; I've been without you long enough!"

The young Utha Mae walked to me with the happiest smile I have ever seen on her face. When she reached me, she pulled me into her arms and hugged me tightly to her.

"Baby, you need to stop all this crying and be happy for me." When she pulled away, I could see my sorrow was dampening the joy she felt. "I can't take you being so sad when I'm so happy."

"I just miss you," I said, realizing the sorrow I felt was completely selfish.

"I know you miss me, but you need to know I haven't really left you. Why, even little Will never really left you when he died. We'll always be watching over you, no matter what."

"Always?" I asked, slightly concerned Utha Mae might see things I didn't want her to see, like moments when Brand and I were alone.

"Oh, not those times," Utha Mae giggled, seeming to know exactly what I was thinking. "But I'll be there when you need me. All you have to do is think of me, baby. But stop mourning. There's no need. I'm as happy as a June bug on a summer day. And we'll all be together when the time is right. He's told me that." Utha Mae looked over at God and smiled.

"Now you go back and have a happy life. That's my last wish for you."

Utha Mae hugged me and turned to go back to her Harry. When she reached the first step of her house, she looked back at me over her shoulder.

"I've met them, you know," she said, completely confusing me as to who she was talking about.

"Met who?" I asked.

"Your children," she answered, a warm smile lighting up her face. "They are something to behold, Lilly Rayne. You take good care of them, like I took care of you."

Utha Mae winked at me and continued walking back into her house.

When I woke up, my tears were gone. I knew Utha Mae was where she was meant to be.

I got out of bed and went to the bathroom. I opened up the medicine cabinet and found my birth control pills. One by one, I punched the pills out of the packet and watched them drop into the toilet. I flushed them down and threw the empty packet into the trash.

The funeral was something I don't think anyone in Dalton had seen for a long time. There were at least as many, if not more, people at Utha Mae's funeral as there were at my wedding. Over a hundred cars lined up to follow us to the gravesite, after the funeral ceremony inside Utha Mae's church. I hoped Utha Mae was watching from Heaven, but knew if she wasn't she was spending some well-deserved time in the arms of her Harry.

Tara was as strong as ever, never letting her emotions get the best of her when we put Utha Mae's casket in the ground. When we went back home, I pulled her aside and told her about the conversation I'd had with Utha Mae the night before.

"I had a similar dream," she told me. "Was it real?"

"Tell me what happened."

"Well, Grandma was dressed in a white robe and this man told me she wanted to talk to me one last time. She told me not to be sad for her because she was where she wanted to be. She said to watch over you, because you would be facing some hard times, but that you would pull through them."

"Describe the man you saw," I said.

From the description Tara gave me, I knew it had been God.

"You're pulling my leg, right?" Tara questioned, after I told her who the man was.

When I shook my head, I thought she might fall over. I suppose realizing you had seen God could be like that, if you weren't used to it happening every other day of your life.

"You know, I never realized my grandma was such a looker," Tara said.

"Or someone who'd ever had sex," I said.

When Tara and I looked at each other, we started to giggle. Before we knew it, we were crying for a completely different reason, and it felt good.

CHAPTER 19.

The day after the funeral, Malcolm came to our house to tell us about the new developments which we had been oblivious to.

"Have you not seen the news recently?" Malcolm asked gently, knowing we had been busy dealing with the aftermath of Utha Mae's passing.

"The news?" I asked.

Malcolm found the TV remote, and searched until he located one of the cable news stations.

A male newscaster was interviewing a woman in Rome, with the Vatican in the background of the shot.

"And who did you see?" the newscaster asked.

"I saw my mother," the woman said, holding the back of a shaky hand to her mouth, in an attempt to prevent a sob. "She looked so beautiful, like she did when I was a little girl."

"And when did she die?"

"Two years ago." The woman completely lost it then, and had to be carried away by a man I presumed to be her husband or boyfriend as the camera zoomed in on the newscaster.

"It's the same thing we've been hearing all over the world for the past couple of days. People are seeing dead relatives and friends, even having conversations with them and holding them. Unfortunately, not all the reunions are happy ones, like the one this woman experienced with her mother. We have heard tales of what I can only call evil spirits visiting their victims and family members, with deadly consequences."

News footage of a bloody crime scene filled the screen.

"It's the end of times," a man was screaming into the camera. "The 'dead shall rise', that's what the Bible says!"

"This scene is the latest in a string of murders attributed to malevolent spirits. The police say they've never had so many unsolvable murders one right after the other."

Malcolm turned the TV volume down to a minimum.

"I don't understand," I said, remembering my own experience with the ghost of Will, Harry, and Utha Mae when she died. "What's going on?"

"I've consulted with the Watchers who are experts in such things, and they all came to the same conclusion," Malcolm said. "The veils are weakening."

Brand's body went stiff beside me.

"Are you certain?" Brand asked. It was one of the few times I'd ever heard true fear in his voice.

"It's the only explanation that makes sense," Malcolm said.

"Ok, you guys are scaring and confusing me," I said. "What are the veils, and why are you guys so scared that they're weakening?"

Malcolm looked around the kitchen and picked up a roll of paper towels. He tore off one towel and laid it on the kitchen island in front of me.

"Think of the universe as being different layers," he told me. "Let's say this first layer is the world you know." He tore off another towel. "This layer represents a multitude of alternate realities, universes similar to your own, but slightly different in some way." He tore off another towel. "This layer represents Heaven." He tore off another towel from the roll. "And this layer represents Hell. Each veil is protected from one another by a strong magnetic field. They're never supposed to meet, but now they are. They're converging in on one another."

"Has this ever happened before?" I asked.

"Never to this degree," Malcolm said. "The universe is in a constant flux of destruction and renewal. Usually, it's kept in balance, with neither one occurring more times than the other, but, according to the other Watchers, there's been more destruction happening than renewal. The energy released during the destruction of a planet or a galaxy has been building up over the past few years, and that's what's causing the veils to thin out."

"When did this start to happen?" I asked. "Do they know?"

Malcolm looked to Brand. "Could we speak in private for a moment?"

"Why?" I demanded. "What are you afraid to say in front of me?"

"Dearest, please…" Malcolm begged, looking away from me, not wanting to meet my eyes.

"Say it, Malcolm."

Malcolm looked up at me, and I knew he didn't want to speak his next words.

"The Watchers have calculated the exact day and time the universe began to fall apart. In your time, it was February 20, 1994."

I stared at Malcolm, sure I had heard him wrong, but knowing in my heart I hadn't.

"That's my birthday," I said.

"Yes," Malcolm said. "It is. You are someone who shouldn't exist, yet you do. Your birth was like throwing a monkey wrench into the gears of the universe. The longer you remain here, the more damage is done."

"But, even if the veils are thinning, they should hold," Brand said. "They shouldn't break."

"No, they shouldn't break," Malcolm agreed, but not sounding convinced of his own words. "They are almost at their weakest points now, but we believe the universe will correct itself and start to heal in time. The universe will adjust around you, dearest, and things should almost return to normal."

"I feel like you're leaving something out," I said. "What aren't you telling us?"

"I've told you everything I know for sure," Malcolm said, "but we are fairly certain Lucifer plans to use Lilly to tear a hole in all the veils while they are weakened. We're just not sure how he intends to harness enough power to do it. It seems to be the only conclusion if you add in the vision Lilly saw when Lucifer touched her. The ribbon of light you saw yourself making in the sky had to be the beginning of the tear in this world. And like we've always assumed; Lucifer will use Lillith's power to phase himself to Heaven to finish the job."

"What will happen if he succeeds?" I asked.

"Complete annihilation," Malcolm said, not trying to hold anything back from me now. "The universe, as we know it, won't exist anymore."

"Well, I'm not about to let that happen," I said, finding strength from an unknown source within myself. I stood straighter, with my shoulders back. "What are we going to do now? How do we make sure Lucifer's plan fails?"

"We're working on it." Malcolm looked pointedly at King Solomon's ring, still wrapped around my thumb. "Are we certain that ring helps you control Lucifer's actions?"

"I can't say for sure, but it seemed to work for me when I last spoke with him at the hospital. As far as I know, he hasn't tried to contact my mother, or anyone else that I know of."

"Well, it either works on him, or he's trying to lull us into a false sense of security," Malcolm said. "Our next step is to figure out what he intends to use as a power source. If we can figure that out, maybe we can destroy it before he's able to use it."

"And if we can't?" I asked.

"The Watchers are all willing to give their lives to keep the universe from being destroyed," Malcolm said. "Lucifer can't fight all of us at once, without diminishing his power with each death. It might be enough to bleed him dry before he's able to do anything. We simply need to figure out exactly when he plans to set his plan into motion to make our deaths effective."

"That's not much of an option either," I said. "There's no way I'm losing any of you."

"It's a last resort maneuver, dearest. Hopefully, it won't come to that. But, rest assured, we won't let him win, no matter what the cost."

I knew I couldn't argue with either of them. Hadn't I just made Brand promise to kill me if Lucifer gained possession of me? We would all do what needed to be done to stop Lucifer. No matter the cost.

CHAPTER 20.

After Malcolm left, Brand took me into his arms and whispered, "Where is the one place you would go if this were our last day on Earth?"

"Besides our bed?" I said, kissing his neck lightly.

"Ok, second place," he said, a pleased smile on his face.

"You'll probably think it's childish."

"No, I won't. Tell me."

"I always wanted to go to Disney World." I pulled away slightly to look at his face. He didn't look like he was about to laugh. Instead, he looked curious as to why I picked such a place. "My mom said she would take me one day, but she never did. I guess it became my holy grail of vacations."

"I took Abby once," Brand said. "Of course, she was already an adult when it first opened, but I'm not sure it matters how old you are there. The atmosphere is charged with the energy of children that makes you feel like a child too. Everything is so new to them. The joy and wonder on their faces reminds you what life should be about."

"Can we go?" I asked, getting excited now. "I mean, I know we're supposed to be facing the end of the world, but can we pretend just for one day that we aren't?"

"Of course we can go. I'll let Malcolm know where we are, and he can contact us if anything comes up. I'll arrange for us to stay on the property. You really can't just go for one day. You would never see anything that way."

"Could we take everyone with us? Make it a real family outing?"

"If that's what you want, that's what we'll do."

"I know I should be more scared about what will happen," I said, "but I'm not. I actually feel hopeful that everything will work out the way it's supposed to."

Brand looked at me in surprise. "The girl who was frightened to jump off my boat to prove she had faith in us isn't scared to face Lucifer in a grand showdown?"

"I know; I'm completely twisted," I said with a half laugh.

"No, you're logical most of the time. Can you tell me what's made you so hopeful all of a sudden?"

"I will, if you promise to hear me out before responding to what I have to say."

"Should I be sitting down to hear this?"

I smiled. "It would probably be a wise thing to do. I'm not sure how you'll take the news, actually."

Brand let me go and sat down on one of the stools at the kitchen island, bringing me in between his legs and cupping his hands behind my back, not willing to have me too far away.

"All right, I'm listening," Brand said, a degree of caution in his voice.

"Do you remember the dream I had, the one you were able to step into the first time you saw the home Malcolm built me?"

Brand nodded, keeping to his word not to say anything until I was finished.

"The little girl you saw, our daughter, I think she's real, or will be real sometime in the future."

"Lilly…" Brand said, warning in his voice.

I placed my index finger against his lips.

"Listen." I reminded him. "When God showed me Lucifer's fall from Heaven, He also showed me our daughter again. He told me she was our wedding gift, Brand. Now, why would He say that if she wasn't real?"

"Am I allowed to speak?"

I smiled. "Yes."

"I don't know why He would say that or show her to you again, but you know what happens when a Watcher has a child with a human."

"Yes, a human. But I'm not completely human. I don't think the same rules apply to me."

"Maybe not, but it's not a risk I'm willing to take."

"When He let me see Utha Mae in Heaven after she died, Utha Mae gave me a message before I woke up. She said she had met our children. Is it possible? Could she have met them in Heaven?"

Brand looked confused, like what I was saying might actually make sense to him.

"It's possible. He could have introduced them to her if their souls have already been chosen." Brand was silent for a while, contemplating what I had just told him.

"Speaking of that time you made me prove my faith in us by jumping off your boat, I think you owe me the same courtesy."

"Lilly, it's not the same. You were never in any real danger then."

"And I don't believe I'm in any real danger now."

Brand sighed, resting his forehead on my chest.

"Could we talk about this again when everything is settled and done, my love? I just don't think I can take the added stress right now." He pulled his head back and looked at me. "I promise we can revisit this topic later, and I will try to have an open mind about it, but right now, all I want to do is spend time with you and enjoy the time we have left until Lucifer acts on his plan."

"I'll drop the subject, for now," I said, a warning of my own in my voice, "but you can rest assured I won't let this go. I've met our daughter twice now, and I felt her little brother moving around inside me. I *will* have them," I said, in no uncertain terms.

"When did you become so feisty?" Brand asked, a smile tugging at the corners of his mouth, obviously finding my new-found attitude cute.

"When I learned to let go of my fears and have faith in our future. I wish you could have the same faith, Brand."

"It's been a long time since I had a reason to have faith in something or someone," he admitted. "I guess I'm just out of practice."

"Then start with me," I said. "Have faith in me to know what's right. I promise you won't regret it."

Brand looked at me in wonder. "Why was I chosen to find you?" he asked more to himself than to me. "Why me?"

"Because, of anyone in this world, you're the only one I can give all of me to."

"But you were in love with Will once, and you still love Malcolm to a point. What makes me different? Did I just come into your life at the right moment? What if Malcolm had met you first? Would you be his wife instead of mine right now?"

"You can't think like that," I said. "I can't even imagine my life any different than it is now. You're like the other half of me. Yes, I do love Will and Malcolm in my way, but the love I feel for them is so small in comparison to what I feel for you. I don't think I would have the will to take another breath if I ever lost you. That's not something I can say for either Will or Malcolm. I could go on without them if I had to, but you? I might as well die the moment you do, because I would be dead inside anyway. *You* are my everything. *You* are my life. Without you, I have nothing."

In one swift motion, Brand pulled me into him, pressing his lips against mine so fervently it left no doubt in my mind he felt the same way I did. When we made love afterwards, we were two pieces of one whole. Neither could survive without the other, because that wasn't how we were built. Destiny had pulled us together, because neither of us would have lived the lives we were meant to otherwise. When I lay naked against Brand afterwards, I couldn't help but marvel at how much my life had changed for the better since the first time I saw him walk into that Physics classroom. Back then, I knew Brand was special on the outside, but now, I knew he was just as perfect on the inside too.

CHAPTER 21.

When I went to tell Tara about our plans to take everyone we loved to Disney World, she squealed in delight and danced around me like there was no tomorrow, which actually *was* one of the reasons we were going.

"So I guess I can count on you coming?" I said, completely joking.

"With bells on my shoes," she replied.

"Brand is making the hotel reservations. We plan to invite Malik as well, and wanted to know what we should do about the room situation with the two of you."

Tara's mouth formed a silent "O".

"Well, to tell you the truth, Lilly Rayne, we'll probably just need the one room for the both of us."

I crossed my arms over my chest. "So, when did this happen? You gave me and Brand a ton of grief about not having sex before marriage. And now you're having wild premarital sex? A little hypocritical of you, wouldn't you say?"

Tara rolled her eyes at me. "We are not cut from the same cloth, girl. I knew if you had sex before marriage, you would regret it for the rest of your life. That's just who you are. Now, me, on the other hand?" Tara said pointing to herself. "I've already been around that block. There wasn't anything to save because I'd already given it away to the wrong person.

Now I know what it feels like to be with a man I love, and there ain't no power on this earth that's going to take that away from me."

"Maybe I should warn Lucifer," I said. "I know how you are when you want something, and it ain't pretty." Mentally, I was reliving the after-Thanksgiving mayhem caused by Tara's unstoppable desire to get what she wanted for Malik.

"You think that might stop him?" Tara said with a smile.

"I know it would stop me," I replied in all seriousness, before falling into a fit of laughter.

The next person I went to see was Will.

We hadn't talked much since Utha Mae's death, and I felt a bit guilty for not checking up on him sooner. When I knocked on his apartment door, I saw the curtain of the front window move, and knew he had seen me standing outside. I waited for what seemed an eternity until he finally answered the door.

"Hey, Lilly," he said, looking a complete mess. His hair hadn't been brushed in at least a couple of days. His facial hair was a good inch long, and he smelled like he hadn't bathed in a week.

"Are you ok?" I asked, immediately concerned. "Are you sick?"

Will shook his head. "No."

We stood there, silently staring at one another. Finally I asked, "Can I come in?"

I wasn't sure Will was going to let me in, but finally he opened the door wider and allowed me entry.

When I stepped into the apartment, I could smell the overflowing trash can and what remained of left over take-out coming from the kitchen area. I immediately found my phone in my pants pocket and called Tara.

"Get over to Will's," I told her. "I need your help."

"What's wrong?"

"Just come over. We need to clean."

When I got off the phone with Tara, Will had already returned to his bedroom and pulled the covers over his head, apparently attempting to hide from the world.

I didn't bother him. It was going to take a while to get his apartment back to normal, and the less he was in the way, the faster I could accomplish it.

When Tara arrived, she looked like she was ready for battle. In one hand, she carried a mop, and, in the other hand, she carried a bucket filled with cleaning supplies. As she stepped over the threshold, she gagged a little, but stood fast against the mess and helped me clean our best friend's home. Once we reached the bedroom, Tara used the wooden handle on the mop to poke at Will, who was still underneath the covers.

Will peeked out with bleary eyes, obviously not appreciating the disturbance.

"Stop it, Tara," he said, annoyed at her poking and prodding. "Can't you guys tell I want to be alone?"

"Considering the way you smell?" Tara said. "You're lucky your neighbors haven't called the police to come and see if there's a dead body in your apartment."

Will pulled the covers over his head and mumbled, "Go away. I don't want you guys here."

In one swift motion, and with more strength than I thought she possessed, Tara poked the mop handle under the comforter and slung it onto the floor. I snatched it up before Will could pull it back onto the bed, and took it straight to the washing machine in the kitchen.

"Now, don't make me do to you what I just did to that comforter," Tara warned. "You stink like the gates of Hell opened wide, Will Allan Kilpatrick. Get your butt out of that bed before you make me come in and snatch that pretty blond hair of yours right off your head."

"Leave me alone!" Will yelled, burying his face in his pillow.

When I walked back into the room, Tara was just about to pounce on Will, making good on her threat when I stopped her.

"Give us a minute, Tara," I said to her. "I have a feeling I know what might be going on."

"Well, if you can't get results, let me know," she said. "I'm sure I can go to Lowe's and buy a garden hose. 'Cause he's getting a bath one way or the other before I leave this place."

After Tara left the room, I put a hand on Will's shoulder, only to have him flinch away from me.

"Will," I begged, "turn around and face me."

I wasn't sure he would, but he finally rolled over onto his side, refusing to meet my eyes.

"You haven't been the same since you had your talk with Utha Mae. What did she say to you?"

Will blinked as if he was finally coming back from wherever his mind had gone to hide, and reluctantly answered me.

"She said she loved me and that she forgave me for taking her Will's life. She said she knew," he looked at me, "that you all knew Will was different after that night at the lake. You just couldn't quite put your finger on what had happened."

Will fell silent.

"What else did she say?" I gently prodded.

"She told me it was my responsibility to make sure Will hadn't given his life for nothing, and that I should protect you no matter what, because that was what I had been sent for."

"I don't understand. Why does that upset you?"

"Because she said it wasn't Lucifer who sent me," he said, looking back at me. "She said God sent me to you."

"You already figured that part out," I reminded him. "I still don't understand why you're so upset."

"It was the way she said it," Will said. "It was like she knew it for a fact. It was something I suspected, but didn't really know. Why would He still care about me, Lilly? I betrayed Him in the worst way. I chose to take Lucifer's side against Him. I hated humans just as much as Lucifer did, and couldn't wait to find the time when we could finally destroy all of you."

"But you don't feel that way anymore," I said. "Utha Mae was right. All three of us knew you were different, but we didn't talk about it with one another. You were still our Will and, changed or not, we loved you. We still love you. You're like the annoying big brother our parents never had."

Will laughed harshly, but it was still a laugh.

"Now, come on and stop feeling sorry for yourself. Take the gift you've been given and prove that you earned it. God didn't send you to us to just wallow around in self-pity. You're too good a person for that. Plus, you have to go somewhere with me and Tara."

"Where?" Will said, rubbing his eyes with one hand, finally coming out of his self-imposed stupor.

"Brand and I are taking the whole family to Disney World to wait out Lucifer's plan."

Will looked at me like I'd lost my mind. "You know how crazy that sounds, right?"

I shrugged. "Listen, if the world is going to end, at least we'll be at the happiest place on Earth. I figure if there's one place Lucifer's power isn't going to work, it has to be there."

"Why would Brand want me there?"

"Because, whether you like it or not, he considers you part of the family too. Yes, the black sheep of the family, but still family."

"You're all crazy, you know," Will said, sitting up in his bed, almost causing me to gag on his body odor.

"Apparently not as crazy as you," I said, waving a hand in front of my face to dissipate the stench. "Now go shower a few times while I wash these sheets. And don't come out of there unless that hairy thing living on your face is shaved off. You're starting to look like Cousin It."

A twinkle of mischief entered Will's eyes, and I knew what he was about to do but felt helpless to stop it. He pushed me down onto the mattress and started to rub his scraggly beard along my cheeks. I tried my best to push him away, but just ended up laughing hysterically. The bristles were too soft to hurt. They only tickled.

When he finally let me go, we both had smiles on our faces like we did when we were children, trying our best to annoy one another. I stood from his bed and kissed what I hoped was a clean spot on his forehead.

"Now go clean up, Will Allen. We've got Space Mountain to conquer."

Brand said he would go talk with Abby, Sebastian, and Malik about going with us, and the last person on my list was my mother.

After Utha Mae's funeral, Brand and I had a long talk with my mother and told her everything. She had already seen my power when I used it on Utha Mae, and needed to know who it was she had married. I was surprised at how well she took everything, and was proud of her when she moved back into her trailer. She said she would file for a divorce as soon as she could figure out where Lucas/Lucifer was.

After Tara and I got Will straightened out, I phased over to my mom's. She answered the door quickly and gave me a big hug.

"Come on in, sweetie," she said. "I was just making something to eat. You want to eat some supper with me?"

We ate my mom's specialty, Hamburger Helper. A gourmet chef my mom wasn't, but she was pretty good at H and H. It was then I realized my culinary skills must have been inherited from her.

"I'm glad you came by," she told me as we sat down to eat. "I thought I owed you an explanation about why I never wanted to talk about your grandparents."

I immediately felt a ton of guilt land on my shoulders. That had been the one point of the explanation Brand and I gave her that we completely glossed over. I wasn't sure how to tell my mother that her father still didn't want anything to do with her after all these years.

"Mom, I already know who they are."

She looked surprised, as she had every right to.

"I actually went to see my grandparents not too long ago."

My mother put her fork down on her plate and sat back in her chair.

"How are they?" she asked.

"They seemed fine. Though, I only talked to Grandma. Grandpa refused to speak with me, but I did see him right before I left."

My mother sighed. "That sounds about right. He was the one who decided I should be shunned from the others. Your grandmother just wasn't strong enough to talk him out of it."

"Why didn't you ever tell me you grew up Amish?"

My mother smiled. "Would you have believed me, or thought I was telling you a lie?"

Thinking on my mother's past, I knew the answer immediately.

"Lying," I said.

"That's part of the reason I never told you. Plus, I didn't want you to think badly of your father for leaving us. At least now we know he was only sent here to give me you."

"I'm sorry you got used like that because of me. Your life would have been so much easier if you hadn't had me."

My mother looked at me like I'd lost my mind.

"Lilly, you're the only thing that I did right. Having you was like having a little piece of your father with me. If I couldn't have him, at least I had you."

"But," I felt myself begin to cry, "you never seemed to want to be around me."

My mother sighed. "I'm only human, Lilly. I had a hard time being around you because you *did* remind me of your father so much. It broke my heart to be around you sometimes, because I missed him so. I know that sounds selfish and awful, but don't you dare think for one minute I never loved you. You're the only thing in this world I do love."

When I broke down in tears, my mother got up from her seat and put her arms around me.

"I'm so sorry, sweetie. I should have said all that to you a long time ago."

When I finally got my emotions under control, I told her, "Well, there's one thing you can do to make it up to me."

"Anything."

"Come to Disney World with us."

My mother gave me the same odd look Will had. "With everything you and Brand are having to deal with, you two decide we should all go on vacation?"

I shrugged. "Well, you know, if the world is going to end and all, at least we'll all have a smile on our faces."

My mother shook her head and smiled. "You are definitely your father's daughter."

"Why? Why would you say that?"

"Because he was the only person I knew who would do something completely insane just to have fun."

It wasn't the way I thought an archangel of Heaven would be described, but it oddly made me feel closer to him in a way. I wasn't sure if I would ever be able to meet him in person, but was thankful my mother was able to see a small part of him inside me.

CHAPTER 22.

The next day we all phased to Disney World. Brand booked us rooms at the Disney Animal Kingdom Villas. I felt like an honored guest when the manager of the hotel came to greet us personally. He arranged to have everyone's bags delivered to their rooms and told Brand that our special room was waiting for us. All we needed to do was go outside the hotel and get into the waiting limousine.

"We're not staying here with everyone else?" I asked as Brand took my arm to escort me out of the hotel.

"No."

And that was it. That was all the explanation I got.

To say I was slightly disappointed I wouldn't be able to wake up and watch the African wildlife surrounding the hotel roam freely by our bedroom window would have been an understatement.

Brand helped me into the back of the white stretch limousine waiting for us outside. As we drove away, I watched the giraffes walking around in the fenced-in area and sighed.

"I thought I would be able to pet a giraffe," I said dramatically, with a touch of a whine.

Brand laughed. "Don't look so disappointed. I promise you'll like where we're staying."

I snuggled up to Brand and just enjoyed the ride with him by my side. We drove up to the Magic Kingdom Theme Park and were met by a man dressed as Prince Charming.

"Welcome to Disney World, Mr. and Mrs. Cole. We're delighted to have you stay with us. Please take a seat in the cart, and I'll take you to the castle."

I looked at Brand. "Why are we going to the castle?"

"Patience," Brand said, apparently pleased that I was absolutely clueless to his plans.

Prince Charming drove us up to Cinderella's castle. We were escorted to a secret elevator that went up to the fourth floor. When we disembarked, we walked into a small foyer that was beautifully decorated with all things Cinderella. There was a circular tiled mosaic of Cinderella's carriage inlaid in the floor beneath our feet. There was also a desk, grandfather clock, and a glass case on one of the walls, housing Cinderella's crown, scepter, and an arrangement of glass blown pumpkins of varying colors. The suite wasn't very large but the space held a cozy, homey feeling. Two queen-size canopy beds butted against the far wall, while the inner wall was home to a fireplace. Above the fireplace hung a picture of Cinderella, and we were told it also doubled as a flat screen TV. The bathroom looked like something you would find in a medieval castle with a deep, almost Grecian-style tub, and separate shower. Hanging over the toilet were draperies that made it look like a throne, which made me giggle.

Once Prince Charming left, I jumped my husband until he fell on one of the canopied beds, and kissed him until he gave me what I wanted. When we lay in each other's arms afterwards, I said, "I didn't even know this room existed."

"Well, now you do, my love. Whenever you want to come here, we can stay in this suite."

I looked up at Brand. "How much does it cost to stay in a room like this?"

"Nothing for me."

"And just what makes you so special?"

"Well, it's true the room isn't generally open to the general public anymore, but if you're a major stockholder in the company, they pretty much let you have anything you want."

"You have stock in Disney?"

Brand shrugged. "I knew a good investment when I saw it. And after I met Walt, I knew he would take the company in the direction it needed to go. I was one of the very first investors. Of course, people think that person was my great-grandfather, not me."

"Oh, yeah," I said, trailing my fingers over his chest, smiling. "I forgot I was married to Methuselah."

Brand rolled me over onto my back and held my arms above my head by the wrists. "Are you calling me old, Mrs. Cole?"

"I believe I just did, Mr. Cole. Though," I lowered my eyelashes halfway, "you could always prove me wrong."

And prove me wrong he did...for the next three hours... in each bed....

When we finally met up with the others, Tara forced me to ride Space Mountain with her. It was the first time I ever heard Tara call on the Lord so much. After that, we pretty much rode whatever we wanted, whenever we wanted. I felt a little bad skipping people who were waiting in line, but Brand assured me it was protocol for someone like him who owned a large part of the company.

Tara was in Heaven when we went to Cinderella's Royal Table Dinner. We were greeted by Cinderella herself, who also escorted us to our private table. We were given a choice of appetizers, entrees, and desserts. I chose to eat the rock shrimp cocktail, grilled swordfish, and the chef's dessert trio.

After we ate, we watched the parade by the castle, and invited everyone up to our room to watch the fireworks show.

Luckily, someone had already been in the room and tidied up. I realized everyone knew Brand and I had been privately busy during our three hours away from them, but I didn't need them to have proof of our physical activity. I knew Tara would have brought it to the attention of everyone, and I wasn't sure how I would ever live through the embarrassment.

While we were walking by the large bronze statue of Walt Disney and Mickey Mouse, by the castle the following day, Tara grabbed my hand like her life depended on it.

"What's wrong?" I asked her, following her gaze to the statue.

Standing there, as if he was alive, was the eight-year-old Will we had lost once upon a time. He was smiling at us. The Will we had lived with for the past eleven years walked up to his young counterpart, and knelt down on one knee in front of him. Tara and I walked over.

"Are you real?" Tara asked.

"With the veils so weak," young Will said, "it takes less energy for me to appear to you guys."

I remembered the newscast I saw when Malcolm first told us about the weakening of the veils.

"Why haven't you come before now?" I asked him.

Young Will shrugged his shoulders. "I don't know. I wasn't sure how you guys would react. I'm still a ghost, you know."

I held my hand out to young Will, testing to see just how real he was. Will reached out and grabbed my hand, letting him know he felt very real.

I knelt in front of him and pulled him into my arms, feeling hot tears roll down my cheeks. I knew I shouldn't be happy about the veils being so weak, but I couldn't help feeling glad I was being given a chance to hold one of my dearest friends again.

Before I knew it, all three of us were giving young Will a giant group hug.

"Thank you," older Will said to him. "Thank you for letting me live your life."

"You're welcome," young Will said back.

The three musketeers were back together, with the addition of our newest/oldest member. We spent the day acting like we were eight years old again, finally having a last chance to play with one another. Young Will left at the end of that day, but he didn't say goodbye; he just vanished. I don't think he said goodbye, because he knew it wouldn't be goodbye forever. We would see him again one day when we all went to meet him instead.

For the next two days, we acted like we didn't have a care in the world. We went to every park and rode every ride there was to ride. Malcolm would come to visit us and keep us up to date on things, each evening when we sat down to eat. I could tell the strain of trying to find Lucifer's power source was taking its toll on him. I felt bad he was working so tirelessly when we were having so much fun.

"I'll have fun when this is over, dearest," Malcolm assured me. "Don't worry about me. Just enjoy your time together. We're certain to figure things out before it's too late."

That night, Brand and I stayed up most of the night, not letting ourselves fall asleep until the early morning hours. When I finally did go to sleep, I had a strange dream. I was floating in space above the Earth, but the world I lived on looked odd to me. It looked like it had been wrapped in a clear plastic bubble that was pocked with holes in various places, but the largest hole seemed to be situated over Antarctica. From the direction of the sun, I saw what looked like an invisible disturbance in space, only visible to me because of the optical illusion it presented of bending the star fields around it. What looked like a shock wave of energy passed over the Earth. The next thing I knew, I was sitting straight up in bed, having a hard time catching my breath.

Brand was already up. I heard the water of the shower going in the bathroom, and laid back down on the bed until my breathing returned to normal. I reached for the TV remote to check on the weather for that day and flipped through the channels, trying to find the local news. When I turned the volume up, the newscaster on the screen had a picture of the sun, with what looked like a large loop of fire streaming from its surface.

"Scientists say the solar storm is the largest in recorded history. They are warning that the resulting flare might affect electrical power grids within the next two days."

I sat there and watched the digitally-produced reenactment of the geomagnetic storm which was to take place, finally understanding what my dream actually meant.

"Brand!" I yelled, finding my robe and hastily putting in on. Brand came out of the bathroom, completely naked and glistening with the wetness of his shower.

"What's wrong?" he asked, looking me up and down to make sure I was physically unharmed.

In any other circumstance, I would have dragged him to bed and had my way with him he looked so good, but now wasn't the time for such frivolity.

"Call Malcolm; I think I know what Lucifer intends to use as a power source."

"It was literally staring us in the face all this time," Malcolm said as he sat on the red settee in our suite's sitting room.

"I wouldn't have put it together if I hadn't just had the dream," I told him, knowing the subtle hint had probably come from God. "So you think that's what Lucifer plans to use, then?"

"It makes complete sense," Malcolm said. "The geomagnetic storm which will pass over the Earth's atmosphere normally wouldn't affect us. But if we take into account your vision of you standing in snow with a tear forming in the sky, he has to plan to take you somewhere in the Antarctic, since that's where the ozone layer is the thinnest, and harness the power from the solar storm to punch a hole in the veils. If he can find a way to possess you and combine your power with his, I don't see why his plan would fail."

Brand took my hand with King Solomon's ring on it. "But we won't let him possess you. Just make sure you keep this ring on."

"I feel like I should hide somewhere he wouldn't think to look for me," I said.

"I don't think it matters where you go, dearest. He would be able to find you. It's in the archangel's arsenal of powers to know where any angel is at any time. Since you're half archangel, you probably stand out like a lighthouse beacon for a lost ship to him."

Nowhere to hide. Nowhere to run. Even the happiest place on Earth wasn't a safe haven.

"Then we wait for him to show up, and we fight," Brand said, squeezing my hand.

"We should go home," I said. "I would like to come back here one day when this is all over. Mickey Mouse might not take it too kindly if we started Armageddon on his doorstep."

Malcolm stood. "I'll gather the Watchers. Where should we meet?"

"Let's meet in my London home. It's big enough to accommodate everyone for a while."

"I don't think anything will happen until sometime tomorrow," I told them.

"Why is that, dearest?"

"Because tomorrow is December 21." I looked at them both, to see if they understood what I was saying. "Maybe the Mayans had it right all along. Tomorrow might actually be the end of the world."

CHAPTER 23.

The Watchers decided they should *all* be at Brand's house to wait out Lucifer. As seemed to be the unspoken rule among the Watchers when a fight was near, they all wore their ceremonial black feather cloaks and tight leather pants. I suppose as part of their war uniform they also had to wear the black leather belt around their waists that held a sword on one side and a serrated blade on the other.

I felt like I was in the opposite of the Playboy mansion, with so many bare-chested men walking around in form-fitting, leave-nothing-to-the- imagination pants.

I thought Tara's eyes were going to bulge out of their sockets at the sight of them all together.

I tried to talk her into staying somewhere else, at an undoubtedly safer place with Malik, but she refused. True to form, she wanted to stay with me through thick and thin.

"Girl, it's a sacrifice I am willing to make for you," she said, eyeing a pair of Watchers pass by the couch we were sitting on in the living room. "Why is it that each one looks just as good as or better than the last one I saw?"

"Seriously, am I going to have to put blinders over your eyes? We're supposed to be in crisis mode here."

"Don't you dare," Tara said in alarm. "I'm just fine, girl. I'm just fine."

I did worry about Tara being in a house full of Watchers, though. I knew with so many of them, a normal human would be hard-pressed to withstand the pull of their overpowering pheromones. However, Brand seemed to be right in his first estimation about my best friend. Her loyalty to me trumped anything the Watchers could do to her.

Brand and Malcolm walked into the room, dressed just like the other Watchers, with Mason walking between them. Even though Brand and Malcolm were formidable in their own rights, you didn't have to be a Watcher to know Mason was their leader. I couldn't quite put my finger on why, exactly, though. True, he was just as gorgeous as my friend and my husband, but he seemed to emit a different aura. Maybe he stood a centimeter taller or was broader of shoulder, I don't know. But he did make you take notice of him, and you knew he wasn't someone you should ever double-cross.

"Can I ask you guys something?" I said.

"You can ask us anything, dearest."

"Why does every Watcher look like a male supermodel?" It had been a question bothering me for some time.

"It was easier to gain the trust of humans in these forms," Mason answered.

"Truly, dearest, wouldn't you rather have someone who looks like us giving you advice than some ancient old man with a balding head and missing teeth?"

"Makes sense to me," Tara said, ogling another set of Watchers passing by.

"Is everyone here?" I asked Brand as he came to sit beside me on the couch.

"Yes, everyone has gathered."

"And you're sure it's safe for Tara and Malik to be here?"

"None of the Watchers will harm them," Mason said. "You have my word on that, Lilly. Plus, the calm your presence brings them makes their hunger go away when they are close to you."

"So," I said, feeling like I should twiddle my thumbs or something, "what do we do now?"

"We wait for him to make his move, dearest," Malcolm said, standing before me, like he would personally rip Lucifer's throat out if he dared materialize in front of him.

"Anybody got an idea on what that move might be?" Tara asked.

"We have to assume he'll try to get Lilly somehow," Will said as he and Malik walked into the room. Will handed me the soda he had gone to get from the kitchen.

Will's presence rankled some of the Watchers, but Mason quickly put an end to their objections. I told Mason I needed my family around me and that included Will, so he took care of things, and made it so I didn't have to worry about any of my friends while we waited.

We all started to stare at one another, and I said the most obvious thing, "Well, this is awkward."

Mason was the first to chuckle, and we all at least got one decent laugh out of the impossible situation we found ourselves in.

We decided to play a game of poker to keep our minds off things. I completely sucked at the game, which wasn't a big surprise to anyone.

"You've never had a poker face," Tara said with a shake of her head, as if she pitied me. "Everything you think is written all over your face."

I took a sideways glance at Brand sitting beside me.

"Oh, no," Tara said, shaking a finger at me. "We don't have time for you and Prince Charming to go find an empty corner, Lilly Rayne. Just get that thought out of your head."

Everyone looked at me, making me want to hide underneath the table.

"Stop picking on my wife," Brand said, taking one of my hands and kissing it. "Like I've said before, she can't help it if she finds me irresistible."

"Could we please not talk about your sex life at this exact moment?" Malcolm begged. "However, since you brought the subject up, do you need any more condoms? I have a large stockpile at home I haven't been using, if you need more. I'm sure the box Abby and Angela gave you is gone by now."

"I've got money, Malcolm," Brand said matter-of-factly. "I can afford to buy my own stockpile."

"Ok, you guys are just making me too uncomfortable," Will said, looking a bit nauseated. He threw his cards into the pile and stood. "Come get me when the apocalypse begins. I think that would be easier to handle than this conversation."

"I think I'm with Will on this one," Malik said, tossing his cards in and giving his chips to Tara, who greedily added them to her own horde. Malik stood, and he and Will walked out of the room, saying they were hungry and going to the kitchen.

"Bring me something back," Tara yelled at Malik. "I don't plan to leave this table until all the chips are mine!"

It always tickled me how competitive Tara was when you played any game with her. Her specialty was, of course, Monopoly, but poker was her second-favorite. I always thought she should try the professional poker tour. She had the best luck at games of anyone I knew.

Sometime around one in the morning, I decided I needed some sleep. I went to use the bathroom and found Tara practically glued to my side.

"What do you think you're doing?" I asked.

"Going to the bathroom with you. What does it look like I'm doing?"

"I'm not two years old, Mom. I don't need your help."

"You are not supposed to go anywhere alone," Tara said. "And I'm not about to just let you go in there without someone watching you."

"No," I said adamantly. "You are not going in, and you are most definitely not watching me go to the bathroom."

"Brand!" Tara called, looking for backup.

Brand phased in beside us.

"What's wrong?" he asked, immediately looking for danger.

"Lilly refuses to let me go to the bathroom with her."

"I think I can go to the bathroom without being abducted. Besides, it's not like I can't phase back here even if someone does try to grab me."

"She's right, Tara," Brand said, coming to my defense. "Lilly can phase anywhere she wants."

"Well, I don't like it," Tara huffed, even though she knew we were making sense. "Go on then, Lilly Rayne. We'll wait right here until you get finished."

Before I closed the door, I silently mouthed, 'Thank you' to my husband. He winked at me and smiled.

His beautiful face was the last thing I saw before I noticed the jewels embedded in King Solomon's ring beginning to glow.

I stared at the ring, completely hypnotized by its luminous beauty.

"Come to me," I heard the voice inside my head say. "Come to me."

Without phasing or having someone phase me, I found myself standing on the snowy plain of Lucifer's vision, surrounded by a massive mountain range.

Lucifer, wearing his human suit of Lucas, stood in front of me smiling.

"That was easier than I thought it would be," he said, holding out a thick white padded coat. "Put your arms in the coat, Lilly, like a good girl. I don't need you to freeze to death when I'm so close to winning."

I did what he said without even thinking about it, like I wasn't in control of my own body. The wind was biting cold, even though the sun was high in the clear blue sky overhead. Lucifer walked around me and began to button the coat for me.

"You know," he began, "when I saw you with King Solomon's ring that night at the restaurant, I couldn't believe my luck. Up until that point, I wasn't sure what I would do to get you when the time was right. It was as if the universe handed me the keys to its own destruction on a shiny silver platter. How did you find it?"

"Horace told us where it was," I said, not having any control over what I was saying. It was like, whatever Lucifer commanded, I did automatically. He must have seen the confusion I felt in my expression, because he began to laugh.

"You have no idea what's going on, do you?"

"No," I answered.

"Who do you think made that ring, Lilly?"

"I don't know."

"It is one of seven rings I made from my heavenly crown, after I fell out of my father's good graces. I kept one ring and gave the other six to the other princes of hell. At any time of my choosing, I can call any of the six to me just as I called you to me."

Lucifer cocked his head to the side as he looked at me. "You look like you want to ask me something. Go ahead and ask; I'll answer anything you want to know. We have a couple of minutes until the end of the universe."

"If it's your ring, how did King Solomon get it?"

"I gave it to him."

"But everyone seems to think God gave it to him to protect his people against demons and jinn. That's what the Watchers believe."

"Of course they believe that," Lucifer grinned at his own imagined brilliance. "I appeared to Solomon, looking quite angelic, if I do say so myself. He, in turn, told a grand tale of a beautiful angel coming to him and presenting him with a ring of protection from God. It's not like the Watchers were privy to things happening in Heaven or Hell. All their knowledge on the subject was second-hand."

"Why didn't Will know?" I asked, not believing for one minute Will would have withheld such vital information from me.

"Will is nothing but a grunt," Lucifer scoffed. "He does what he's told like a good worker ant. He hasn't seen the six princes of hell since I left them in charge of things there. So, no he had no idea the ring was mine either. I suppose that should be something of a comfort to you. He never betrayed you."

"But why did you give Solomon the ring?"

"I ordered everyone to stay away from Solomon while he had possession of the ring, but, in truth, it was my way to weed out the weak. Those who thought they knew better than me, and wanted to take possession of the ring for themselves, went after it, only to find themselves trapped with Solomon for all eternity. Only someone with a pure soul could have taken the ring from them. I guess I really shouldn't have been surprised you were the one who was able to get it. Lucky for me you kept wearing the ring, which made it possible for me to call you to me."

He smiled, and I died a little inside.

"Why are you doing this?"

"So I can win. I thought that would be obvious."

"But you'll die too. Why would you want to?"

"Death is better than living on this God-forsaken planet with you little monkeys. You can't imagine what it's like to have the one person you love the most order you to bow down to creatures completely beneath you in every possible aspect. I'm finally going to do what He should have done a long time ago. If I have to sacrifice myself in the process, so be it. Think of it as giving the universe a chance to start over. He'll have a clean slate to begin again."

"Why are you so jealous of us?"

"I'm not jealous!" Lucifer became livid, his face turning red. "It's hatred I feel, not jealousy. Now, shut up so I can do what needs to be done."

I tried to make my body do something, anything, but I couldn't even twitch my little finger, much less phase myself somewhere safe. In the back of my mind, I could hear Tara tell me, "I told you so, girl." If I had let her come into the bathroom with me, she probably would have ripped the ring off my finger when it began to glow, saving me from being under Lucifer's control.

Even though I knew the circumstances I found myself in looked hopeless, I didn't lose faith that everything would work out in the end. A vision of my daughter floated in the ether of my memories. Her face was crystal-clear in my mind, like she was standing right in front of me. I knew I would survive this day somehow, because I had too much to live for.

Something that looked like a circular rainbow formed in the sky overhead. I heard Lucifer laugh, and the body of Lucas Hunter collapsed to the ground. Lucifer stood before me in his true form, looking much like Uriel had, completely translucent, only casting a slight shimmer against the white snow, but I could feel his presence now, no longer hidden by the skin of a human body.

I stood helpless as he floated closer to me, intent on possessing my body to tear the universe apart. The world around me faded to black, as if it was a scene in a movie, and all I could hear was silence.

CHAPTER 24.
(Brand's Point of View)

I watched as Lilly closed the door. Her soft lips moved in a silent 'Thank you' to me. I couldn't repress my smile or miss an opportunity to wink at her secretly. I stood there, staring at the door, marveling at how the meaning of my life had changed in such a short period of time.

My wife. My love. My life. Lilly had become all those things to me, and I couldn't imagine trying to live in a world where she didn't exist. It was a concept I refused to even consider as a possibility.

"You two are too cute sometimes," Tara said to me. "I swear I've never seen Lilly so happy."

"I will always strive to keep her happy," I promised Tara. "I hope you know that."

"Yeah," Tara said, a slow smile spreading her lips. "I know that, Prince Charming."

"Brand!"

I turned to the voice of Will calling me from the front of my home, instantly knowing what he was going to tell me. I could sense the presence of the others just as well as he.

I grabbed Tara and phased her to my home in Lakewood.

"What the…"

"Stay here," I told her. "It's not safe for you back there. I'll send Malik as soon as I can."

She looked at me stunned, only one word issuing from her lips, "Lilly…"

"We'll protect her," I promised, before phasing back to the front door of my London home.

I found Will standing just inside the house at the open door, staring straight ahead to the front lawn. All of the Watchers stood behind him in the foyer. When I turned to look at what was coming, I saw a multitude of fallen rebellion angels like Will staring back at us, with only one thing on their collective minds: war.

"How many?" I asked.

"All of them," Will replied.

"Well, I guess he's playing for keeps this time," Mason said as he and Malcolm came to stand with us.

"This should be fun." Malcolm smiled. "I haven't had a good fight since the last war."

"But I don't think Lucifer is here," Will said. "I can sense him anywhere when he's not in a human body, and even if he were here in the Lucas form, I should be able to sense him if he were that close."

"Could this be a distraction?" Mason questioned.

"Where is Lilly?" Malcolm asked.

I phased to the bathroom. Lilly was gone, but there wasn't a phase trail. I refused to let panic set in. More than likely she had just stepped out and I just missed her leaving. I went back to the others.

"She's not where I left her," I told them. "But there isn't a phase trail there either. She has to be somewhere in the house. Help me find her."

We phased all over the house, calling her name. When I came across Malik, he began to ask me what was going on, but I didn't have time to tell him. I phased him to Lakewood to be with Tara, and continued to search for Lilly back in London.

I phased back into my den, knowing how much she loved the couch there. More often than not, she would seek it out and curl up on its soft leather to nap on.

I didn't find Lilly there, but I did find Will.

"Any luck?" I asked him.

Will turned to me. The fear in his eyes told me something was terribly wrong.

"I feel him," Will whispered, before grabbing my arm and phasing us.

The sun glared off the hard-packed snow all around us. A calm biting wind yawned against the open plain. In the distance, the jagged black edges of a mountain range could be seen.

"No!" Will screamed, falling to his knees in front of me.

I followed his gaze and watched helplessly as Lucifer, in his true angelic form, approached Lilly. Why wasn't she phasing away? Why was she just standing there, allowing Lucifer to come closer to possess her? I knew in those split seconds something was wrong, but had no idea what.

The body once belonging to Will Kilpatrick crumbled to the snow, lifeless. I watched as the fallen angel, who had possessed Will so long ago and who had fallen in love with a human, flew across the ice with unimaginable speed propelling himself against Lucifer, gifting me with the few precious seconds I needed to phase to Lilly.

I grabbed her arm and attempted to phase us back to London, but something counteracted my power.

"Lilly!" I yelled at her, shaking her to wake her of whatever trance Lucifer had placed her under. "Lilly!" Still no response.

I looked up into the far reaches of the sky, and saw Will and Lucifer in a firestorm of battle.

"Do you really think just because you love her it makes you stronger than me?" Lucifer taunted Will.

"Her love for me has given me something you were never able to get after we were exiled here," Will yelled back, knowing he was in a losing battle, but doing what he could to buy me time to figure out how to phase Lilly out of harm's way.

"And what exactly did her love give you?" Lucifer asked snidely.

"A reason to die."

Lucifer laughed menacingly. "Well, far be it from me not fulfill your final wish."

I watched as Lucifer used the power all archangels possess to turn Will into a pile of black ash on the pristine white snow below.

As I kept attempting to phase Lilly to safety, to no avail, Lucifer descended to the snow beside me.

I felt him use his power against me, a power he had over all angelic beings to control their bodies and break their will, to fling me a few yards away, forcing me to my knees and making me lift my head to watch him.

"I want you to watch what your God has made me do," he said to me.

I tried to break the bonds of his power keeping me where I was, forcing me to act as a silent observer to my deepest nightmare as he entered the body of the woman I had intended to die with.

Secretly, I had already made the decision to ask Lilly to end my life with her archangel powers when she was close to death. Spending an eternity without her would have been my own personal Hell on Earth. I assumed she would resist the idea at first, but knew her love for me would make her end my torment before she left me forever.

The face I loved looked at me now with fire in her eyes, and the malicious smile of Lucifer laughed at my torment. I watched as Lilly's vision of herself came true. Lucifer raised her arms to the sky, now possessing the combined power of two archangels. The air around me crackled with the force of that power as streams of fire shot from Lilly's palms, tearing through the sky above to harness the added strength from the sun's solar storm as it passed over the Earth. A ribbon of white light appeared in the sky, continuing to grow wider. I watched in horror as two planets, one blue and one orange, appeared within the opened tear. The first tear to end the universe had been made.

The promise I made to Lilly begged me to go through with what she wanted. I knew I had promised her, if Lucifer found a way to take control of her, I would end her life before the universe could be destroyed. Her soul would no longer be in her body now, already pushed out by Lucifer. But that knowledge didn't make it any easier for me to do what I knew needed to be done.

Being preoccupied with destroying the universe, Lucifer's power over me was now divided, not being strong enough to keep me under his control while destroying the world. I gripped the hilt of the serrated blade hanging at my side, filled with an overpowering hatred. I would not let Lucifer desecrate Lilly's body. I would fulfill her request to end her torment, and stop Lucifer before he had a chance to phase into Heaven and destroy everything my father loved.

I quickly phased to stand in front of Lilly, her face contorted by Lucifer's malevolence, no longer recognizable as the woman I had given my heart and soul to. In one swift motion, I pulled my dagger from its sheath and raised it above her heart, swinging down towards her chest with all my might.

CHAPTER 24
(Lilly's Point of View)

I found myself sitting on the swing on the front porch of my Colorado home. I tried to think what my last waking memory was, and realized it was of Lucifer in his angelic form floating towards me, intent on possessing my body, but I never actually saw him do it. Before he reached me, I completely blacked out.

"You did well."

I looked beside me and saw God sitting on the swing, smiling at me.

"But he won. I wasn't strong enough to stop him."

God smiled. "Search your heart. Do you really think he won?"

I sat there, thinking back over the last scene I remembered.

"I said your heart, Lilly," God gently reminded me, "not your mind."

I took a deep breath and closed my eyes, trying to do as He suggested.

My heart swelled with so much love and hope it brought tears to my eyes. Without Him having to tell me, I knew without a doubt Lucifer had not been completely victorious. Somehow, by some miracle, he failed to destroy what God had made.

I opened my eyes, "How?" I asked.

"Your faith in your family and the love you share with Brand stopped him. It's something I had hoped Lucifer would have learned by now, after spending so much time on Earth."

"What did You hope he would learn?"

"That love, not hatred and jealousy, gives you the strength you need to make anything happen. It's a lesson you taught to many of my children, one in particular.

God looked to the other end of the porch and I followed his gaze. Will stood there, smiling at me. I jumped out of the swing and ran to him. He held his arms out to me and hugged me tightly to him.

I felt the warmth of his love for me like a warm blanket, protecting me from the cold.

But, why was Will here?

I pulled away from him slightly.

"Why are you in my dream?" I asked.

"Because I'm dead, Lilly."

I felt my body start to tremble. "Does that mean I'm dead too? Are we actually in Heaven?"

Will shook his head. "No, you're not dead. You have a long life to live. He just let me come say goodbye to you before I move on."

I felt God standing behind me and turned to Him.

"Your love and that of Tara and Utha Mae taught Will the true reason I treasure human life so much. In the end, he sacrificed himself trying to save you, a mere human, who he would have destroyed an eon ago and never thought twice about."

I looked back at Will. "Where will you go now?"

"Back home," he smiled. "I get to go back to Heaven because of you, Lilly. It's the greatest gift you could have given me."

"I'll miss you," I said, taking him in my arms for what I knew would be the last time for a long while.

"I'll miss you, too, but time is different in Heaven. It won't be as long for me as it will be for you." Will hugged me close before letting me go. "Promise me one thing," he said.

I nodded. "Anything."

"Promise me you won't cry over me after I leave. I'm finally happy, Lilly. I want you to be happy for me too."

"I can promise I'll try not to cry much," I said, "but I'll still miss you."

Will smiled. "I guess that'll have to do. I love you, Lilly Rayne. Enjoy your life. That's the greatest gift you could give to me."

Will disappeared.

I turned to God. "If I'm not dead, why am I here?"

"I wanted you to meet the reason Lucifer didn't win."

God pointed out past the porch, towards the lush green lawn in front of the house.

I took in a sharp breath, feeling light-headed as the reason for Lucifer's failure smiled at me.

CHAPTER 25.

I grabbed Brand's wrist, just as he was about to plunge the tip of his dagger into my heart. The fire emanating from my hands died down, and I looked at Brand's tear- streaked face. I felt the presence of Lucifer still inside me, but felt him be unceremoniously pushed out by a pure soul.

Brand's eyes were drawn to Lucifer, now standing outside my body. He immediately looked down at me, daring to hope that what he was seeing was real.

"It's me," I said.

The dagger fell from his hands onto the snow as he pulled me into his embrace, crying tears of happiness now, instead of sorrow.

"That's not possible!" I heard Lucifer scream behind me, like a child who had just lost his favorite toy.

I turned to face him, still basking in the warmth of my husband's love.

"Haven't you ever heard the phrase 'love conquerors all'?" I asked, dropping my hand to my belly.

"But the curse," he began to say. "You should be practically dead with that thing's spawn growing inside you."

I heard Brand's sharp intake of breath behind me. "Lilly?"

I turned back to my husband, and brought his hand to my stomach.

"I guess you're getting your Christmas gift a little early. I would like you to meet our daughter," I said to him gently, letting the realization of my condition sink in.

Brand fell to his knees in front of me, resting his head against my stomach, and holding me tight. I felt his body tremble as he cried.

"But that's not possible!" Lucifer stormed.

"That's quite enough," I heard a familiar voice say beside me.

I turned my head and saw God. He was looking at Lucifer, like a father getting ready to discipline his child.

"So, you chose humans over me yet again," Lucifer spat. "Typical."

"I had hoped your time here would have taught you something about the strength they possess. I suppose it will take a while longer for you to realize how wrong you are about them... and me. I never chose them above you. That's just what your jealousy of them led you to believe. I still love you, Lucifer, but I don't condone the way you've been behaving. You were one of my greatest triumphs, but you also turned out to be one of my greatest disappointments. Now, leave, and let me talk to my other children about what needs to be done with the mess you've created."

Lucifer disappeared as ordered, and the snowy plain before me was instantly dotted with black as the Watchers appeared.

I felt myself gasp. Most of them were covered in red, and I knew it was blood. They all fell to a knee as one in front of God, everyone except for Malcolm.

Malcolm phased in front of me, and I threw my arms around him, not caring that the white coat I wore would now be red.

"Are you all right?" I asked frantically, reluctantly pulling away from him to see if he was missing any limbs.

"Yes, dearest. I'm fine," he held my face in the palms of his hands and kissed me lightly on the lips. When he pulled away, he looked over at Brand.

"I couldn't help myself," he said, in way of an excuse for his boldness.

"Not even you could spoil today for me," Brand said.

Malcolm's eyes finally found God.

"You," God said to Malcolm, "out of everyone, have surprised Me the most. I thought you were lost to Me for good when you started to drink human blood. I'm thankful to Lilly for bringing you closer to me."

"Can You forgive a sinner like me?" Malcolm asked, obviously not expecting a favorable response.

"I can forgive any sin with true repentance," God answered. "But, it doesn't seem to be Me you need forgiveness from. You are your own worst enemy, Malcolm. You allow your guilt to eat at you, not allowing yourself to realize how much you've changed. I will always be able to forgive you, but first you must find a way to forgive yourself."

God looked out at all the Watchers. "I know many of you feel the way Malcolm does. Until you are able to forgive yourselves for what you have done, I don't see a way to bring you back to Me fully. Fortunately, Lucifer provided you with a way."

I looked at God, completely confused.

God looked up at the white ribbon of light floating like a white sash in the sky. "The Tear Lucifer made today will take a

237

lot to heal. When the time is right, you will be given the knowledge as to how to repair the damage Lucifer caused to the universe. In the meantime, I ask that all of you do what you were sent here to do in the first place: serve humanity. Teach them what they need to know in the trying times to come. The world as they know it doesn't exist anymore. Their reality has been shaken to the core, and many of them will never recover. They will have to face the fact that they are not alone in the universe, and they will need you to guide them. Help them face their fears. Let them lean on your strength in their greatest time of need."

God took two steps forward. "Mason, stand before me."

Mason phased, still kneeling on one knee in front of God.

God placed one of his hands under Mason's chin, encouraging him to stand in His presence. I watched as He traced the scar over Mason's eye with the tips of his fingers, much like I did the first time I met the leader of the Watchers.

"I see the old scar has not yet healed," God said, not taking any joy in the fact that Mason still wore the proof of His wrath.

"No," Mason said. "I fear it will never heal."

"It can be healed," God said. "But you have to allow it to happen. Your guilt keeps it as deep as when I first made it. When you find a way to forgive yourself, it will begin to fade. That is My promise to you." God put his hands on Mason's shoulders. "You must lead the Watchers once more during the dark days ahead. You will be the one who finds a way to close the Tear and help bring peace back into the universe."

"Will You help us?" Mason asked. "Will You give us the power to close it?"

"I already have," God said, lowering His arms back to His side. "The answer is here on this Earth. But you will have to figure out how to find it and then how to use it. Only then will you all feel as though you have done enough to be forgiven. I will help if I see you are being led astray, but ultimately you will have to figure things out on your own. Without the struggle, you will never feel like you have done enough, and I fear this may be your last chance at redemption."

"I will lead them well this time," Mason promised. "I won't let them be led astray again."

"You are not solely to blame for the first fall," God said. "I should have known you would all eventually fall in love with the humans. How could you not, from working so closely with them? I release you from that promise to Me; especially considering that type of love is what saved the universe in the end."

God turned to Brand and me. He walked up to us and placed His hand over the hand Brand still had resting on my stomach.

"Your daughter will be strong-willed," God warned us, smiling at the irony. "But I guess I shouldn't expect any less from one of your children." God looked at Brand and was silent for a while, as if he was studying something about my husband. "I know the answer to this question, but I will ask it so Lilly can hear it for herself." He paused, making sure I was listening. "Brand, if you could have one wish which only affects you, what would it be?"

Without hesitation, Brand said, "To be human."

As he said the words, I remembered the moment Brand told me that same wish once. I knew it was something he desperately wanted, granting us a true life together, but I felt trepidation in my heart over the possibility of it happening.

What if Brand didn't see me the same way after he became human? A vision of the paintings Brand did of me flashed through my mind. Tara had been right that the paintings were an idealistic version of me, not the real way I looked. What would Brand see when he looked at me through human eyes? Would he still see the woman he fell in love with, or would his view of me change? Would he still love me the same?

God nodded his head at what Brand wished for. "Then your wish is granted, as long as you can forgive yourself for your past."

"Abby…" Brand said, letting his guilt over his daughter's circumstance resonate in his voice. It would be the one thing he would always feel guilty about.

"Only the children who have drunk human blood will retain the curse," God promised him. "Those who have been protected by their fathers and abstained from their natural instinct to drink human blood all these years will be granted a normal, human life from this point forward."

God turned to the other Watchers. I could hear some of them sobbing over the lost opportunity to save their children. "But," God told them, "to those of you who allowed your children to hunt humans for fun and kill for sport, I will grant you a second chance to prove your children deserve redemption. You must show them you were wrong in dooming them to live with the curse, and have them serve humanity by your side. If you do this, I will lift the curse from them also, in time."

God looked back at Brand and me. "Can you forgive yourself now?" He asked.

"Yes," Brand said. "I can."

God nodded his approval.

I felt Brand put his hands on my shoulders to turn me to face him. I almost resisted, not wanting to see his disappointment in how I really looked. I refused to meet his eyes, for fear of what I would see there.

"Lilly," Brand said, his voice trembling. "How can you be even more beautiful?"

I looked up at Brand's face and saw he wasn't just saying it to hide what he might have truly thought. He did believe I looked more beautiful through his now-human eyes than I did when he was an angel.

I threw my arms around his neck, feeling the power of pure joy fill my heart.

"I will see you again in time," God told us. "Live a full life together. Love one another and nothing will ever seem insurmountable."

God disappeared then, leaving in His wake a new sense of hope and purpose to everyone present.

Still holding onto Brand, I looked up at the sky, and wondered what the Tear had done to the world. Even though it scared me, I knew whatever damage Lucifer had caused, God would stay true to His word and help the Watchers heal the wound. It was just a matter of time.

EPILOGUE

I stood in our home in Colorado, looking out the picture window at the snow-capped mountain and lake beyond. My hands rested on the large bump of my belly as I felt my son move to gain a more comfortable position inside me.

"Give me your hands," I told Brand as he came to stand behind me. I put his palms on top of my belly, just as our son moved again.

"He's strong," Brand said in my ear, nibbling at the tender flesh, "just like his mother."

I smiled and leaned back against my husband, feeling eternal bliss like I always did in his presence.

"Mommy!"

We turned at the sound of our daughter's excited voice as she ran down the stairs from the second floor towards us. She was almost three years old now, with a head full of chestnut-colored hair like mine and beautiful grey eyes like her father's. Brand let me go as he bent down to pick her up, holding her against his side.

"Mommy, is it time?"

"I don't know," I said to her, unable to repress a smile. "You better go to the kitchen and ask Aunt Tara and Uncle Malik that question."

Caylin wiggled out of her father's arms and ran headlong to the back of the house to find the kitchen.

Malcolm was still crouched beside the large blue spruce Christmas tree in the living room.

"Are you sure you have a gift for me under here, dearest?" he asked, scanning the tags on the presents. "I still don't see it."

"It's there, Malcolm," I said, for what had to have been the hundredth time that day. "But you can't open it until tomorrow morning. That's the rule."

Malcolm sighed heavily and stood up. He turned to face Brand and me.

"All I seem to be able to find are gifts for Caylin," he halfheartedly complained.

"I've been a good girl, Uncle Malcolm," Caylin said, walking back into the living room with a half-eaten cookie in her hand.

"Did Aunt Tara give you that?" I asked, already knowing Tara had bribed my child with sweets once again.

"She said supper wasn't ready," Caylin answered, with pieces of the sugar cookie dribbling out of her mouth as she spoke.

"It's almost ready!" I heard Tara yell from the kitchen. "We're just setting the table!"

The front door of the house opened, and Abby and Sebastian walked in, stomping the snow off their boots in the entryway.

Brand and I went to greet them. When I hugged Abby, I had to carefully maneuver my belly alongside her own protruding one.

"I love you both," Abby said, hastily kissing us both on the cheeks. "But your grandchild has been pressing on my bladder all the way up here." Abby waddled off to find the bathroom.

Malcolm came and gave his son a hug. "You should have let me phase you here," Malcolm told him. "I don't know why you insisted on risking my grandchild's life driving in this snow."

Sebastian smiled. "We're trying to live the way humans do, Dad. And humans don't phase everywhere they want to go."

"Have it your way," Malcolm said, throwing his hands up in the air. "But when the time comes for my grandson to be born, I'm phasing us all to the hospital. Your driving isn't that great in the best of situations. I am not about to let you risk his life when you can't even think straight."

"Come on, y'all," Tara said, walking from the back of the house, with Malik right behind her. "Supper is ready."

Just before we went to the dining room, the phone rang.

"Go ahead," I told everyone. "It's for me."

When I picked up the phone, my mom yelled, "Merry Christmas, sweetie!"

"Hey, Mom. How is everyone doing?"

"Oh, your grandpa is as ornery as ever, but your grandma is keeping him in line."

"Even after God himself visited them and told them everything, he's still giving you attitude?"

"It's just the way he is, sweetie. I don't take any of it personally. I'm just glad he let me spend Christmas with them this year. It's been so long. And your grandma wants you and Brand to come visit after her newest great-grandbaby is born. She said she missed seeing Caylin as a baby, so she's not going to miss seeing…Oh, have you decided on a name for him yet?"

I smiled. "Yes, we're going to name him Will."

"Will," my mother repeated. "That's perfect."

When I walked into the dining room and saw my family gathered around the table, discussing who was the most worthy of the prized turkey leg, I couldn't help but smile.

My dream really did come true.

The End

AUTHOR'S NOTE

Thank you so much for reading *The Watchers Trilogy*, If you have enjoyed *Forgiven*, book 3, please take a moment to leave a review. To leave a review please visit:
Forgiven,

Thank you in advance for leaving a review for the book. I hope you have loved it as much as I do.
Sincerely,

S.J. West.

THE NEXT IN THE WATCHERS UNIVERSE

THE WATCHER CHRONICLES

Based in the Watcher Universe, *The Watcher Chronicles* is my second series. The first book is titled *Broken*. This series takes place 15 years after the Tear is formed and deals with its aftermath. The main character is named Jess, and the story is told from her perspective. Many of the characters from *The Watchers Trilogy* will pop up here and there, especially Mason, Malcolm, Lilly, and Brand. This series is targeted for the +17 and older crowd, due to mature themes.

As a thank you for purchasing the Watchers Trilogy, I have included in this book the first two chapters of *Broken*.

But first, if you are below the age of 17, I have released a duology based on Brand and Lilly's daughter, Caylin. If you are interested in that series, it is called *Caylin's Story* and the first book is titled *Timeless*.

Timeless, book 1 *of Caylin's Story.*
Exclusively on Amazon, FREE on KU.

BROKEN SNEAK PEEK

Now, please enjoy this sample of *Broken,*
Book 1 of *The Watcher Chronicles.*

Exclusively on Amazon, FREE on KU

BROKEN. CHAPTER 1

The world my parents knew doesn't exist anymore. On the night they were taken from me, the people of Earth learned definitively that we are not alone in the universe. A permanent ripple of white light now laces the sky like a silky ribbon of fate, reminding any remaining disbelievers that their lives could be irrevocably changed in an instant. Day or night, you can see the tear, which has literally transported people off of our world, like my parents, and exchanged people and creatures from alternate realities and distant planets into their place.

All our scientists have been able to tell us is that, what we perceive as a tear in the sky is actually one end of a wormhole. But none of them can explain where the tear came from or how it chooses its victims. Even with our advanced modern science, no one can find a way to stop the wormhole from opening and ripping our loved ones from our lives, casting them out into the unknown.

"Don't get your hopes up, Jess. You know the chances of them ever coming back are slim."

I look at my best friend, Faison, in the dim light cast by the moon and tear in the sky. Her perfectly braided auburn hair hangs over her right shoulder against the emerald green of the scrubs she is wearing. Faison is the classic version of a true southern belle, a status in our circle of friends I could never quite seem to achieve no matter how hard Mama Lynn, the woman who raised us, tried to make me into one.

We are sitting on a red and black plaid wool blanket in the middle of my parents' land. On the night of their disappearance, my parents and I had been looking up at the sky because we were actually going to be able to see the Aurora Borealis in the Deep South. It was supposed to be an event caused by the after-effects of a large solar storm, which no one would ever see again for a thousand years.

December 20, 2012, just before Santa had a chance to visit seven-year-old me, is the date I lost my parents.

At exactly seven o'clock in the evening, the ripple appeared in the sky and opened to reveal two planets, one blue and one orange. When I reached out to my parents for comfort, thinking the world was about to end, I found only empty warm spots on the blanket where they had been laying only moments before.

Every year since then, the ripple has opened at the exact same time and date as it first happened. Sometimes those who were chosen from our planet would return to the spot they were taken from. So, every year, I come back to my parents' home, hoping to win the lottery of their safe return.

I glance down at my phone and see it's a minute until seven. I reach out for Faison's hand. She clasps mine tightly; neither of us knowing if one, both, or neither of us will be chosen to travel through the tear this year.

The tear opens, showing only blackness on the other side. For fifteen years, we have seen various worlds and distant star constellations through the ripple, but never absolute darkness. The other side of the tear looks void of anything, a great expanse of nothingness. I suddenly consider the absurd possibility that we won't have to deal with any new tearers this year. The idea almost makes me laugh. The odds it would take for us to get that lucky don't exist in the real world.

"What do you think is comin' through?" Faison asks, her hand squeezing mine tighter with justifiable worry.

"Your guess is as good as mine," I say, reaching for the plasma pistol in front of me with my free hand. "But you're safe with me."

"I know I am, Jess." I hear the tease in Faison's voice just before she says, "Even if you are a hundred and twenty pounds of nothin' and can't scare a fly."

I shake my head in feigned disappointment, keeping my eyes on the tear as it closes. "Geez, no respect for Watcher agents these days; not even from the best friend of one."

"Well, if you actually ate something every once in a while, maybe you wouldn't look like a bag of bones. I don't know how tearers are supposed to be frightened of someone who looks like a brown-haired Barbie doll."

I just sigh and stand up, pulling Faison swiftly to her feet with a jerk of my arm.

"Listen, I know you don't like me being an agent, but it's what I've chosen to do with my life. Mama Lynn understands why I have to do it. I don't know why you refuse to."

Faison crosses her arms in front of her ample bosom. If I look like Barbie, Faison's curves make her look like a Playmate of the Year.

"Mama Lynn thinks the world rises and sets just for you. Of course, she wouldn't second guess what you decided to go and do with your life. But I know why you chose to join the Watchers. You think it'll help you find a way to get your parents back."

"You don't know it won't," I say defensively.

It's an old argument between Faison and me. I know she doesn't think working for the Watchers will help me find my parents, and I can't deny she might be right. But the odds are fifty-fifty as far as I'm concerned. As long as there is a chance I can get them back, I'm going to take it, no matter the cost.

"I need to get back to the station," I tell her. "I'm lucky they let me come here this year as it is. Rookies don't usually get to take time off on this night."

Faison bends down and picks up the blanket from the grass, folding it into a neat square.

"Call Mama Lynn and make sure she's ok first," Faison instructs. "Then you can drop me off at the hospital. They asked all the nurses to come in for the first few hours after the tear opened."

I scroll down my contact list to Mama Lynn's number, and tap her name twice to place the call. She picks up on the second ring.

"Jess?"

"We're both fine," I immediately reassure her. "Are you ok? Did anything happen at home?"

"No, I'm fine. George came over to keep me company while it opened. But you two be careful out there," Mama Lynn says, "and tell Faison to call me when she gets to the hospital."

"Yes, ma'am. I will."

"Love you, kids. You watch your back. Who knows what came through this time."

"I know. I'll be careful. Just make sure you stay inside and keep the doors and windows locked. Don't let anyone try to come into your house until the Agency is able to do a threat assessment. In fact, why don't you get George to stay with you tonight? That way I won't worry about you."

"You tell me that every year," Mama Lynn says, with a smile in her voice. "I'll ask George to stay with me just so you don't worry. I love you girls."

"We love you, too."

"Oh, Jess?"

"Yes?"

"Don't forget we're all supposed to go see Uncle Dan tomorrow evening. They don't think he'll make it much longer," I hear the strain in Mama Lynn's voice, as if she's trying not to cry. "I sure would appreciate it if you and Faison would go up there with me this time and say your goodbyes."

"All right, we'll go with you," I tell her, even though I feel like the loss of Uncle Dan is simply granting us one less asshole in the world.

"I know the two of you had a falling out before his accident," she says. "And I still don't need you to tell me what happened, but maybe you could find a way to forgive him for whatever it is he did before he passes away."

That's never happening, I say to myself but not to Mama Lynn.

"See you tomorrow, Mama Lynn."

"Ok," Mama Lynn sounds disappointed, but I know it's better than her knowing the real reason I can't mourn the loss of Uncle Dan.

When I end the call with Mama Lynn, I tell Faison, "She wants us to go pay our respects to Uncle Dan tomorrow."

"Pfft, the sooner he dies, the better off we all are," Faison says. "Especially you."

"Sometimes," I say, pausing to get my thoughts together, "I want to tell her what her brother did, but then I realize it wouldn't do any good. It would only cause her pain."

"But maybe you need to tell her," Faison urges. "Maybe it's time you told someone else besides me."

"You know the only reason I told you was to make sure you never went over to his house alone."

"I know, Jess," Faison puts her free hand on my arm. "And I know what you did to protect me from him."

"I love you," I tell her. "And if he had laid a hand on you, I couldn't have lived with myself."

"I wish we had told someone back then what he was."

"We were kids," I say in way of an explanation. "You don't expect someone you trust to hurt you on purpose."

"I know, but…"

"Let's just forget about it," I say, putting one of my arms around Faison's shoulders. "Come on. We both need to get back to work."

By the time I drop Faison off at the hospital where she works, I've already received a call from the head office in Memphis about disturbances caused by the new tearers in the northern part of Mississippi where I'm stationed. I'm given directions to a home in Tunica where a man reported a tearer holding his daughter hostage, demanding he be sent back home.

It isn't uncommon for tearers to become a tad psychotic when they reach their final destination. Being taken completely away from your own reality against your will can do that to a person. Most tearers end up accepting the government's assistance in setting them up in a home of their own and finding jobs for them. It isn't much different from the witness protection program. Some tearers never acclimate to their new homes, though, and have to be dealt with by Watcher agents like me.

Being an agent is a fairly thankless job. The general public fears us because we are a law unto ourselves. All Watcher agents are placed under the jurisdiction of one Watcher. There are five Watchers in the U.S. alone and a hundred and seventy-four more stationed around the world. No one knows where the Watchers came from or who or what they are exactly. All we know is that the governments of the world trust them completely. They look human, but we all know they aren't. Some speculate they're demons bent on destroying us, while others think they're our saviors sent in a time when the world needs heroes. All I know is that they're different, just like the tearers are different. And I know they were living on our planet long before the ripple ever appeared.

Since I was a small child, I have unknowingly been aware that there are people living on our planet who don't belong.

My father is one of those people.

I didn't realize what I was seeing at the time. I just thought the faint golden halo which perpetually surrounded my dad meant he was special. When I was old enough to ask him why he glowed and no one else I knew did, he simply told me it was because I could see the truth of things. He asked me not to let anyone else know what I could see and I never did, not even Mama Lynn or Faison. It was my secret, and I was thankful he advised me to keep my peculiar ability to myself.

It wasn't until I saw my first tearer and Watcher that I realized my father was right. For some strange reason, I *could* see the truth of things. Tearers don't glow blue like Watchers. Those who are brought to Earth through the tear glow red, making them stand out in a crowd for my eyes. As a Watcher agent, my unusual talent comes in handy. It helped me rise through the ranks of the organization faster than any other agent my age. No one else in my class has a class one rating in identifying tearers; only me. Some of my colleagues think I am a tearer, but the Watcher I work for knows better.

When I reach the house on Bankston Street, I park in the driveway and make a quick survey of the surrounding area. The house is a regular ranch-style brick home. There's a cedar play set in the lot beside the house, a red F150 double cab parked in the garage, and a white steepled church across the street. I can hear frantic yelling coming from inside the home, but the voices are too muffled to make out the exact words.

I step out of my Watcher-issued black Dodge Phoenix when I hear the distinct pop of a Watcher phasing in behind me. All Watchers have the ability to teleport wherever they want, whenever they want. It comes in handy.

"So what's the situation exactly?" I ask, turning to face the Watcher of my jurisdiction while I put my Kevlar vest on over the black leather jacket of my Watcher uniform.

Isaiah Greenleaf stares in the direction of the house before answering me.

The first time Faison saw Isaiah, I thought she was going to faint. She called him the prettiest black man she'd ever seen. Mama Lynn said he was pretty enough to be a movie star. But, the strange thing is, if you were to round up all the Watchers in one room, you would have a hard time deciding which one of them was the most gorgeous. They all have an unearthly beauty that would have separated them out from us regular humans anyway.

"Jonas Hunt, his wife, and daughter, were gathered around their dining room table, holding hands and praying when the tear opened," Isaiah tells me as his gaze finally turns in my direction. "When it closed, the wife was gone and a tearer sat in her place. The tearer freaked out, like most of them do, and put a knife to the little girl's throat, demanding to be returned to his home. That's all I know."

I grab my plasma pistol from the passenger seat and slide it into the holster on my right thigh.

"Ready when you are, boss."

Without another word, Isaiah and I make our way to the front of the house and ring the doorbell. It's standard protocol to announce our presence before actually entering a situation involving a tearer. Taking a newly-deposited tearer by surprise isn't wise because you never know what you're dealing with until you meet them.

We don't wait for someone to answer the door. That would be ridiculous, considering the situation. Isaiah opens the door a crack and yells, "Watcher Greenleaf and Agent Riley coming in!"

Isaiah pushes the door completely inward, revealing the entire situation in one glance. Directly across from the front door through the living room, the dining area of the house is in plain view. The tearer is a man of average height and build with brown hair, wearing jeans and a plain white T-shirt under a thin blue jacket. An ominous red glow only I can see pulsates around him. Yet, something seems odd to my eyes. The red is a darker hue than usual for some reason.

The tearer is holding a small girl of about five in one arm, while pointing the edge of a long kitchen knife against her throat. The father of the girl stands anxiously on the opposite side of the table, helplessly watching his daughter sob uncontrollably.

"Please, help her," the father begs us, chancing a glance in our direction with frantic eyes.

With the cool assuredness only Watchers seem to possess, Isaiah walks through the living room to stand beside the distraught father.

"Everything will be all right," Isaiah says. His silky voice is like a healing balm meant to bring calm to the tense situation.

"Send me back home," the tearer demands, the hand holding the knife visibly shaking. "I want to go home now!"

Isaiah looks at the man. "You know we can't do that. You've more than likely had this type of thing happen on your world, too. The same rules apply here. No one controls the tear."

"My wife," the man's voice trembles with grief, "my kids. They need me!"

"What's your name?" Isaiah asks.

"Owen."

"Owen, if there was any way we could return you home, we would. But holding this man's daughter hostage isn't earning you any points on this planet. I'm not sure where you come from, but I feel sure if someone was doing this to your family, you wouldn't stand for it."

Owen's eyes fall to the knife in his hands just before he lets it drop to the floor and releases his hold on the girl. The girl immediately runs to her father.

Owen sits on the kitchen floor, completely dejected. "What am I supposed to do now?"

I step up to his side to do what I've been trained for.

"Come with me. We can help you start a new life here. You're not alone."

Owen looks up at me, his eyes void of hope. "Without my family, what's the point?"

"Maybe someone from where you came from is here, too. You'll never know until we get everyone's information into our database." I hold out my hand to him. "Come on. Let's see if we can find your family."

A spark of hope lights Owen's eyes. He takes my offered hand and stands to follow me out of the house.

Isaiah stays behind to make sure the Hunt family is all right, and gives them our number if they want free counseling. I know from firsthand experience that the counseling will be useless. No one can help you get over the fact that your family member was sucked through a wormhole to points unknown. At least if they had died naturally, you would have something physical to prove they once existed, a body or ashes, something to mourn over. Having someone ripped from your life without explanation, and not knowing where they are or if they are even still alive, is a hundred times worse.

I help Owen into the backseat of my car and head towards the Tunica Watcher Station. When I glance in my rearview mirror, I see him staring out the window at the flat farmland on either side of Hwy 61. During the winter, most of the Delta looks like a barren landscape in some post-apocalyptic movie. With the trees bare of leaves giving the illusion of skeletal figures, I can only imagine what our unearthly guest thinks of his new home.

"Do you mind me asking the name of your planet?" I ask. It's the first question all tearers are asked. That way, we know whether or not they are alien or simply from a parallel universe.

"Earth," he replies, never taking his eyes off the world outside.

"This is Earth, too. What was your Earth like?"

"Nothing like this one."

"What's different?"

The man meets my eyes in the rearview mirror. A passing car's headlights illuminates his face for a fraction of a second, but that's all I need to see that his eyes have turned completely black and glossy, like pieces of marble.

"They weren't as gullible as you."

Before I know what's happening, he thrusts his arms through the Plexiglas which separates the front seats from the back, passing his hands and arms through the –inch-thick plastic like it isn't even there. I slam both feet on the brakes just as his fingers are about to wrap around my neck. The force of my rash move causes the car to skid off the road, slamming us headlong into a power pole along the highway. The airbag deploys from the steering wheel column and slaps my face like someone just kicked a soccer ball into it. As quickly as it inflated, the airbag deflates, giving me time to unlatch my seat belt and stumble out of the car.

I feel disoriented from the impact, but have enough sense left to draw the plasma pistol from my thigh holster and point it at the car.

The back passenger door blows off its hinges, soon followed by Owen.

"Hands over your head!" I yell, trying to keep the gun steady in my hands while I try not to pass out.

"Now, why would I do that?" Owen walks steadily towards me, no hesitancy in his actions.

"Stop where you are or I'll shoot! This is your last warning!"

Owen doesn't stop; I know if he reaches me, I'm dead. I shoot.

The ball of plasma bounces off his face and dances off into the night sky, exploding into a shower of light like a sparkler on the Fourth of July.

Before I even have a chance to get off another shot, Owen has one hand around my throat and uses his other hand to yank the pistol out of my grasp. I desperately try to pry his hand away from my throat, but it's like his fingers are welded to my skin.

"Now just be still," he whispers in my ear. "This won't hurt much as long as you don't try to fight me."

The words are anything but comforting. Owen brings my body closer to his like he's about to hug me. I feel more than see the right side of my body begin to meld with Owen's left side, like two candles melting into one another. I grab him by the shoulders and desperately try to push him away, but the added pressure only causes me more pain.

"Stop resisting," he murmurs, as though he's receiving pleasure from the process.

My mind rejects what I'm going through. I feel like someone who's stepped into quicksand, without anything around to use as a handhold. I don't know what's happening, and I'm not completely sure I want to.

His shoulders begin to tremble beneath my hands, causing my whole body to vibrate like a tuning fork. He finally starts to scream as loud as I am, and thrusts me away from him, causing me to fall ungracefully onto the ground. When I look back up at him, I see that half of his body is missing, the half mine occupied only moments before.

"What did you do?" he shrieks, like I should have all the answers.

My eyes feel like they're about to bulge out of their sockets as I continue to stare at him, unable to move or even take in a breath of air to fill my burning lungs.

Owen falls down on the one knee he has left, screaming in agony before exploding into a pile of black ash.

I hear the distinct pop of a Watcher phase in behind me. I assume it's Isaiah, and I relax, comforted by the fact that he will know what to do next, because my mind is a maelstrom of confusion.

I finally find it possible to take in a deep breath, but impossible to say anything to Isaiah, who is strangely silent and still behind me. I turn my head to look up at him.

It's not Isaiah.

I scramble to my feet to face a Watcher I've never seen before. Everyone in America knows what the five Watchers who help protect us look like, and this one isn't one of the five. I know what many of the Watchers from overseas look like, and can't seem to place him as one of those either.

In the dim light of night, his pale face glows softly. His grey wool button-down coat flutters in the wind around his legs. Like all Watchers, he is handsome but, unlike other Watchers, his face isn't perfect. A deep scar marks his face, running from right above his left eye to below his cheekbone. An imperfection no Watcher I've ever seen has.

His eyes stare into mine for a moment before moving to the pile of ash still lying on the ground behind me.

"Who are you?" I demand.

"Mason Collier," he replies. His eyes slowly travel back to me. "More importantly," he pauses, tilting his head and narrowing his eyes in on me. "What are you?"

BROKEN. CHAPTER 2

"What am I?" I repeat, feeling slightly offended by the question considering who is asking it. "Shouldn't that be my question to you?"

The corners of Mason's mouth twitch like he wants to smile. "Touché, agent?"

"Riley. Jess Riley."

He's silent for a moment looking me up and down in one glance, like he's trying to detect anything special about me.

"Has anything like this ever happened to you before, Agent Riley?"

I take a deep breath and say, "No," while sliding my pistol into the holster on my thigh. The steely weight of it against my leg brings a strange sort of comfort to me. "I can't really say I understand what just happened to be honest. I was just doing a routine transport of the tearer to my station when he attacked me."

Mason crosses his arms in front of him. "He wasn't a tearer. He was changeling."

"Which is what exactly? An alien?"

"No, it's a type of demon that is almost impossible for even someone like me to detect."

"A demon?" I ask, thinking he's making some sort of joke. "There's no such thing."

"You say that like you know it for a fact," he comments, tilting his head at me. "Why?"

"Demons are mythological creatures. If demons are real, then there would have to be a God too."

This time it's Mason who looks completely confused. "You don't believe in God?"

"If a benevolent God actually existed, He would do something about that." I point directly above us to the Tear.

"What if He's leaving it there for a reason?"

"It would have to be a pretty damn good reason."

I don't feel like having this discussion with a complete stranger. Mama Lynn's already tried to persuade me God had a purpose for putting the Tear in the sky, but none of her Bible thumping religious mumbo jumbo ever convinced me the God she loves and believes in so blindly could have a good enough reason to take my parents away. I can't place my faith in a higher power that could be so heartless and cruel for its own nefarious purposes.

"Greenleaf is the Watcher for this part of America isn't he?"

"Yes. I actually thought you were him when you phased in behind me."

Mason holds one of his hands out to me, and I automatically shake it thinking he intends to leave me and search for Isaiah to inform him of my situation. Instead, I instantly find myself standing in the middle of Isaiah's office at Watcher Headquarters in Memphis.

I stare at Mason with eyes wide and yank my hand away from his before he has a chance to whisk me off somewhere else.

"I didn't know you guys could take someone else along with you," I say, feeling like I need to explain why I might look like a startled rabbit.

"We don't share the knowledge with many people," Mason tells me.

"Why not?" I ask, walking over to the glass wall of Isaiah's office which looks out over the Mississippi River. I feel a need to put as much distance as I can between me and Mason. "Afraid people will start bugging you for rides?"

Mason smiles sardonically. "Something like that."

I hear the distinct pop of a Watcher phase in and silently let out a sigh of relief when I see Isaiah's reflection in the glass.

Isaiah's eyes are immediately drawn to Mason like magnets to metal. My mentor for the last year does something I have never seen him do before. He instantly drops to one knee in Mason's direction and bows his head. It's the first time I have ever seen a Watcher show complete humility towards anyone.

Mason walks over to Isaiah. His gate reminds me of a white tiger I saw once in a zoo. Confident isn't exactly the right word to describe it. It's more like he knows he is the most powerful being in the room but lacks the arrogance usually associated with such a fact.

Mason steps up to Isaiah and places his hand on my mentor's head.

"Rise, Isaiah," Mason's words are gentle, like he's talking to a trusted friend.

Isaiah stands to his feet and meets Mason's eyes.

"May I ask what has brought you here?" Isaiah's voice holds a note of uneasy reverence, a warning to me that Mason's presence bodes danger.

"I came to tell you I'm recruiting one of your agents." Mason briefly looks over at me before returning his attention back to Isaiah.

Finally noticing I'm in the room, Isaiah stares at me with a confused frown on his face.

"Why do you want Jess?" Isaiah asks.

"She just killed a changeling demon without even trying or knowing what it was. I think she might be useful in helping us solve the puzzle we were asked to deal with."

"She killed a demon?" Isaiah asks in surprise, obviously sure he heard Mason wrong.

Mason nods once.

Isaiah looks back over at me. "What are you, Jess?"

My temper flares at the question.

"I'm getting really tired of being asked that like I'm some sort of freak. Isaiah," I take a step forward, "what's going on? You don't really believe that man from the Hunt's home was a demon, do you?"

"What happened exactly, Jess? Tell me everything."

I tell Isaiah what there is to tell of my story. He listens to each of my words closely, like he doesn't want to miss a single syllable.

"Then Mason showed up and brought me here," I say, finishing a story that sounds completely absurd to my own ears even though I was the one who lived through it.

Isaiah is silent after my tale, which causes me more worry than anything else.

"From your file," Isaiah finally says, "I remember reading that your parents were taken through the Tear when you were very young."

"Yes, when I was seven."

"So, they were among the first to be taken?"

I nod.

"Did you go live with relatives afterwards?"

"No. The government wasn't able to find any family on either my father or mother's side. I was put into the foster care system like a lot of other kids who lost their parents that night. I got lucky though and was adopted by the foster parent I was placed with."

"Then, you don't have any living relatives?" Mason asks.

I shake my head. "Not that I know of."

Isaiah and Mason glance at one another like what I've said confirms something they are both thinking.

"What is it?" I ask, not appreciating being left out of the loop, especially when I'm at the center of it. "What do the two of you think I am?"

"We've only encountered a human who can kill the way you did once before," Isaiah says. "Jess, did your parents have any friends who used to come over to the house? Any work colleagues? Anything at all that you can tell us about the people they associated with?"

I shake my head realizing for the first time how sheltered life with my parents had been.

"How did they make their money?" Mason asks.

"I was just a kid," I reply. "I didn't worry about things like that."

"Did they work from home or go somewhere to work?"

I thought back through my childhood trying to piece together what memories I had of my parents.

"I don't remember them ever working. I was home schooled by my mother, and my father was always in the house. I never saw him leave home to go to work. I guess he could have worked from home or something, but I honestly don't know. What I do know is that whatever they did to earn money must have been lucrative."

"What makes you say that?" Isaiah asks.

"Because when I turned eighteen a lawyer came to see me and told me I was a millionaire."

"Why weren't you given the money when your parents disappeared?" Mason asks. "With that sort of trust fund, you should have stayed out of the foster care system."

"He said my parents set up the account and conditions of disbursement when I was born. I guess in all their planning they never thought they would be sucked up by a wormhole and leave me an orphan," I say defensively on their behalf.

"Even so," Isaiah says, "all those taken through the Tear are declared legally dead. All of their financial wealth should have been given to you."

"They're not dead," I remind him.

"To this world they are," he in turn reminds me. "All of their financial property should have reverted to you."

I shrug. "All I can tell you is that after the government liquidated their assets, I was told I had a little over a hundred grand. I don't know why my parents didn't have more than that in the bank. All I know is that the government deposited the money they could find in a savings account for me and the bank was directed to make good on the taxes on my parents' house and land since I refused to sell them."

"So, you really don't know anything about your parents past," Mason states.

"No, I guess I don't," I answer, keeping the secret about my father to myself. I know that's what they're fishing for: the real reason I'm different. More than likely the reason I was able to kill this so called demon.

"Could either of you have killed that thing?" I ask, doing my own sort of fact finding.

"We can't kill demons," Isaiah answers. "That's why we're trying to figure out how a regular human could have. Has anything out of the ordinary ever happened to you before now? Can you think of anything else that's different about you, Jess?"

I shrug my shoulders not willing to trust them completely. My father told me to keep my secret to myself, and that's exactly what I've done all these years. I've always assumed my father would have explained why I could see 'the truth of things', as he put it, when I was old enough to understand. He simply wasn't given the chance. But I wasn't going to divulge the information to them so readily, not until I understood what I was first.

"Not much else I can tell you other than what you already know from my file," I say and leave it at that. Lies get more complicated when you try to elaborate on them. I figure the less I say the safer I am.

Both Mason and Isaiah look at me as if they know I'm holding something back from them, but neither seem ready to call me out on my small lie.

"Well, I'll figure out how you killed the demon," Mason says, completely confident in his statement. "In the meantime, I still want you to join my group."

"Which does what exactly?"

"We're trying to find a way to seal the Tear."

"Seal it?" I look to Isaiah for confirmation. He nods his head, though something in his eyes tells me he's not confident Mason will ever be successful in his task.

"How do you intend to seal the Tear?" I ask Mason. "And what makes you think I can help?"

"I'm not sure you *can* help," he admits. "But there is definitely something unique about you, and considering the type of creatures I usually end up dealing with, you might prove to be useful to me."

I feel slightly offended at the way he makes his statement. I cross my arms over my chest and automatically take a defensive stance. "What makes you think I want the Tear closed?"

Mason frowns. "Weren't you the one who blamed God for not closing it just a few minutes ago? I assumed you would be more than willing to help."

I shake my head slowly. "No, I never said I wanted it closed. I said I blamed Him for not doing something about it."

"Your logic is confusing," Mason admits. "Can you explain exactly what the difference is?"

"I want my parents back. I can't have that if the Tear is closed. If there is a God, then I blame Him for letting it be put there in the first place. The world's got enough problems without having something like that hanging in the sky and randomly destroying people's lives."

Mason takes three slow steps towards me. "What if I promise I'll do everything I can to help you find your parents?"

"Mason…" I hear the note of caution in Isaiah's voice and instantly know he doesn't think Mason can fulfill such a promise.

"You don't know it can't be done," Mason tells Isaiah almost harshly.

"Have you ever been able to do it?" I ask, my arms dropping to my sides, daring to hope after all these years that I might actually have a way to get my parents back.

"Not yet but that doesn't mean it's impossible."

I look to Isaiah and see the creases of his troubled brow. My mentor looks me in the eyes unwilling to voice the warning I see on his face. When I look back at Mason, his earnest expression makes me want to believe in his promise. He is giving me hope. It might be a fool's hope, but it's the only time anyone has ever offered me a real opportunity to find my parents and not just sit around and wait once a year hoping they make it back home to me by chance.

"I'll help you," I hear myself tell Mason. "I'll join your team."

Mason holds out his hand as if he wants a handshake to seal the deal. Without hesitation, I place my hand into his and instantly find myself standing somewhere that isn't Isaiah's office.

I'm really gonna have to stop shaking his hand.

Thank you for reading the sample of Broken. If you'd like to read more you can visit amazon and get your copy today.

Broken, Book 1 of The Watcher Chronicles.
Exclusively on Amazon, FREE on KU.

ABOUT THE AUTHOR

Once upon a time, a little girl was born on a cold winter morning in the heart of Seoul, Korea. She was brought to America by her parents and raised in the Deep South where the words ma'am and y'all became an integrated part of her lexicon. She wrote her first novel at the age of eight and continued writing on and off during her teenage years. In college she studied biology and chemistry and finally combined the two by earning a master's degree in biochemistry.

After that she moved to Yankee land where she lived for four years working in a laboratory at Cornell University. Homesickness and snow aversion forced her back South where she lives in the land, which spawned Jim Henson, Elvis Presley, Oprah Winfrey, John Grisham and B.B. King.

After finding her Prince Charming, she gave birth to a wondrous baby girl and they all lived happily ever after.

As always, you can learn about the progress on my books, get news about new releases, new projects and participate on amazing giveaways by following me:

FB Book Page: @ReadTheWatchersTrilogy
FB Author Page:

https://www.facebook.com/sandra.west.585112
Website: www.sjwest.com
Amazon: http://bit.ly/SJWest-Amazon
Newsletter Sign-up: http://bit.ly/SJWest-NewsletterSignUp
Instagram: @authorsjwest
Twitter: @SJWest2013

If you'd like to contact the author, you can email her to:
sandrawest481@gmail.com

THE WATCHERS TRILOGY

Printed in Great Britain
by Amazon